Flu Shot

by

Kendrick Lacey

DREAMCATCHER PUBLISHING
Saint John • New Brunswick • Canada

Copyright © 2004 Kendrick Lacey

First Printing - February 2004

All rights reserved. No part of this publication may be reproduced or transmitted in any form or by any means - electronic or mechanical, including photocopying, recording or any information storage and retrieval system - without written permission from the Publisher, except by a reviewer who wishes to quote brief passages for inclusion in a review.

DreamCatcher Publishing acknowledges the support of the New Brunswick Arts Council.

Canadian Cataloguing in Publication Data

Lacey, Kendrick - 1950

Flu Shot

ISBN - 1-894372-35-2
I. Title.
PS8623.A34F58 2004 C813'.6 C2004-900969-9

Editor: Yvonne Wilson

Typesetter: Chas Goguen

Cover Design: Dawn Drew, INK Graphic Design Services Corp.

Author's Photo: taken by Mary Ellen Nealis

Printed and bound in Canada

DREAMCATCHER PUBLISHING INC.
105 Prince William Street
Saint John, New Brunswick, Canada E2L 2B2
www.dreamcatcher.ca

To my wife Dominique who, when I declared my intention to write a story, said, "How exciting!" and who continues to support my every endeavour.

ACKNOWLEDGEMENTS

Thanks to Jeanne Caissie, Dr. Tanya Wood, Gerry Aldwinckle, and Lynda Aldwinckle for their sympathetic yet honest critique of the first readable draft.

Thanks to DreamCatcher for taking a chance on a new author, and to Editor-in-Chief Yvonne Wilson for gentle but firm guidance.

And particular thanks to Robert Caissie, a fellow writer, whose own early literary steps fanned to life one of my creative embers. Just to talk writing with you, Robert, can drag a half chapter from my numbed brain.

PS. To the citizens of my village: None of the characters in this story are real people. Their good traits are based on what I see around me. Their bad traits are purely fiction.

CHAPTER 1

15 October

York Lancaster crouched motionless in the crotch of a century old sugar maple, waiting. At last he detected the faint tread of a single white tailed deer hoof on almost frozen leaves. His bow and a nocked arrow were cradled in his left arm. His right leg burned from knee to ankle because of the forced immobility, but he resisted the urge to adjust position. The slightest unfamiliar sound at this point could be the signal to send the approaching buck whirling into the thicket to the right.

York was savouring his morning. The woods were never truly quiet except maybe on a calm midwinter day when you'd swear that you could hear the sun rising. On an autumn day, such as this one, there was little stirring at first glance; but with concentration and with a knowing eye nature's undercurrent rises to the surface and spills all around you. The gentle rub of one birch sapling against another, the rushed arrival of a couplet of chickadees into the fir thicket, the far off call of a squirrel startled into an insistent chatter. He was just where he wanted to be; alone, reliant on himself, unconcerned with others.

York was right handed, drawing the bowstring with his dominant hand. That made the area to his right difficult to cover and he was forced to wait for the buck to enter the killing zone before he could attempt any movement. York did not hunt for trophy or for sport. He hunted to put food on the table. He did not like to kill but he was determined to provide for himself, to rely on nobody for his day to day life.

Most human carnivores deluded themselves that their protein just appeared, wrapped in double layered plastic on sparkling grocery store shelves. But he had seen the reality of the abattoir. He had seen the terror of the moaning bullocks and the pandemonium of the slaughter house floor. There was no cruelty in a well-directed arrow or well-aimed bullet in the tranquil woods at dawn. He forced himself to take responsibility for the killing, for the blood, and for the ending of life. He refused to hide behind the plastic.

The first shadow of motion alerted his right eye. It was just the hint of movement, not real action. The burn in his right calf whispered for attention. The sound of his eyes and head swivelling to the right seemed impossibly loud in his own mind but would be inaudible to the deer.

The buck stepped once more and froze. York remembered that deer did not necessarily know they were watched but rather acted as if they always were. The buck gazed through the undergrowth to his left then peered around the yellow birch to his right. He sniffed the early morning crispness, and then lowered his head to browse on an alder twig.

Suddenly, the double take. Better than any slap stick comedian, the deer jerked his head up to detect the movement of a predator attempting to take advantage of his possible moment of inattention.

York was no virgin in these woods. He had observed these magnificent animals during many seasons, sometimes hunting, sometimes not. To him these movements were profoundly predictable. He remained rock steady. His right leg shouted for ease but he pushed it farther back on the list of priorities. His jacket now was binding a little around his left arm but should give plenty of slack when he lifted the bow.

The buck had apparently completed its comedy routine of feints and double takes and it started to move again, hesitatingly at first then more quickly. This was neither a casual stroll nor a determined feeding. The buck was on his way home. He had likely fed throughout the night, resting occasionally and even bedding down for a few hours. Now at first light the buck made his way to his likely refuge, to the cedar swamp in the low ground to the north.

York's nose itched. Was it a sneeze in utero? No, just an itch. His bladder gave the first signal of future demands. He remained frozen.

The buck stopped. He repeated his slapstick routine, then after sniffing the air again, urinated in a hard stream onto the partially frozen earth. With his front hooves he pawed the ground into a scrape and then reared up onto his hind legs and laid his facial scent glands against the overhanging branch above. This buck was declaring his territory, his two square miles. With the coming rut this would be one of many scrapes that would announce to the doe population that he was in control.

York remained motionless while the buck completed the scrape. He signalled the fingers of his right hand to flex and extend, making sure that they were ready for further orders. He repeated the action with the left fingers and hand, forcing himself to take note of the texture of the bow and arrow, all of this without perceptible movement. His right leg now screamed for relief but the strain would soon be over and he could attend to his personal comfort.

The buck moved again, advancing but still at not more than a walk. York sensed restlessness in the buck that he could not explain. There was no wind but the deer acted as if there was something on the air. In the distance a squirrel chattered angrily.

York blinked through the pain in his right leg knowing that he had several minutes before it would endanger his perch in the tree. To move now would ruin the hunt, but he felt rushed by the palpable agitation so obvious in the buck.

The buck flared his nostrils again. The first stirrings of fight or flight were apparent to York. The buck searched for any visual danger then again exercised his nose. He stamped his left forefoot, as if daring the unknown danger to declare itself so that it could be recognised.

York tensed his left forearm, activating the muscles so long immobilised. He willed the buck to take two more steps, just two more. The bow swivelled in his left hand and the arrow began to line up from the buck to York's shoulder. The right hand inched upward in anticipation of fingering the arrow and bowstring. He was above the field of vision of the buck. In seconds the shot would be his.

The buck leapt to his right and backwards and the white flag sprang into sight. A stirring of the dawn breeze had apparently filled in some critical detail for the animal, and he left the killing zone like a coiled spring suddenly released. The buck did not saunter when he smelled danger, he ran. Several short sharp steps to gain some room, a half dozen bounds in a different direction, staccato turns amongst the firs and he was gone. A single flash of a white tail was the last goodbye.

York was stunned. What had he done wrong? He knew that he had not been seen. He knew that he had not been heard. He could have been smelled but that was unlikely since he was twenty feet above the ground and his scent should have carried well away before reaching ground level. He could feel the dawn breeze on his cheek. Perhaps the vagaries of air movement had betrayed him. Maybe he should have been higher and maybe should have been less clean.

Suddenly, with a chill running down his spine, he understood what had happened. At first there was just a suspicion of rotting onion, and then the full pungent and sour odour engulfed his nose. Anyone who had smelled it once would recognise it again. Armed with a traditional bow and three small shafts, he sat alone in the tree as the air became ripe with bear.

The bear was a fully mature male that from above looked like a plodding ebony sedan. This was not the smaller sow or the two yearling cubs that York knew were in the area. This was an outsider, a magnificent animal but also a fearsome animal.

York disliked bears. As a youngster, while hunting with his father, they had startled one. The bear reared, bellowed, and then rushed them. York ran to the nearest tree and started to climb. The crack of his father's rifle forced his gaze back to the bear, and to his father standing over it.

Later that day York's father spent hours teaching York about the species, how to live with them and, when needed, how to kill them. "Never try to outrun or outclimb a bear," he had cautioned. "They have four feet and you have only two. They are designed to run and climb, designed much better than you for those tasks. If you have to resort to running and climbing then you are dead."

York still had the rifle that had killed that bear, a .45-70 calibre that chambered a shell the size of your thumb. Today it was locked up at his cabin.

His right leg agonised for release as he stared directly below him. The massive black bear standing there had spooked the deer into the deep woods. Because of the bear, York would not have venison hanging in the woodshed tonight.

He watched the beast snort, sniff the air loudly, and then lumber toward York's tree. Reaching the base of the tree it used its coarse aged bark for a back scratcher. The tree, despite its maturity and size, shuddered and swayed and he had to hold on to avoid being thrown to the ground.

His right leg was now silent and that concerned him more than the pain. Asleep, it would be practically useless if he had to flee. Three small arrows were all that stood between him and that monster.

The bear seemed satisfied that its itchiness was quelled. It moved away from the tree but immediately sniffed the air again, throwing its head from side to side. York watched it advance into the killing zone then stop beside the buck's scrape. With lips curled back, it snuffed and snorted then reared up onto its back legs and pawed the air with its huge front paws. The bear then thundered a roar that reverberated through the forest.

York used the bear's racket as an opportunity to move, an opportunity to change his position and relieve the strain on his deadened right leg. As the blood began to flow again into his calf and foot, the agony swept over him and he grabbed for the trunk of the tree.

In his new position he was now dangerously unbalanced but at least with each passing second he became less helpless if the bear should notice him. He toyed with the idea of shooting an arrow at the bear while it was in the killing zone. The bear might not even know where its attacker lurked. He could get off three shots in five seconds if he had to, a bit longer with more exact aiming. Maybe he would get lucky.

Lucky, he thought. Lucky doesn't even enter the equation. He was not hunting the bear. He did not need its coat or its meat. And with the weapons that he had in his hands, he was vastly outclassed. Those huge paws and butcher-knife claws overshadowed his arrows. If he could remain undetected then the confrontation was unnecessary and the bear would move on. He would likely never see the bear again.

Then he watched the bear depart as quickly as it had arrived. Not the elegant flight of the buck; the bear bulldozed directly through the fir thicket and was gone. Its crashing and thrashing lingered and then faded out of earshot.

During this time York massaged his right leg back into shape. "Some morning," he said aloud. "All I wanted was meat for the winter. I end up with nothing and I could've gotten myself killed in the meantime." Then as an afterthought, "Who would care? The world could explode tomorrow and who would think of me?"

York climbed down from the tree. His quiver and bow dangled from the thong at his belt. As his toes touched ground, he instantly recovered his bow, nocked an arrow and stood silently looking, listening, and smelling. The odour of bear still lingered but only the gentle breeze disturbed the forest.

Satisfied that he was alone, York worked his way westward toward the wood line a couple of hundred metres distant. Although he knew the route like a city dweller knows the sidewalk leading to his house, he took note of the occasional fluorescent tape fragments that he had arranged partially concealed along the route. He had placed the markers so that they did not reveal the path but rather provided reminders at key locations. His tree stand location was well scouted and very effective during the bow-hunting season and he did not want to betray its position to prying eyes or to some trespasser stumbling through his woods.

As York approached the edge of the wood line he halted well back inside the cover of the trees and scanned the open field, forcing his eyes to move from right to left. Since he had joined the army fourteen years ago this technique of searching ground had become second nature to him.

He could still hear his sniper instructor explaining that most languages were viewed left to right and the brain learned to skip over things, filling in blanks and making assumptions while reading. The same routine occurs with looking. The eyes and brain also filled in things and skipped over details when searching ground. He knew that if he wanted to see absolutely everything that he had to scan in just the opposite direction, from right to left. He had to force his eyes to see, and the brain to acknowledge, every facet of the scene in front of him. For many years his life had depended on it.

Perhaps my life doesn't depend on it in this situation, he thought, but the old military habits died hard. Those habits were part of what made him self-sufficient, allowed him to manage on his own. All that he wanted in this life, he told himself again, was to be left alone.

After he completed the scan of the field, he then concentrated on the woods bordering the open area. No movement. No unusual shape or shine. He checked the field on the hillside past the opposite woods. Satisfied that all was as it should be in front of and alongside of him, he once more glanced to the rear then set off directly across the field. When he reached the far side he swung to the right and along the edge of the forest.

As he approached the crest of the hill, and the building came into view, he eased into the woods and carefully scrutinised his cabin, his oasis. A wisp of white smoke curled from the chimney. All was quiet.

He strode quickly through the orchard and alongside the vegetable garden, feeling a momentary pang as he passed the half dozen sunflowers that had sprung up uninvited along the western row. Victoria had always planted flowers amongst the vegetables and she had adored sunflowers. It had always seemed a little inefficient to York, but it gave her so much joy that he had never teased her about it. When he planted the garden this year he had not planted sunflowers. Neither had he planted them the previous two years but they always seemed to spring out to taunt him.

As he started around the corner of the cabin he heard a footstep grate on the front porch. Hackles raised, he nocked an arrow and swung around to the front of the building. A young man in a black suit and tie paused on the front porch. No one else was in sight.

"What are you doing here?" York snarled.

The man-in-black jerked around, dropping the handful of papers that he had carried. "Ooh! I'm sorry, I... I... I...," he spluttered.

"You still haven't answered my question. What are you doing snooping around my cabin?" York hurled words back at him, as he advanced toward the man.

"I'm, I'm from the Church of Jesus Christ of Latter Day Saints," he managed to stammer out as York moved closer to the porch. "I'm here to tell you some good news and to bring you these readings." He pointed to the papers still scattered on the porch.

"Mormons!" York spat out the word. "I'm not interested in any proselytising. Who sent you here to find me? How did you know that I was here?"

"Nobody, Sir. I mean nobody told me that you were here, Sir. It's my duty to make contact with everybody in this area, and at the last house I noticed that the power lines kept going, so I followed them here."

York halted, lowered the bow, and scrutinized the man-in-black. The boy-in-black was probably closer to the facts, since he could not be more than seventeen. His shoes were dusty and well worn. His suit was pressed but threadbare in spots.

A little compassion forced its way to the surface. "The nearest house is over five miles down the road," York said.

"Yes, sir. I've been walking almost an hour and a half since the last house."

Five miles in an hour and a half. The lad was not lazy, that was for sure. "And the road goes no farther. You'll have another five miles back." He looked the young man straight in the eye.

"Yes, sir. Since I'm here, sir, may I talk to you about my calling?"

"No you may not," York parroted back. "I'm not interested." He paused when he saw the young man lick his dry lips. "Are you thirsty, son?"

"Yes, sir."

York stepped past him, opened the front door, and hung bow and quiver on the rack inside. Crossing to the sink by the front window he filled a mug with cold water. Walking back to the front door, he caught a glimpse of himself in the mirror on the wall. A chuckle escaped him. His face and hands were coloured green, black, and brown with camouflage paint. He must look to the young Mormon like something out of a horror film. He strode outside and thrust the mug toward the young man.

"I've no interest in your message, lad, but I'll not see you thirsty or hungry. Did you have breakfast this morning?"

"Yes, sir. I had toast and milk at about five o'clock." He drained the mug in two long swallows.

York glanced at the sun. He estimated the time as shortly before noon. The sun was already low in the southern sky, heralding the approach of winter.

"There are apple trees around back. There are still Cortlands for picking. Those are the redder ones. The Northern Spy are not ready yet, although if we get a good frost tonight they'll be pickable. They keep better if they've had a couple of good frosts on the tree."

York rebuked himself for being so conversational. "Pick some apples for yourself then come back for another drink of water, and then be on your way."

York went inside, grabbed some soap, then thought better of washing his face. Let the kid remember that he wanted to be left alone. He refilled the mug and went back outside.

"I have four, sir, if that's OK," the boy said as he came around the corner of the cabin. He held out two apples in each hand.

York passed him the mug again. The young man put the apples in his suit coat pockets, then drank the water, and started picking up the papers on the porch.

"Eat the apples slowly over a couple of hours," York instructed. "Less chance of a stomach ache. And forget you were ever here."

"Yes, sir, and God bless you."

York grunted and went into the house securing the door behind him. "Yeah, I'm really blessed," he muttered.

He went into his bedroom, stripped off his clothing and turned on the shower. He immediately stepped into the spray. It was well-water cold and he steeled himself to the shock before it gradually warmed. He scrubbed off the camouflage paint and the other accumulations since yesterday at this time. You did not go hunting freshly showered if you wanted to get close enough to get a bowshot. He brushed his close-cropped hair, and dressed in jeans and flannel shirt.

Unlike the stereotypical single man's bedroom, his was neat and tidy. The rose-decorated curtains seemed a little out of place amongst the other furnishings. The king size bed was natural for his burly six-foot frame. The hardwood floor was swept and polished. He went to the front door to retrieve his hunting gear. Protruding from the quiver was a small sheaf of papers.

I guess I underestimated his determination, York thought to himself. You have to admire someone who keeps his mind on the mission. He unrolled the papers, a series of tracts published by the Mormons. He tossed them on the counter to use later to start the fire in the wood stove. He locked his bow in the arms cabinet and then hung his jacket in the woodshed attached to the cabin. There the jacket would be free from the usual scents of man, scents that could cost him a buck tomorrow.

York switched on his small television. The Health Reporter was schmoozing with the anchorwoman about some new type of flu that could be a problem in the future. They were discussing flu shots and possible epidemics although it sounded as if they said the word wrong. Every year at this time the topic was the flu but he had never heard the word "pandemic" before.

CHAPTER 2

30 October

Two weeks later found York in the cold woodshed. The winter's wood, well aged, was meticulously stacked along the outer wall in the shed. This was a community where the cut of a man's woodpile meant more than the cut of his suit, and York's woodpile was solid and self-supporting. But he would have laughed derisively if anybody suggested that he cared what others thought about him, or his stack of maple and beech.

York wielded his belt knife with confidence, skinning the buck that had hung in the shed for the last six days. With the meat in the freezer and the garden harvest canned or frozen, he would have the basics for a comfortable winter.

"Damn it," he cursed as he felt the outside edge of his hand sliced by a shard of bone. This had been a bow kill and there should have been no broken bones. The buck must have broken something as it fell. Just what he needed now. Winter would not wait for healing and he still had work to do.

When was my last tetanus shot? he thought. Discharge from the army was three years ago and his last shots had been quite a few years before that. He could sew up the wound himself. Special

Operations training included lots of unusual skills but getting the tetanus shot was another matter.

"Screw the army," he snarled, as he wiped off the belt knife and wrapped a clean cloth around his hand. He went into his cabin to wash his hands, and change into a clean shirt before travelling to the clinic.

He drove the year-old Jeep TJ out of the shed that he used as a garage and a wood shop. The soft-top was open on the sides. A quick glance at the sky confirmed that there would be no rain or snow today. He slipped the transmission through the gears, the wrapped right hand a minor inconvenience as he shifted. As he passed Shamus MacGregor's place, his closest neighbour was moving his small herd of Highland cattle into the fields next to the farmstead, closer to the barn as winter approached.

York fixed his gaze ahead, not glancing left or right until he had passed MacGregor's farm. Only then did he resume his careful examination of the terrain as he sped down the road. In the rear view mirror he could see his trail of dust, as wide as the road and ten feet high, as he sped along the dry gravel toward the main highway.

In fifteen minutes he was approaching the village of Spencer. The medical clinic on the edge of the built up area served the seven hundred occupants of the village as well as another three thousand in the catchment area. He passed the old Presbyterian church and the legion hall and then slowed for the fifty-kilometre speed zone.

The clinic parking lot was full as usual as he swung into the yard. He registered and took a seat in the corner, picking up a pamphlet in which to bury his head. He was more interested in avoiding conversation than he was in education. It was an information booklet about flu shots, encouraging the elderly and those with chronic disease to get annual immunisation.

"York," Doctor Simpson called from the edge of the waiting room after a few minutes. "Come on in. What did you do to yourself?" he asked as they walked to the procedure room.

"Deer bone cut my hand while I was skinning the carcass. I could sew it up myself but my last tetanus shot was probably nine years ago."

"You probably could sew it up yourself, and likely with quarter inch rope, and without freezing." The doctor grinned. "But why don't you let us finesse it a little?"

Doc Simpson had an easy going competent way about him that made illness or injury a little easier to bear. He always treated York with respect and kindness but also with an old-lost-friend sort of approach that made York uncomfortable. He had done nothing to encourage friendship.

Working as swiftly and competently as York had with the skinning knife, the doctor soon had the wound cleaned, closed and dressed.

"Doc, what's the story on these flu shots that I was reading about?"

"You are not in the high risk group, York, so it's not that important for you, although I think almost anyone can benefit. The shot is given in the fall after the laboratories have produced the serum for the most likely strains that year. Because the flu viruses change very quickly the shot is only good for one year."

"Yeah, I heard something about that on CNN last week. They were talking about an epidemic or something."

"Well, there's not a lot of flu in North America yet this year. It will start to appear about a month from now."

"They were talking about planning for a big one."

"Oh, I know what you were hearing, pandemic planning. There is a track record of major world-wide flu outbreaks three or four times every century." The doctor walked over to the sink in the corner and washed his hands. "The worst in the past century was in 1918. They called it the Spanish Flu. It caused over twenty million deaths world-wide; some say forty million and there are some who insist that the true number was one hundred million."

York gave a low whistle. "A hundred million? Even twenty million. Shit, Doc, that's almost the population of Canada."

The doctor rolled down his sleeves and slipped his watch back onto his left wrist. "We're overdue actually and many countries are trying to plan what to do when it happens."

"Won't they just give everybody flu shots?"

"There are two major problems. When a pandemic occurs it's because the virus has had a major change, not just the little changes that occur year to year. There is little or no immunity in the population as a whole. In addition it will take six months or more to start pumping out shots in any quantity." He turned to York. "Do you carry an immunisation record with you? There's nothing on your chart."

"No, it was with my military medical records but I know that it's been at least nine years for my tetanus shot and likely longer."

The doctor took a green card from a stack inside a cupboard, and then made some notes on the card and in the chart.

"Why so long to get flu shots, Doc?"

"There are no laboratories in Canada to produce serum. We get all our flu shots from the US or France. If I were a betting man, I'd bet there wouldn't be a lot of extra supply for us if we need it. Besides it takes a lot of time to make the serum, for technical reasons." He handed the green card to York.

"What's this?"

"That's an immunisation record. Keep it in your wallet so you know next time you're due for a tetanus booster."

"Doc, if there's no flu shots, aren't there antibiotics?"

"Antibiotics work for bacteria not viruses. There are a few antivirals but they are not that effective. They're expensive and they're not stocked in large amounts."

"But they are available?"

"In small quantities, yes." He walked to the door of the procedure room. "I'm going to ask Elizabeth to come in and give you the tetanus shot."

"Doc, I'd appreciate it if you'd give it yourself."

"I'm really busy, York. I know Elizabeth is your sister but this is just a shot in the arm, not your butt. And she's a good RN."

"Doc, if you can't do it yourself, then I'll have to drive to Georgetown to the clinic there."

Doctor Simpson pondered him and then shook his head. "OK, you asked for it. I give a terrible needle. It may be none of my business but..."

"You're right, Doc, it is none of your business. I appreciate you sewing me up but what's between my sister and me isn't part of it. So leave it there, please."

Doctor Simpson injected the deltoid muscle of York's left arm. "Fifteen minutes in the waiting room. Let me know if you have any reaction," he said, and left the room without looking back.

York waited as directed then left without a word. He felt guilty that he had treated Doc Simpson the way he had, then he shrugged it off. My business, he thought. I can manage this on my own.

York strode to the Jeep, slipped behind the wheel and churned up some gravel as he pulled out of the parking lot. He was in a big hurry to get back to his own turf. The mention of his sister had stirred up uncomfortable feelings that he did not wish to address; and immersing himself in his preparations for winter would help take his mind off of that.

Preoccupied as he was he almost rendered himself locally famous. One of the curves on Route 373 was banked in the wrong direction and there was no warning sign. "Everyone knows that you have to be careful there," he was told. The corner was locally named in honour of the last person to go off the road there. It was presently Coburn Curve or some such thing; named after the postal driver who had graced the ditch last winter during a snowstorm. York eased off the gas in time to avoid mishap. He had no wish to call attention to himself in such a manner.

He parked the jeep and headed back to the woodshed. He finished skinning the deer but his hand throbbed and he gladly left the completed carcass hanging. He would finish butchering it tomorrow. He headed for the garden to dig some parsnips and turnips, and carried a half-bushel basket of vegetables into the woodshed.

Back inside the cabin he lit a fire in the woodstove, using paper and kindling from the large crock on the floor. He found himself holding one of the tracts that the boy-in-black had left earlier. "Preparing and Storing Food," its title read. Odd topic for a religious pusher, thought York. He skimmed over the information, then tossed it back into the crock, and put water to boil on the wood stove to make a coffee.

Hot mug in hand he sat down at the computer and started a

Google search for Influenza, 1918, and several other related topics. It was six hours later when he stretched himself erect and left the screen to put together a simple supper.

York was very disturbed by what he had found on the computer. He was a man accustomed to planning: planning his day's work, planning his garden, planning for emergencies. But this type of flu outbreak appeared to be a problem almost beyond any preparation. He was staggered by the magnitude of the problem. In some countries of the world the death toll had been as high as twenty-five percent. How would you deal with one in four people dead?

The computer seduced him back that evening. He spent another four hours surfing the influenza topic and then endured a restless sleep peppered with apocalyptic dreams.

The next morning York was up early but not refreshed. His right hand hurt and he had been chased all night long by faceless figures spreading diseases. Part of the time he was in his own cabin but part of the time he was back in Afghanistan. He bathed and dressed his wound. No sign of any infection. He lit a fire in the woodstove to drive away the chill. As he did, his gaze fell again on the tract that he had tossed among the fire lighting materials.

He dug out the paper and sat down at the computer again. He typed in the URL on the tract and started to search. What he found should not have surprised him, as he knew that survivalists all over North America stockpiled freeze dried foods and military surplus equipment. But here was a large religious organisation, a church, which recommended a one-year supply of food and essentials for everyone. This philosophy was no doubt born in the turbulent and persecutory beginnings of this group but seemed out of place in the land of plenty.

The recommendations he found were not for freeze-dried sirloin and Crème Brulé like he had seen before on the survivalist websites. The Mormon recommendations were for staples of grains and lentils and other basic foods. The site also included links to other web sites where these items were available. Other links were to venues for hand cranked grain grinders, water purifiers, and high nutrition supplements.

York bookmarked a few web pages, shut down the computer,

had breakfast, and was in his garden before the sun came over the tree line. It was 31 October and last night's frost had killed the sunflowers and finished off the foliage on the root vegetables. He found peace walking in his garden. Providing for himself and not having to rely on others was his greatest satisfaction in life. The root vegetables needed to be covered with a thick layer of mulch so that they could be dug up all winter. Some of his earlier harvest was stored in his freezer and some was processed and canned. "I'd make a good farm wife in my grandmother's time," he chuckled to himself.

He set a ladder into a tree and picked the last of the Northern Spy apples. All the time that he was working, his mind churned through the details of the flu pandemic that he had researched. As his hands flew, his mind translated the evidence from the past into the reality of today.

It was chilling to consider attack rates of thirty to fifty percent and mortality rates of up to twenty five percent. Twenty five percent! That would be seven or eight million dead in Canada alone. Surely they would take care of it since the events of the past were so well known. But "they" had not taken care of things when he was captured in Afghanistan. No, if there were going to be preparations then he must look after that himself.

He stored the apples in the woodshed and headed for the computer. Was he being crazy? Maybe he had been living alone for too long. I wish that I had you here to talk this over with, Dad, he thought. You always had the common sense approach.

What would others say if they thought that he was worrying about an influenza pandemic? That sealed it. Who cares what others think? He would move away from the rest of the pack and would make preparations while the others were acting like so many lemmings.

York headed to a website that he had bookmarked earlier, a Canadian site to avoid border and customs hassles. He ordered a year's supply of basic foodstuffs for one person then after a pause changed it to two people, and then because of discounts for bulk buying, he changed it to three people. The supplies had a shelf life of five to seven years and he would learn to use the products so they would not go to waste. At another site he ordered a grinder, water purifier and replacement purifier cartridges, and a crank powered radio and battery charger. All of these things had delivery time of two to four weeks so he might as well get things rolling. Concurrent activity was the efficient way to get things done. He could continue planning while these things were in the pipeline. Besides, it would likely never happen, and certainly not this year.

* * *

Ten days later he was back at the clinic to have his wound checked and have sutures removed. He at least owed it to Doc Simpson to comply with his follow up instructions. It was 6:30 PM and he was the last to be seen that day.

The doctor examined the area carefully and, satisfied with healing, removed the sutures.

"York, it obviously upset you last time you were here when I mentioned your sister. If there is anything that I can do to help I would be very willing. Sometimes just talking about things can make it a little easier."

"Look, Doc…" York forced himself not to lash out at the physician. "I know it's part of your job and I know that you're just trying to help, but I don't want to talk about it."

"Well I do," announced Elizabeth emerging from around the corner. "And before you accuse the doctor of setting you up, he thought that I was gone. When I saw your name on the list for today I hung around in the staff room so that I could see you."

"Well I have nothing to say, Elizabeth, so just drop it."

"No, I won't drop it. You are my brother and you're worth the trouble to me. Now I'm sorry that I sold your house but we all thought that you had died in Afghanistan. We even had a death certificate."

"You had a death certificate?" Doc Simpson stared wide-eyed at Elizabeth.

Before York could object she sped on. "He was in the Army, Special Forces. He was captured at an ambush in Afghanistan. He was held by a bunch of Taliban that escaped to Pakistan. They kept him prisoner for almost two years. Heaven knows why they didn't just kill him. It certainly wasn't his shiny disposition that kept him alive."

York snorted.

"York won't talk about his ordeal. As I understand it from our other brother, York escaped one night. He killed six people on the way out, spent two weeks in the wilderness with nothing but a knife, made his way back to allied forces, and managed to convince them that he was who he said he was."

"Yeah, that was the hardest part," York growled. "But it was nothing compared to coming home. I almost wish that I hadn't."

Doc Simpson swivelled his head from one to the other as if watching a tennis match. York saw him start to speak but Elizabeth silenced him.

"Because everybody thought that he was dead, had proof that he was dead, we all moved on with our lives." She glanced at York then appeared to steel herself. "His fiancée Ashley was devastated, as we all were, and we kind of all rallied around. One thing led to another and almost two years later his fiancée married our brother Russell; a month before we got word that York was alive."

Doc Simpson made a sympathetic sound and looked at York. York resented the pity that was so obvious in his eyes.

"Go on, Sis," York hissed. "You've started so you might as well finish. Tell him what you did to welcome me home. Tell him what you did to my house."

"I was the executor of York's will. None of us wanted the old house. Mom and Dad had been gone five years. York lived there, but there was nothing there for the rest of us except bad memories. So I sold it. It's the big Victorian-looking house above Shamus MacGregor's place out on The Old Connector Road, the gravel road that turns off a few miles before your lane."

"I still live at the end of that road," York interjected. "I get the pleasure of driving by the house every time I go anywhere. She sold it two weeks before I came home."

"You know I didn't do it on purpose, York." Elizabeth stamped her foot. "We thought you were dead."

"Couldn't the sale be cancelled or reversed, for heaven's sake?" asked the doctor. "After all he was away fighting for the country."

"Don't think I didn't try from the moment that I heard he was alive, and before York even got home. I even tried to talk to the president of the company that bought it. What I got for my trouble was a cease and desist order. I was threatened with charges of harassment by the company lawyer if I didn't stop my attempts."

"Did you try when you got home, York?" asked Doc Simpson.

"No, I just rolled over and played dead," York scoffed. "Of course I tried, but what my sister had wrought, no man could put asunder."

"So you blame your sister for this?"

"Yeah, and I blame life. I blame relying on other people. I blame volunteering. I blame helping other people. I've learned my lesson and now I rely on myself alone."

"What about your brother? Do you get along with him?" Doc Simpson stopped as Elizabeth gave him a frantic glance.

"Oh I get along with him really well. First he steals my fiancée then he gets me court martialled."

"York, that's not true!" Elizabeth shouted. "He didn't steal her and it was that Colonel that court martialled you because you were insubordinate to Russell in front of him and the other soldiers. You had to take your anger to work, and there are still some things that the Army won't tolerate, even from its heroes."

"Yeah, well screw the asshole colonel, and screw Russell. Doc, have you had enough of this for now 'cause I'd like to go home."

"I understand, York. I thought that I'd heard it all in twenty years of practising medicine, but this is too bizarre. I'm sorry that those things happened to you. If there is anything that I can do to help then give me a call, anytime."

"Yeah, well I'll keep that in mind, Doc. I'll leave now so the two of you can talk some more about me."

York grabbed his windbreaker and stalked out of the clinic. It was very cold outside and there was a skiff of snow in the air.

CHAPTER 3

3 November

A few days later, York stepped outside the cabin to look at the weather. Snow had begun as a few tiny flakes, perfectly formed, falling, then clinging to any cold surface. The filigree of each of the points acted as barbs on a hook, securing the flakes to his jacket sleeve. York had a momentary impulse to try to catch a flake on his tongue then dismissed it as frivolous. The individual flakes turned into a flurry, quickly covering the stain of muddy tracks that criss-crossed his driveway. The flurry softened the hard edges of the cabin and the white birches that stood along the lane.

He walked to the south side of the cabin and gazed into the distance. The snow already obscured the most distant ridgeline a full twenty kilometres away; and the evergreens at the far end of his south field were now indistinct. The garden mulch was fading from straw yellow to white as more accumulated. He watched as a single blue jay pecked at a tiny apple at the top of the nearest Northern Spy tree. A slight breeze swirled the snow and, as if disturbed from its leisure, the snow intensified. The individual flakes were now lost in the steady snowfall. The distant evergreens were almost vaporous, and York turned back toward the front of the cabin, leaving the solitary blue jay to its work.

He closed the large doors of the detached shed on the western side of the cabin. He puttered around inside for a few minutes topping up the anti-freeze fluids in the Jeep and laying out shovels by the door. He secured a shovel and a set of corrugated traction strips to tie-down points on the floor of the Jeep. Becoming mired in snow could be the first step to disaster and York had no wish to die for want of a tow truck.

York left the shed carrying two dozen four-foot stakes with reflector tape on them. The snow had become heavy and steady. He worked his way down the lane to the north, setting the stakes into the ground at key locations so Shamus MacGregor could clear snow from the driveway without becoming stuck in the ditch. By the time he reached the bottom of the hill, the temperature had begun to drop noticeably. He blew on his hands to warm them then started the long walk back up the slope. Despite the dropping temperature the snow intensified again. He could not see the crest of the hill, and the increasing wind was chill. There was a bit of ice in the snow and it stung the right side of his face.

By the time he reached the cabin there were almost five centimetres of snow on the ground and it was apparent that this was to be the first of many major storms this winter. York went inside, lit the fireplace in the gathering room, and set about rounding up the items for his winter survival kit to be loaded in the Jeep. Everything went into a rucsac that he had retained when he left the army. He packed extra clothing and survival candles, flashlight, glow sticks, survival rations, a belt knife and matches in a waterproof case. He then carefully buried his compass in the side pocket, cushioned in a thick pair of socks.

He looked out the kitchen window when he heard the wind rattling against the north side of the house. Lots of heat loss tonight, he thought. He spent the rest of the day reading and listening to music and went to bed early.

He awoke several times in the night as the snowstorm mutated into a full-blown blizzard. The wind raged at the cabin. The power went out. He was no doubt isolated by the snow and the wind and the cold. This held no fear for him, but pity help any poor soul caught out on a night like this.

* * *

He heard a banging outside the cabin and he crawled out of bed. The first light of day was cutting the blackness of night and he could see movement at the shed. There was no power for the outside lights but the door to the shed appeared to be thrashing against the wall, likely unhooked by the wind. He slipped into outdoor gear and headed out to fix the problem. The snow at the front of the cabin was drifted a metre deep and he waded to the shed as if struggling upstream against a current.

The door had not unhinged but the latch was broken. He pulled the door closed and lashed it in position using cordage hanging inside the shed. He selected a small snow scoop and went back out into the storm and cleared snow from the front door and the woodshed door. Clear exits were important for safety. He did not want to find himself trapped inside in case of fire. The wind was abating as he finished his labour and went back inside the cabin.

He fired up the woodstove, made coffee and breakfast, and then went back outside to clear the snow away from the shed doors. He would want to get the Jeep out later. A trip to town would provide a replacement for the broken latch.

The snow was falling in huge flakes now, a sure sign that it was coming to an end. "Big flakes, little snow," he said aloud, and then walked to the back of the cabin and the spectacular view. The sun was just starting to break through the clouds in the east. The trees were laden with snow and everything was pristine and white. The storm was typical for this part of the country, lots of snow and wind but a threat only to those who were unprepared. A small gust of wind swirled the big flakes around him and he found himself in the centre of a snow globe that some giant child had just shaken and then set on its feet.

He went back inside and found that the power had returned. About an hour later Shamus appeared at the top of the hill mounted on his faded red Belarus tractor. The farmer cleared the snow from the driveway area and then headed down the hill again, blowing snow as he went.

York went to get the Jeep. The temperature had risen above freezing, and snowmelt was dripping off the roof. He grabbed his survival kit from the cabin and tossed it in the back of the Jeep. As he pulled out of the shed, shifting into four wheel drive, he had a momentary pang that he had no one to share the moment with, nobody to tell how great he felt on a day like this.

After he had replaced the door latch, he would continue his preparations for the flu, the flu that would never happen.

* * *

Three weeks later, on a trip to Fredericton, York left the FedEx office with a Jeep crammed to the roof with supplies. He had no wish to encourage delivery vehicles at his cabin and had therefore arranged for his order to be available for pick up at the depot. He also had no wish to telegraph to the world that he had large supplies of food at his house. The supplies came in thirty-plus cardboard cartons, each containing several industrial size food cans.

"Don't want to forget a can opener." He grimaced as he spoke aloud the caution he had seen on the website.

He wheeled through the city, crossed the bridge and headed north into wooded, hilly countryside heading back home toward Spencer. The terrain was covered mainly by mixed evergreen and deciduous forest and punctuated occasionally by a hayfield and farm buildings. He loved the feel of the countryside. The whole area was criss-crossed by small streams in deep gullies, and from the road he could see narrow trails leading into logging areas, gravel pits, or hunting camps.

York enjoyed the country and he felt more comfortable in the woods than he did in a crowded city. After an hour's drive he swung onto the Old Connector Road. There was a mixture of mud and snow where the plow had cleared away last night's snowfall. It was a month before Christmas.

If his first name had been Ebeneezer he would have shouted,

"Humbug!" at the thought of Christmas. Instead he snorted indifferently, and slowed to avoid a snowshoe hare that threatened to bolt in front of the vehicle.

Because of his preoccupation with the rabbit he was not paying attention as closely as usual, and his gaze fell on the old Victorian house on the hillside to his front left. His house; the house that had been sold out from under him. He always looked anywhere but on that hillside as he drove this stretch of road. For a few seconds he held that gaze then slammed his eyes to the front and focused on the road ahead. Only as he turned into his lane did he relax his death grip on the wheel.

He met Shamus MacGregor halfway up the hill. Shamus was using the snow blower attached to his tractor to clear York's lane again. York backed down the hill and loitered at the bottom. As MacGregor finished the task York slid out of the Jeep and went over to the tractor, fishing some bills from his wallet.

"Thanks, Shamus. Here's for this time and next time as well, in case I miss you."

"Thanks, laddie." He pocketed the money. "Have you seen a beat up white pickup around?"

"No, I haven't," said York. "Why?"

"Some break ins over on the Oak Ridge Road. Some people think that there was a white pickup around that didn't belong in the area. I'm suspicious of who it is. One of the local drug dealers has just been let out on parole. He used to drive a white pickup, and he and his buddies are bad business."

"I'll keep my eyes open. Thanks again for plowing me out." York stopped halfway back to the Jeep and returned to the tractor. "Shamus, I've been reading a lot of stuff about a possible flu epidemic. If you're interested, I'll give you the information."

"The flu is it, Laddie? I don't think it's a big priority for me. I've got a sick heifer and one of my windmills is acting up. I'll leave the flu for another year."

"OK, just thought I'd ask." York ambled back to the jeep.

He drove up the lane and pulled into the shed, and then he unloaded the Jeep and spread his cargo onto the kitchen counters and table.

York took stock of everything that he had, made a note of other things that he thought would be useful, and then carried the supplies back out to the Jeep. After assuring himself that he was not being watched, he drove down into the field toward the entry trail to his tree stand. He carried on past that trail into the low ground beyond and drove in behind a trio of bull spruce trees, large evergreen trees with branches extending all the way to the ground.

Only when you were behind these trees could you see the other narrow trail that led into the woods. The trees shielded his actions from view. He did not want to leave any tire tracks that might attract curious eyes down the trail, so he hand-carried load after load the kilometre and a half into the woods to the rundown shack that he alone knew existed.

It had been a sugar shack in years gone by and he and his fiancée Ashley had made plans to revive it for the same purpose. They had planned to buy a new evaporator to replace the old stove that stood in the middle of the shack. The plan was to harvest maple syrup and sugar from the huge stand of rock maples that surrounded it.

Five years ago he had cut an immense pile of wood and banked it against the walls in preparation for the following spring and sugaring-off. Then his routine of Special Forces training had come to an end as the Afghan conflict had emerged. He went to war, and the training became operations for real.

He returned to find his life changed forever. The empty piece of land, that he previously saw as a forestry and maple sugar site, had now become his home. He built the cabin where he now lived. With Ashley married to his brother Russell, there was nobody to share in the fun of sugaring. He had covered the firewood stacked around the shack, to protect it from the elements. It would have been sinful in his eyes to allow it to rot and waste.

His new girlfriend Victoria made it plain that she had no interest in making sugar. York found that one sugaring season led to another, with no trees tapped and no sap boiled. Maybe he would make a little sugar this spring.

He stacked the food in the rafters as far from prying eyes as possible. He would have other trips to make here if this were to be his fall-back position. For a moment he wondered if these were the first signs of paranoia.

As he wheeled the Jeep out from behind the evergreens, he could see the old Victorian house on the far hillside to the west; the house that had been his parents' and then his. He quickly rescanned the area to see if he was in any danger of being seen. Taking a different route through the field he returned from the shack to his cabin. No track discipline required here. He was not worried about somebody detecting his presence in the field. His concern was that somebody would detect a well-worn route to the shack.

* * *

York continued his preparations for winter. He ordered more foodstuffs with long shelf life, adding canned cheese and some spices for variety. He picked up shipments at FedEx and some at the post office. He put a water purifier and grinder and some basic kitchen utensils and tools in the sugar shack. He packed metal items with desiccant and wrapped them in plastic.

He took his father's rifle out of the arms cabinet, along with several boxes of cartridges. He packed them in grease, wrapped them in oilcloth and buried them carefully in the dirt in front of the stove in the sugar shack. Now he knew he was paranoid, but he also didn't want to get arrested for improper storage of firearms. Better totally undetectable even if it meant not immediately available.

He bought some multivitamins and made an appointment to see Doctor Simpson.

"Hi, York. Good to see you again."

"Hi, Doc. Look, I'm sorry if I was kind of short at that last visit. It's been a tough time for me. There was no reason for me to be that way with you. You've never caused me any grief."

"I understand. You know it's kind of hard on your sister too."

"Well, we can talk about that later. I came to ask for help with a medical kit."

"What kind of medical kit?"

"You will probably think this is stupid but hear me out before you say no. You know that I spend most of my time alone and I would like to have some medicines as well as some dressings and equipment that I can use if I have to. Also I've been thinking about that flu pandemic that you told me about; and I believe in being prepared."

Doctor Simpson frowned. "York, using medications is not like a cookbook and they can be dangerous if used for the wrong problems. In addition, although I believe in preparedness, hoarding medication is not the way to prepare. If everybody hoarded medication there would be nothing for those who need it."

"I've thought of that, Doc. I would never treat myself if I could get to you. This is a 'just in case'. And think about the medication this way. You told me that the antiviral medicine was seldom prescribed so there was not that much made. If I buy some now, that means that more will be put into the pipeline now. If it's ever needed, then I'll be one less person you'll have to find the medicine for. It's different than hoarding if you plan far enough ahead."

Doctor Simpson looked pensive for a moment. "York, those medications have a short shelf life, only a year or so. You'd be wasting your money."

"Doc, I don't have much to spend my money on anyway. I'm willing to pay that as an insurance premium."

"OK, let's talk about what you would need in an emergency."

* * *

The next day York went to the Pharmacy in Fredericton and purchased the supplies. He told the inquisitive pharmacist that it was for a logging camp and he was just picking up the supplies for the doctor. "We don't see much demand for these," said the pharmacist as he placed the Tamiflu antiviral in the bag.

CHAPTER 4

24 December

The first real mention of an epidemic was early on Christmas Eve. The news broadcast reported widespread outbreaks of a flu-like illness across North America. High fever, pain, and a deadly pneumonia wracked the victims. That broadcast was amended later in the day to include similar situations in some of the major cities in Europe.

York stayed in his cabin that day. He received a call from Doctor Simpson inviting him for Christmas dinner the following evening. When he mentioned that Elizabeth would be there as well, York quickly declined. After a brief exchange York told him that he would drop off a couple of deer steaks for him at the office next week, then said goodbye.

The winter was a good time for York. He had his wall of books, the computer for Internet surfing and a beautiful view to the south out of his cabin windows. He considered it a time of rest. No wood to cut, no garden to plant or tend, no unwanted visitors. He thought briefly of the Mormon lad from earlier in the fall.

The snow began to softly fall outside the window.

* * *

Two days later the news deteriorated. There were deaths from the flu in Hong Kong. The Chinese government appeared to be trying to suppress information from the interior of the country but it didn't have quite as good control on the media in the former British colony. Business telexes, email, and faxes reported widespread illness in Hong Kong and also throughout China. This was echoed from news reports from the more open societies of Japan and South Korea.

Europe reported widespread influenza and the Centres for Disease Control in the United States was trying to determine if the strain was part of the expected annual influenza, the strains that the flu shots this year were designed for.

The CBC National News reported hospitals in major cities inundated with patients suffering from the flu. Emergency rooms were jammed with acutely ill patients. One hospital in Toronto reported that the waiting time to be seen in its emergency room was about twenty hours. Hospital wards were full. Almost every bed was occupied by a patient with chronic disease, suddenly made worse by contracting the flu. Patients with cardiac problems, asthma, and other lung diseases appeared to be the worst hit; but a surprisingly high number of young, otherwise healthy people were thronging to the emergency departments.

A government spokesman proclaimed that the long delays and hospital overcrowding were because of the holiday season and that the situation would stabilise as the doctors and other health care workers returned to work after the Christmas break.

York gave a mirthless chuckle as he listened to the radio. "And what if the doctors and nurses have the flu?" he said aloud. "Does this guy think we're morons?"

* * *

As each day passed the influenza news became more of a headline. On New Year's Day there was almost no news except the flu.

On CNN the familiar format was missing. A few of the usual faces were still there but the presentation was a single anchor at a time reading the news reports. There were no splashy correspondent interviews from around the world, only a couple of stock video shots of hospitals in Atlanta showing lines of people outside the emergency departments.

Major population centres across the world were badly hit with tens of thousands falling ill each day. The cities of Europe had the most accurate figures. Paris reported over one thousand deaths today; Rome at least four hundred. London's report was most shocking to York. There had been more deaths in that city on this single day than had occurred on the worst day of bombing during the Blitz of World War II.

A mid-air collision had occurred at Chicago O'Hare airport, apparently because the local air traffic control centre had been left only partially staffed because of sudden illness. The CNN anchor finished the 6PM broadcast by reading a list of their personnel that had died from the flu. It was a long list.

York's local radio station carried announcements of cancellations as well as businesses that were closed. The mayor of Fredericton requested people to stay away from crowded locations. Theatres were closed. A message from the Department of Public Health gave instructions for treating the flu and also advice to stay away from the Emergency Room unless absolutely necessary.

The Canadian Broadcasting Corporation internet website advised that all aircraft were grounded in Canada with the exception of emergency flights controlled at national government level.

* * *

The following day, as the news got worse in the media reports, York called the clinic in Spencer. The line was busy but when he got through the receptionist said that there were only a couple of people sick in the area. They were hoping that this would stay confined to the big cities.

* * *

On the 3rd of January CNN reported that the President of the

United States had ordered a state of emergency and that all US military units were mobilised to protect the country in case of enemy attack while the outbreak lasted. The Secretary of State denied reports that this was a bioterrorism attack but said the FBI continued to investigate.

Local CBC Radio reported sporadic outbreaks of the flu in New Brunswick and in the other Maritime Provinces. In Canada there was a widespread influenza outbreak but mainly in the cities. For the first time in weeks, however, York heard the word again. The radio announcer used the word "pandemic".

York watched with fascination as the situation around the world deteriorated. A breaking news story on CNN reported that a Nippon Airlines 747 was in the skies near Seattle, Washington and was denied permission to land. A passenger calling on a sky phone had told CNN that it had flown from Tokyo carrying 300 passengers who paid 20,000 dollars each. The passengers were Americans trying to escape the flu in the Far East. The airliner was refused entry to American airspace, threatened with being shot down by intercepting F-15s. An unidentified source at the Pentagon had apparently stated that "they had no proof that there were Americans on board, and the aircraft was likely full of flu-infested foreigners."

Transit systems in New York, Los Angeles, Boston, Washington, Toronto and Vancouver were in shambles. These cities, the hardest hit in North America, were the hubs for international flights. Hundreds of transit employees were ill. Thousands more refused to report to work for fear of getting infected with the flu. Buses, trains, and subways ground to a halt. Some were abandoned half way through their routes as staff left their posts as close to their own homes as possible.

Taxis were non-existent on the streets of big cities. Some cars, driven by toughs wearing surgical masks, were available to carry passengers for exorbitant amounts.

Three fires burned out of control in Los Angeles because there were not enough fire fighters to fight them all simultaneously. Police and fire departments reported that illness was rampant amongst their members but thankfully criminal activity was equally decreased.

A follow up report on the Nippon Airways 747 was that the

aircraft had been diverted to Vancouver international Airport. A controller there had heard the calls from the jumbo jet and had given it instructions to land at Vancouver. The passengers were still on the airplane under armed guard while quarantine was being arranged.

Well at least they didn't get hung out to dry like some of us did, thought York.

* * *

The next day, the radio station transmitted flu-related emergency instructions almost continuously. Reception centres were being set up to handle influenza patients that could not be cared for at home. There were few patients in the Fredericton area so far but these measures were being implemented to handle the outbreak if it occurred.

"Oh sure," said York aloud. "I've heard this before. There's no attack expected but fix bayonets anyway. Oh by the way, what's that sound coming over the hill?"

* * *

The following day York had a call from the FedEx office in Fredericton advising him that there were some boxes for him. They had been there for two days but they were short handed at the depot and had not been able to process them. The office was closing at 5pm indefinitely the caller said. Airline grounding and possible upcoming restrictions on movement had put them out of business.

The weather forecast was for heavy snow but York could see there was nothing in the air as yet. The sky had that blue grey appearance that promised something memorable to follow. He tossed a couple of deer steaks into a cooler. I'll drop these off to the Doc on the way back, he thought.

The roads were clear as he wheeled the Jeep down the highway. There had been no snow since the early storm in November. He turned on the radio. No music, and he had heard enough about the flu for now so he slipped a disc in the CD player. Halfway to Fredericton, as he came over a hill, he saw the flashing lights and stood on the brake pedal. He checked the speedometer. Not much over the limit. His speed was not the concern of the police on this occasion. A van was off the road and a tow truck was pulling it out. He stopped beside the Mountie as directed.

"It's going to be a couple of minutes, Sir, just until the tow truck gets clear."

"What happened?" asked York.

"Don't know. Heart attack maybe. The roads are good and the car wasn't really damaged a lot. More like it just ran off the road and stopped. The driver was dead. Kind of young for a heart attack though."

York switched off the CD and switched the radio back on. When the truck was finished he followed it down the road toward Fredericton. Two ambulances passed him going into the city. He noticed that one of them was the ambulance based in Spencer.

Traffic was light in Fredericton although there seemed to be lots of activity around the SuperFood store. He could see that there wasn't a parking spot in that lot, and people were lined up at the entrance to the store.

He went first to the FedEx depot. No waiting lines here but no help either to carry the small heavy parcels to the Jeep.

"What's in there, rocks?" asked the clerk.

"Metal parts," York replied as he signed the manifest.

He carried the last one to the Jeep, set it on the passenger seat and drove the vehicle to the end of the parking lot where he would not be disturbed. He opened the parcel carefully. Inside were 250 yellow coins, gold Maple Leafs, the most pure gold that could be purchased, and minted into a beautiful coin by the Canadian Mint. Each coin was an ounce of pure gold. There were four boxes in total. He opened a second box and placed the coin holders in the briefcase along with the first. The other two boxes he secured in the lock box at the rear of the Jeep.

He drove to his bank and, briefcase in hand, walked in to the service desk. A couple of minutes later he handed over his key and followed the attendant to his safety deposit box. He offered to lift out the box himself. No sense anyone knowing even the weight of the container. He entered the privacy room, opened the brief case and transferred the contents into the safety deposit box. The gold coins joined the silver ones already there. He took out two stock certificates then briefly fingered a small diamond ring that lay loose in the box. Then, annoyed at himself, he closed the box and rang for the attendant. It was a heavy lift replacing the box and he did his best to make it appear effortless. He accepted his key back and left the bank.

He next crossed the bridge to the south side of the river and pulled into the parking lot at the brokerage office. He asked for his financial planner at the reception desk. The receptionist looked askance at his rough clothing and less-than-elegant boots.

Randall on the other hand greeted him warmly and not just because he was a customer. Randall had been in the army for twenty-three years and they had soldiered together for many of those years. Two years of back pay in a combat zone as well as some smart investments had made York a moderately wealthy man. The money from the sale of his house had helped as well. York frowned slightly at the thought.

"What can I do for you today, York?" asked Randall.

"A few changes to my portfolio," he replied as they paraded down the hallway to the private offices.

Randall ushered him into the office and closed the door. "You know the market is down right now because of this flu thing, York."

"I know, but I see this thing as more than just a short term glitch. I just converted a lot of cash, money market and bonds into gold coins." He paused to watch for a reaction. Randall's brow knit a little but he continued to listen. These two certificates I'd like to sell at the market and convert the proceeds into the longest government bonds that you can get for me."

"Any more surprises?"

"Rebalance my mutual funds with 60% in government bond funds, and 40% in blue chips; the stuff that people need to eat and drink and burn."

"Do you want to hear any comment from me or is your mind made up?" Randall asked.

"I always want your advice as long as I don't always have to follow it," said York. "You've never lied to me or tried to snow me. I value your opinion."

"Well, you're going to lock in some losses because the market's so low right now, but you're basically talking about a very conservative portfolio. I'll come back to the gold. You will remember that I've been trying to get you to shift some of your stocks into bonds for the last two years. You of course have stuck with a very aggressive portfolio and made a lot of money; at times very lucky money I might add. Why the sudden shift?"

"Randall, I firmly believe that this flu thing is not just a typical flu. I've researched it and asked questions about it and I think it's going to change the world, just like the September 11th thing only more so. I think there is going to be global turmoil and I think it's going to last a long time. After you've executed my trades, get on the Internet and search on the 1918 flu, not just the official reports but some of the anecdotal and social history ones. Then extrapolate that into today. That will explain the gold."

Randall was silent for a moment then nodded. "I will, and maybe I'll make a trade or two myself."

York took a piece of paper and a pencil from Randall's desktop and wrote "Tamiflu" on it. "If you've got a good doc, see if you can get some of this today. Not to take today but maybe later this winter. If you don't need it I'll pay you back later."

York asked about Randall's wife and kids and they traded a few reminiscences about past escapades. The bad always seemed to disappear into the background as they remembered the good times. York found himself laughing out loud. They had shared some tough experiences and the bond would be lifelong.

York left the brokerage and headed for the bridge and out of town. He swung inadvertently on to Prince Street and when he realised where he was he pulled to the curb in front of a legal and real estate office. He stared at the dirty brick building for a while then shrugged his shoulders and sped away from the area.

He took the long way home and stopped at the clinic in Spencer to deliver the deer steaks. He was shocked at the line-up at the door to the clinic. As he approached the door the line-up parted and two men and a woman exited. The woman was screeching and the two men were trying to calm her. York slipped through the resisting crowd explaining that he was not here to seek medical care just to make a delivery.

Inside, the scene was bedlam. The waiting area was packed with people coughing and moaning. An ambulance crew was wheeling a stretcher out the back door. Its cargo was muffled with an oxygen mask and strung with plastic tubing. The receptionist was talking to four people at the entrance desk as an elderly man sagged in their arms. The doctor rushed from one examining room into another, followed shortly thereafter by Elizabeth.

York took the cooler to the office where the doctor usually did paperwork and found a place for it beside the coat rack. There were stacks of charts on the desk, probably two hundred. York slipped out the way that he had come in, unnoticed by those too busy or miserable to care.

His thoughts turned back five years to Afghanistan. He saw again the lines of emaciated refugees, the piles of corpses, and heard again the supplications of those crying for help.

He quickly left the parking lot. He had done his part for mankind. He had fought and almost died, had given two years of his life in a stinking cage, and had returned to find his life stolen from him. He would now look after himself for a change.

As he arrived at his cabin, his gloomy mood started to lift. This is where he was meant to be, at home, alone, at peace.

He carefully secreted the two boxes of gold coins into hiding places in the cabin. Cash or gold was of no use if you could not get at it in an emergency. He was just coming from the basement when the lights went out. He had secured the last of the coins in the arms cabinet in the basement and had brought up some strawberry jam and home canned beans. He lowered the trapdoor in the kitchen floor. The brass latch fit so perfectly into the hardwood under one of the chairs that it disappeared from casual view.

He lit an oil lamp on the kitchen wall. There was still daylight at half past five but it would not last long. He made a meal and then as he was doing the dishes the power came back on again. He was used to power outages, as you had to be in the country, but they usually happened during windstorms when a tree would fall over a line. The weather this evening was calm.

When he awoke next morning the clock by his bed was flashing 12:00. He had reset it before he went to bed so the power must have been off again overnight. He reset the clock against his wristwatch. Seven twenty. He rose with the daylight these days, seldom needing to set an alarm. Those days of alarm clocks were gone. Now he was able to tend to his own needs and those needs seldom required an alarm.

He went first to the television, even before he attended to the stove. The world continued to be attacked by flu. “Maybe we are the modern day dinosaurs,” he said aloud. “And maybe we have just caught sight of our asteroid.”

CHAPTER 5

6 January

All the next day, York thought about what he had seen in Fredericton and Spencer. There were a lot of people ill and probably some had died. The woman being led crying from the clinic was not weeping about the long waiting line. That afternoon he switched on the television to catch the events around the world. The local station was off the air, replaced by a stationary notice of unspecified technical difficulties.

He switched to CNN which reported a worldwide influenza outbreak, with the screen trumpeting PANIC PANDEMIC at each return from fillers and commercial breaks. Deaths were mounting around the globe. The Centres for Disease Control had identified the virus and stated that it was a new bug with a major shift in its makeup. Efforts were now underway to create an immunisation serum. The announcer looked horrified as he read the next part of his script: "A flu shot was probably four to six months away."

York heard the CBC satellite station report that the attack rate for Canada was at least twenty five percent and still growing. One in every four Canadians had developed the flu with more to come. The Prime Minister was in hospital and two of the ten provincial premiers, those of Ontario and British Columbia, were dead. There was no accurate count of the death toll so far, but an estimate of at least six hundred thousand was widely touted.

This new influenza apparently afflicted all age groups. It struck rapidly often turning apparently well people into helpless invalids in less than a day. Symptoms were diffuse muscle and joint pains, respiratory distress, and vomiting. It was the respiratory problems that were causing the greatest difficulty, with those affected often developing a fatal pneumonia. With lungs full of fluid, the stricken patient died gasping for breath.

When the reporting became tedious he switched off the TV and turned on the local radio station. There was no programming except news and quiet music. The announcer repeated the messages for people to stay home, to go out only to buy food or to go to work if they absolutely must. There was a plea for people to only buy the food that they needed, a plea not to hoard supplies.

That's a futile effort, he thought. At least society doesn't have to worry about feeding me. My needs are already out of the pipeline and someone else will eat because of that.

He put a Debussy CD in the player and sat back in front of the fireplace with a book. He drifted off to sleep, and when he next opened his eyes he knew instantly that it was not a natural awakening. Something had drawn him from his sleep and he froze, trying to identify the intrusion.

It was dark and his watch showed just before seven. The low rumble of a motor could be heard in front of the house. He eased out of the chair and could see a vehicle in the driveway. Angry that his solitude had been broken, he catapulted into the kitchen, swatted the light switch and ran for the front door.

The vehicle, now recognizable as a truck, spun its wheels and started down the lane. York switched on the front yard floodlights and the truck was plainly visible, a white pickup with a rusty tailgate. It disappeared quickly from view over the crest of the hill.

He jumped into his boots leaving the laces flapping, grabbed his jacket, and rushed out to the shed. He soon had the Jeep hurtling down the lane after the truck. He wanted a licence plate number and he wanted to have a chat with the driver.

There was a little snow in the air and he noted the ring around the moon as he sped down the road. He barely kept the Jeep on the road at the curve in front of Shamus's farm. Careful now, an accident will get you nowhere. York craned his neck forward as he drove, expecting to see a glow of taillights at each curve but finding only darkness. When he reached the main highway, there were no vehicle lights visible in either direction. The snow was a little heavier now and the moon had completely disappeared along with the truck.

York slammed his hands on the steering wheel, a curse on his lips. He turned to the right and accelerated toward Fredericton, unwilling to give up the chase quite yet. After twenty minutes of empty highway and increasing snow he turned back. He passed the entrance to his road and continued to the north still determined to look for the vehicle.

About three kilometres farther on, he saw a dark figure trudging along the shoulder on the opposite side. The figure stumbled a little and did not seem to be aware of the Jeep that approached from behind. York stopped beside him and saw that it was the young Mormon kid, still in his well-worn dark suit and tie; only ear muffs and a scarf as concessions to winter.

"Hey kid, do you want a lift?"

The boy started and walked toward the Jeep. He fell as he walked in front of the vehicle and York started to get out to help him. The kid braced himself against the front bumper, struggled to his feet, and was soon crawling into the passenger seat.

York scrutinised him and recognized that he was ailing. His eyes were glassy and there was vomit at the corner of his mouth. York released the clutch and headed toward Spencer.

"How do you feel?" he asked.

The kid whispered, "Not too bad." Then as he looked at York, "Hey, you're the guy with the bow and arrows. I could hardly recognize you with a clean face."

"Yeah, that's me. Are you still walking the roads this time of day?"

"Not supposed to be. I was dropped off this morning and they were supposed to pick me up a couple of hours later, but that was six hours ago. I don't know where they are." He coughed. It was a wet wracking cough that for a minute did not appear ready to stop. When the cough was over he continued. "A little while ago a truck stopped and offered a ride then pulled away when I got close."

"What kind of truck?" York asked. "What colour?"

"It was white, I don't know what kind."

"Did you see the licence number? How many people were in it? Which way was it heading?" York interrogated him further. They were approaching Spencer where he would drop the kid off at the clinic.

The kid's breathing rattled again as he fought a cough. "There were three men in it drinking. One of them threw an empty beer bottle at me as they drove off, same way we're going. I didn't see a license number."

Well at least I'm now heading the right way, York thought. He slowed as they came into the village and pulled into the clinic. There was no line up today, much to York's surprise, although there were lots of vehicles in the lot. The lights were off and the sign on the door read, "CLOSED TEMPORARILY. SERVICES ARE AVAILABLE AT THE EMERGENCY RECEPTION CENTRE AT THE SCHOOL".

York powered back onto the road and then a mile later skidded into the school parking lot. The lot was full of cars and trucks. Two ambulances were in the yard, one leaving. He led the young lad through the front door and followed the large red signs to reception. As they passed open classrooms he could see people sprawled on cots, and in some rooms huddled on the floor. The sound of coughing, crying and retching was oppressive. The air reeked of vomit.

Reception was in the gymnasium. He recognised the clinic receptionist behind the first desk. The gym was wall-to-wall cots and there was a low murmur of moaning from the humanity occupying them. On the far side of the room he saw Elizabeth moving from cot to cot. She has guts and staying power; that much I'll say for her, he thought.

To his right, two men were carrying a stretcher through one of the fire exits. The figure on the stretcher was covered with a sheet and beyond them York saw two other shrouded bodies in the back of a red half-ton.

He put his hand on the kid's shoulder and guided him to the reception table. The boy was shivering violently under his hand. "Can you help this lad out?" he said to the woman working there.

She started to ask the boy questions and York gazed around the room again. A hand touched his arm and he turned to see the doctor at his side. "Jesus, Doc, what is happening?"

"You of all people should know, York. You're the one who wanted to be prepared for the pandemic. Were you prepared?"

"Yeah, I guess I was physically, but not for this. It wasn't this bad in Afghanistan. There were more refugees but not this sickness."

"Well I want you to know that I followed your unspoken advice, York. I ordered antivirals for the clinic staff and we have all had to use it already. We've all had the influenza but were able to fight it off. What we don't know is whether we have now developed immunity, or whether we might get it again."

"Are there a lot of people dying?" York asked.

"Yes there are. I think we're up to twenty-eight so far here, probably more. They sent us a few courses of antiviral from Public Health. It was meant for the clinic staff so we could keep giving care to the rest. Since we had our own we could use what they gave us for others, but that was gone days ago. We try to ease suffering and some of the people get better on their own. We're almost out of intravenous fluids and bronchodilators."

"So they basically get better on their own or they die, and you keep them as comfortable as possible?"

"That's about it." The doctor shook his head. "Everything about me wants to make people better, but all I can do is hold their hands as they die."

"Can't they do more in Fredericton?"

"We're probably better off than they are," said the Doctor. "The sense of community here is very strong. See all these people working here? They're just volunteers, helping in any way that they can. They go to where the elderly live, or those that live alone, to see if they are able to look after themselves. They carry out dead bodies and wash linen. They make broth and mix fluids to rehydrate those who are retching their guts out. About half of the people helping here are recovering from the flu. If they are not at home helping family then they are here helping others." York could see tears on the doctor's cheek as he spoke.

The doctor answered questions from two of the helpers then walked over to a cot along the near wall where he was being called. York watched him listen with his stethoscope then pull the sheet over the face of the young man on the stretcher.

"In Fredericton they say it is a different story," said the doctor as he walked back to York. "There are just not enough people to help with the sick and there are apparently bodies lying in the street. I guess the big cities in central Canada are hellish."

"Man, how long can this go on?"

"I don't know," said the doctor "but I think that it's going to get worse before it gets better. More and more people keep getting sick, and as people die there are fewer to care for the ill. It's not just the elderly that are at risk like it is with the annual flu. This year the flu is taking everybody, like that young lad that came in with you. He probably has a fifty percent chance of survival."

York glanced over where the kid was leaning against the reception table. He then looked back at the doctor. "Doc, I'd like to help but I can't work here and do this. It's not where my head is. I'll go out and fight a bear for you but I can't hold a puke bucket."

"That's OK, York. It's not for everybody. Your time will likely come later and I'll call on you then, or your neighbours will."

"Doc, has my sister had the flu?"

"Yes she has. She had the antiviral and is recovering at the moment. I honestly don't know how she keeps going. She is very weak and is running on empty right now. If the influenza comes back she will not survive it. I also don't know if I could go on without her here."

York studied the doctor's face and saw an intensity that surprised him. "Well you look after her, Doc," he said.

"Why don't you go over and talk to her, York? It would mean

a lot to her."

York stood motionless for a couple of seconds then pivotted toward the door. "Tell her I said hello, Doc," he said as he strode toward the door. "Call me if you think I can help you." Then he stopped in his tracks and returned to the gymnasium and walked over to the kid who was now sitting on the floor by the wall.

"Hey kid."

The young man looked up and York crouched down beside him. York held out his hand and the kid slowly took it with a very weak grip.

"Kid, I want to thank you. The papers that you left for me when you were at my cabin are what made me prepare for this flu epidemic. You have made a difference in my life and I want to thank you."

The kid smiled weakly and his grip became a little stronger. "Maybe when this is over I can come back and talk to you some more," he said.

"You've got it, kid. You can come by my place anytime, and talk about whatever you want. Get well soon."

York released his hand and it dropped limp at the kid's side as he began another paroxysm of coughing. York got to his feet and without looking back fled the gymnasium.

Outside in the cold he stood on the packed snow of the parking lot and took several deep breaths. The wind was now whipping around him and the freshly fallen snow was at least fifteen centimetres deep. He went back to the entrance and held the door for a middle-aged couple struggling up the stairs and into the school. They whispered a thank you and disappeared into the school. York wondered if they would come out together again.

York considered his options. There was still the white pickup, and according to the kid the truck had been coming in this direction. He climbed into the Jeep and swung onto the road, yielding to an ambulance leaving the lot. It was snowing heavily as he headed north out of the village. After about ten minutes he realised that there was little or no chance of seeing anything. The snow made it impossible to even see vehicles in dooryards. He swung around and headed back through the village. As he passed the school he was tempted to go in to speak to Elizabeth but he dismissed it. He wanted nothing to do with the environment in the school and he convinced himself that he and his sister had nothing to talk about.

He switched on the radio as a means of diverting his attention. The latest news was bizarre. A supertanker full of crude oil was aground in the city of Saint John. It had apparently steamed at full speed into the harbour, probably on autopilot and the crew all dead of the flu. It was fully ashore and spewing crude into the water and the nearby streets. The harbour was in flames and the Harbour Hotel was also totally engulfed. With fire crews decimated by the influenza the whole city was in danger. Several ships tied up in harbour were on fire and there was concern about the burning oil spreading to the pipeline terminal just down the coast. The environmental disaster was only eclipsed by the potential destruction of the largest city in the province.

CHAPTER 6

7 January

York was blinded by the worsening snowstorm reflecting his headlights back into his eyes. Even with low beams the snow was mesmerising and when he momentarily switched to high beams it was like driving into a white wall. He crawled along the unplowed road lacking even the yellow centre line to provide guidance. The wind flapped the reinforced canvas top against the roll cage that cocooned him. The noise overwhelmed the radio so he switched it off. He didn't need the distraction anyway.

Halfway home, he thought, and slowed even more, anticipating Coburn Curve. There was a delay as the road continued straight ahead. A minute, two minutes. "Guess I'm a little premature," he said aloud.

Then suddenly he felt the slope of the road change and the looming darkness of the tree line appeared in the feeble penetration of the headlights. He braked and eased through the sharp left curve. This was not a night to end up in the ditch.

As he straightened out on the far side of the curve, something flickered in his field of vision then was gone. Was that a light? Right side of the road, low down. No, must have been his imagination. Eyestrain from concentrating in what was now a full-blown blizzard.

Must have been his headlights reflecting on the snow.

Headlights! That was it. That could have been a headlight from a car in the deep ditch. The wind roared at him as he tried to think. There was nobody on the side of the road. If there were a car off the road the driver would have climbed out of the ditch to get help. If the driver could.

"No, it was likely just my imagination," he said to himself as he sharpened his attention on the road slipping by.

Without another thought he braked, checked his mirrors, and made a three point turn in the middle of the road, careful not to stray too close to the ditch. Not so long ago someone, many someones, had given him up for dead. Maybe there really was a headlight in the ditch.

The wind effect eased a little on his new heading; it was coming from behind. He approached Coburn Curve again crawling to a stop just before entering the curve. A light! Yes, there was a light in the ditch now on his left. He put his headlights on high beam, switched on fog lights and emergency flashers and pulled as far off the road to his right as he dared. "I don't need to have another mad fool ram into me," he muttered.

The wind threatened to pull the door from his hand as he slid out. He braced himself then ran across the highway. The tire tracks that he had made passing by just a couple of minutes ago were obliterated.

He slid into the ditch guided by the single headlight beacon. He could see now that a compact hatchback was nosed up against a power pole. The passenger side headlight was not working. The grill and hood were retooled into a pyramid of metal that was barely visible in the reflected light from the headlight.

He opened the door, struggling against the snow in the ditch and against the shrieking wind. There was a driver still belted in. The smell of vomit was foul. Drunk, he thought.

"Hey, can you hear me?" he shouted. No response. "Hey, hey." York shook the driver roughly. No response. York dug out his pocket flashlight and quickly scanned the rest of the wrecked car. Nothing. Just the driver. This was taking too long. He still had to get home to ride out the rest of this storm.

He stashed the flashlight in his pocket and buttoned the fastener. He would need both hands. He tripped the seatbelt release and dragged the driver from the car. A neck injury was possible but at this point the greater danger to both of them was from freezing to death. He bent over and hoisted him onto his shoulder into a fireman's carry and started up the slope. At least he doesn't weigh a ton, he thought, as his feet sank deeper into the snow that had been thrown into the ditch by the plow.

As an afterthought he turned and squatted beside the car and switched off the remaining headlight. At least no other sap would be tempted to stop and struggle into the ditch. On a night like this a Good Samaritan could end up stone cold dead.

York half climbed and half fell up the side of the ditch, homing on the light show from his Jeep; a blazing light show that was shrouded by the blizzard. He reached the roadway, now almost knee deep in wind blasted snow. He dashed to the Jeep and wrenched open the passenger door. Taking care to avoid smashing the driver's head against the roll cage, he dumped him unceremoniously into the seat then struggled to get the unconscious man into a position for a seat belt. They were not home free yet and he did not want an unconscious body landing on him if they went off the road.

The wind ripped his own door from his hand as he got back into the Jeep. He heaved it closed and reduced the high beams. After another three-point turn he switched off the emergency flashers and started for home.

As he turned onto the Old Connector Road he realised that he had followed his instincts and turned away from the clinic and the school, wanting to avoid the nightmare that was there. He also realised that the driver beside him still reeked of vomit. York shuddered. Maybe it was not inebriation but rather influenza that had caused the vomiting; and he had been in close contact with the driver.

The lane into his cabin would not have been passable to any vehicle with less ground clearance than the Jeep. The heavily lugged tires bit into the snow and he was able to make it all the way to the front door. He carried the driver into the cabin and positioned him on the bed in his bedroom. York went back to park the Jeep, then piled wood into the airtight fireplace in the main room. The wind had sapped the heat from the cabin and he would need to replenish the fire more than once overnight. "Guess I won't have a bed to sleep in tonight anyway," he said to himself.

York re-entered the bedroom and pulled the coat and watch cap off the sleeping driver. "Lord Almighty," slipped out as he realised that the driver was a woman.

* * *

By daylight the wind had dropped to a wail. York lit the wood stove and put on a kettle. There was no more snow falling. It was just being rearranged by the wind. He always liked the morning after a storm, that secure feeling inside the cabin and the unrelenting white outside.

He walked toward the bedroom with apprehension. The door was open, as he had left it to allow heat to enter the room. The driver was on the bed covered by a heavy quilt and she had not moved since he had covered her last night. As he approached her he knew that something was wrong. Her breathing was laboured and her face had a mahogany hue. The vomit odour was still prominent and she had debris on her face.

York dialled the number for the clinic. It rang through to the school, and then rang nine more times before it was picked up. A coarse male voice answered.

"Is this the clinic?" York inquired.

"Yes. What do you want?" the voice demanded.

"There's somebody sick here. She has a head injury and she's not breathing right. The snow is too deep to get the ambulance here and I need to know what to do."

"Look, I'm just answering the phone while the doctor and nurse are busy," replied the voice. "I can read out to you the directions for treating the flu."

"No, this is different," York said getting a little exasperated by now. "Let me talk to the doctor."

"He just laid down half an hour ago. He's been up for thirty six hours," explained the voice. "The nurse is here and she said I'm not to call the doctor without talking to her first."

York paused so long that the voice said, "Are you still there?"

"I'll talk to the nurse then." It came out practically as a whisper.

A minute passed and then Elizabeth answered. "This is the nurse."

"This is York. I need to talk to the doctor."

"You'll have to tell me what it's about, York. If I don't let him get some rest, there will be no doctor."

"There is a sick woman at my place. I picked her up last night. Her car was in the ditch. She's been unconscious since then and now her breathing is really wheezy."

"All right, hang on. I'll get Josh."

"Yes, York?" Dr Simpson said a couple of minutes later. The fatigue was obvious in his voice.

York outlined the events of last night and the woman's condition this morning. He answered questions as best he could and waited for instructions.

"York, you're going to have to do the best that you can there. She likely..."

York interrupted, "Doc, can't you send the ambulance for her? Or somebody on snowmobiles or something?"

"Now listen, York. There is no ambulance. The roads have not been plowed. Several of the local snowplow drivers are sick. One of them is dead from the flu. The highways department says that the main routes will not be open until at least tomorrow, so at least until then you're going to have to manage on your own. I'll help you." A pause then, "Are you ready for instructions?"

"OK, Doc. What do you want me to do?"

"She likely has the flu as well as whatever injuries she suffered in the crash. Do you have any of that antiviral medication that I gave you the prescription for?"

"Yes, I have it."

"Well, if she dies of the flu then the other injuries won't matter. Give her the medication and if she survives the flu then we'll worry about the rest. Dissolve the medication in a small amount of water and see if you can get it into her a few drops at a time."

"Anything else?"

"Give her fluids if you can. Keep her clean and warm but not too hot. Call back if you need help. You are one of about a thousand doing the same thing in this area. Wait just a minute."

Another voice came on the line again. "York, take care of yourself. This flu is deadly," said Elizabeth. "We have fifty-seven dead here already and there are still a hundred more here very sick. Try to protect yourself."

"OK," York grunted and hung up.

He stood by the phone for a minute. "Damn! All I wanted was to be left alone."

York shook his head then set about following Dr Simpson's instructions. He prepared the medication and managed to get the woman to take it. At first he gave her too much and set up a coughing fit that he thought would kill her. After that, with supreme patience, a couple of drops at a time, he completed the first of two doses for that day. She still smelled of vomit and then, as York adjusted the quilt, he realised that there was an odour of urine that had not been there last night. "Keep her clean and warm," the doctor had said.

York kicked the nearby chair against the wall then looked unblinking at the woman on the bed for a full minute, and then left the room. He returned a couple of minutes later with a basin of warm water and a stack of towels. "At least you're not going to remember this," he whispered to the woman and he began to strip off her clothing.

His sister might have done a faster job, but York did a thorough job. He tried not to look at her breasts as he washed her from head to waist. He kept her covered where he was not washing. He pulled off her pants and socks then finally he stripped off her underwear throwing it into the malodorous pile by the bed. As he completed the washing he removed the towels and manhandled her as gently as possible in under the sheets.

York added the quilt to the pile, scooped it up and headed for the washing machine. He was sweating. Was it from the exertion, or from his discomfort with what he had just done, or was he getting the flu? Dr Simpson had said that it was vital to get the antiviral medication on board as soon as possible after getting the flu. He would have to pay attention to his own condition.

*　　*　　*

York continued to provide unskilled but compassionate nursing care. He talked to Dr Simpson a couple of times the next day, tended the fire, and followed the tale of the flu pandemic on the Internet. There were lots of “page not available” error messages, likely where servers and nodes were not tended. The picture, although chaotic, was terrifyingly clear. The flu was sporadic still, but some areas had been hit hard. The Centres for Disease Control announced that this was an unusual strain that was not expected, and was not covered by the annual flu shot. Lots of other less scientific sites were calling it anything from the long talked about pandemic to a bioterrorism attack. One page from a religious fundamentalist group was preaching fire and brimstone and the Second Coming.

*　　*　　*

Two days later, York carried medicine into the bedroom. He almost dropped it when the patient opened her eyes and stared into his face.

“Hello,” said York.

“Where am I?” asked the young woman. “Why am I here?”

“You’re at my cabin. You had a car accident and I found you in the ditch. Do you remember the storm?”

“No, wait yes, I couldn’t see and then there was a snow bank. That’s all I remember.”

“The storm turned into a blizzard. I saw your car in the ditch and pulled you out and brought you here. You’ve been unconscious for three days. You’ve had the flu as well.”

“Where is this?”

“Near Spencer, just off Highway 502.”

“I have to get to St Andrews,” she said and started to get up, then clutched the blankets to her throat. “Where are my clothes?” she shouted. “What have you done to me?”

“I haven’t done anything to you. You were covered with vomit. And what do you think your bladder and bowels have been doing for three days,” York retorted. “I cleaned you. Your clothes are right there on the chair.” He pointed to the crisp folded pile beside her.

York stalked out of the room, angry that he had been accused of something odious. “That’s what I get for helping.”

He heard the door close behind him and he went into the main room. A little later he heard another door, and then the toilet flush.

She came to the door of the room, fully clothed and tightly buttoned. “I’m sorry if I upset you, but it was a shock,” she offered, her voice obviously weak as she leaned against the door. “Can you tell me how to get to my car, or a cab or a bus?”

“We are still snowed in. We have to wait for someone to blow out the lane.”

“Can I walk out?”

“The nearest house is five miles. The main highway is ten. Your car is ten miles down that highway, probably buried in snow and wrecked, and the nearest cab or bus is in Fredericton.”

Her eyes turned to the leather couch in front of the fireplace where blankets and pillow signalled York’s bed space for the last few days. She tottered to a nearby chair and sank into it. “I’m sorry, I’m really sorry. I’m just confused.”

“Are you hungry?” asked York. “The doctor said you need to get in fluids.”

“Did a doctor see me?”

“No, I talked to him on the phone and I had medicine here. He told me what to do.”

She didn’t say anything for a while then she whispered, “I’m very thirsty and a bit hungry.”

York got up and headed for the kitchen. “I’ll make some oatmeal. Your medicine is in the bowl there. I’ll talk to Doc first and see if you need any more. There’s milk and juice in the fridge.”

York dialled the clinic and his sister answered. “Can I talk to Doc, please? The woman here has woken up.” There was a pause, and then the doctor answered. “Doc, she’s awake,” York said. “Does she still need more of the medicine?" He received the updated instructions, then at the doctor's request handed the phone to the woman.

"Doc wants to talk to you."

She walked over and took the phone. "Hello."

York busied himself in the kitchen making thin oatmeal porridge and trying to provide some privacy, but he could not help but overhear.

She answered several questions and explained how she felt, answered several more then said "Cat Stevens." A pause then "I know, I know, but that's not the reason. Thank you, doctor." There was another pause as she listened, then she said goodbye.

"The doctor says that I owe you my life," she said. "And I'd like to thank you. May I stay here until the road is clear?"

"Of course," York said. "There's no other option. It should only be another day or two. I'll call and see when Shamus can blow out the lane."

"May I... may I take a shower?"

"Sure. Towels are in the cupboard in the bathroom. Help yourself to anything that you need."

She emerged a half-hour later towelling her hair, in bare feet. She managed a smile that seemed to be almost as infectious as the flu.

"You never told me your name," she said.

"York Lancaster."

"That's unusual."

"No more unusual than Cat Stevens," he retorted.

"Touché," she said. "I got my first name because I was conceived while my parents were vacationing on Cat Island, one of the out islands of the Bahamas. How about you?"

"My mother was a history buff, British history. The War of the Roses was fought between the house of Lancaster and the house of York. I guess she couldn't resist. My sister's name is Elizabeth of course."

They fumbled with small talk that became more relaxed as they shared breakfast, and York was surprised when he noted that two hours had passed. Shamus showed up later that day to blow out the lane. York made supper and the two slipped back into an easy conversation that ended well after dark.

"I'm feeling a little tired," said Cat. "I'll take the couch tonight and you can have your bed back."

"No, that's OK, I need to tend the fire. It's going to minus 30C tonight and the cabin will get pretty cold if I don't. I can do it easier and get more sleep if I bed down by the fireplace." He lied, unsure of why he did.

"Can't you just turn up the thermostat?"

"There is no thermostat," he explained. "I heat with wood as do a lot of folks in the country. It's cheaper than electricity or oil and more reliable. The trade off is inconvenience and more work."

"Can I put wood in the fireplace?" Cat asked. "I don't know anything about fires but I can learn."

"Why don't you let me worry about it tonight and we'll talk about it tomorrow."

She paused then said, "Can you take me to my car tomorrow? I really do need to go to St Andrews."

"No problem. I'll wake you up early tomorrow."

"Goodnight," she said as she turned toward the other end of the cabin.

CHAPTER 7

12 January

York arose with the sun. He filled the woodbin and swept the floor. Then in windbreaker and boots he shovelled the walkways and in front of the shed.

The snow was drifted three feet deep in spots but in others the ground was swept bare by the wind. An unruly band of finches swooped into the trees around the cabin, searching for seed in the increasing light of the day. It was amazing to him that those tiny birds, protected only by a few feathers, could withstand almost anything that winter could throw at them.

He entered the shed and started the Jeep, turning on the defrosters to clear the ice and frost remaining from the dash home through the blizzard. The snow would clear off the jeep in a few minutes. The very last remnants of the blizzard would be gone later today when he could unload his impromptu houseguest. It would be nice to sleep in his own bed again. It would be nice to go about his daily routine, without having to worry about someone else or explain things to someone else.

He moved the Jeep to the front of the house then walked around to the south side of the cabin. The garden now had a heavy blanket of snow over the mulch that he had piled three feet deep. The root vegetables would be protected and should remain available to him all winter.

York returned to the kitchen and lit the woodstove, and put the kettle on the hot spot. Soon he had made strong coffee and had fried some bacon. The breadbox was almost empty, enough for two for breakfast, but he would have to make bread later today or tomorrow.

"You know, bacon and fat will clog up your arteries," she said from the doorway to the bedroom.

"That's fine," he retorted. "I've been as good as dead lots of times. It didn't seem to make much difference."

She walked into the room and then glanced out the window over the sink. "I'm sorry. I didn't mean to criticise. I was just making conversation."

"No problem. There's cereal and some tinned fruit in the cupboard right there if you would prefer, and the bread is whole wheat."

"I'll just have some of the coffee that smells so good. Ron doesn't like it if I put on too much weight."

York poured two mugs of coffee. "Black? Sugar? Milk?" he asked.

"Do you have any Sweet and Low?"

"No. Sorry. Only all natural products," he replied.

"You're making fun of me, aren't you?"

"No, not really. Usually the three things just seem to come together. I'm too fat; food is bad for you; no chemicals in my body."

"Look, I'm sorry. I'll be out of your way as quickly as I can."

"No problem. I'm sure Ron will be happy to see you."

He turned away to take up a plate of bacon and bread, angry at himself for mentioning Ron, whoever Ron was. They finished eating in silence, and then he placed the dishes in the sink.

"Can I help clean up?" she said.

"I didn't think the place was that dirty!"

"I meant the dishes. Your house is not dirty. It's cleaner than I keep mine."

"No, that's fine," said York. "Do you want to go find your car?"

"Sure," she replied, and then stepped into the main room

seeming to want to take one last look around. She got her light jacket off the rack at the front door and waited to leave.

York banked the fire in the fireplace and opened the draft on the wood stove to let it burn hot as it finished the fuel. He wanted no flu fire fuelled by creosote to burn down his cabin. He let Cat out the front door then walked to the back, slipped on his boots and locked up as he left.

In the Jeep and in silence, Cat swivelled in her seat to gaze back at the cabin as it fell behind the crest of the hill. Then she sat facing stiffly forward.

"Thank you again for looking after me, York," she started. "I felt very safe in your house. You're a special person."

"No problem."

After a few minutes she said, "What's that beautiful old house up on the hill?"

York gripped the steering wheel. "The old Lancaster manor house."

"Did your family own it?"

"My family lived there. Then I owned it. Then my sister sold it while I was away. It belongs to a software company from Toronto now."

"Why did your sister sell it?"

"She thought I was dead."

"That's terrible. Could she just do that?"

"Well, she did. She had a death certificate. They thought that I was dead in the war in Afghanistan."

"Oh, I see."

The silence returned and they continued to her car. The damaged vehicle was still there, nosed up against the power pole. With the flu still running rampant, and people seldom venturing outside their houses, he had known that there was little chance that anybody would disturb the vehicle.

The two of them clambered down into the ditch. It would take a strong tow truck with a long winch cable to twitch it out of its resting place. He reached into the car and turned on the lights. There was still battery power. He switched them off again and looked around the interior of the vehicle.

"There's a garage in the village that has a tow truck," he said. "They'll be able to haul this out."

He closed the door and walked around the car to check the other side, and then returned to stand beside Cat.

"If you're lucky the car will still run and they can bang the hood into shape enough to get you where you are going. There's only one headlight. You'll need a new one eventually, but if you travel by daylight the one light won't be a problem."

"OK," she said, looking a little bewildered.

"Do you want to get anything out of the car?" he asked. "I took a quick look in the backseat the night I found you. I didn't see anything but I wasn't looking very carefully right then."

"No, I had everything in my jacket," she said holding her jacket out with her hands in her pockets. "The registration and insurance are in the glove compartment."

"You didn't have a parka or boots, or a winter emergency kit, or anything like that?" he asked.

"No, I was just driving from Miramichi to St Andrews. It's only four hours."

York shook his head and turned toward the Jeep. "Let's go find a tow truck."

They drove into Spencer and past the medical clinic. The parking lot was full of cars and pickups that were still covered with snow. There was a refrigerator semi-trailer backed into the lot as far as the snow had been plowed, and the driver was unhooking the cab, wearing a mask on his face.

At the garage there was a scrawled sign on the pump. SELF SERVE. PUT THE MONEY IN THE MAIL SLOT. York fuelled up, topping the tank as high as possible. He walked to the station door and slipped a twenty-dollar bill into the slot. He shouted through the glass to the owner that he could see sitting inside.

"We need a tow for a car in a snow bank."

The owner shook his head. York held up a wad of bills. At this point he felt that almost any price was worth it to be on his own again. The man stirred from his seat and approached the window.

"Where is it and what is it?" he shouted.

"Small car eight kliks down the 502 toward Fredericton," York answered. "Bring it back here and bang out its hood. That's all."

"Three hundred," said the man.

York scowled. "You know that's way more than it's worth," he shouted.

"That's the price. Take it or leave it."

"All right, I'll take it," said York.

"In advance."

"No way. You know who I am, and that I pay for what I buy; but I'm not stupid. When you deliver the car back here then I'll pay up."

"That's the deal, take it or leave it," said the man.

"I leave it," said York pivoting on his heel toward the Jeep. He wasn't sure exactly what he was going to do next to get his houseguest on her way but he was not going to roll over and play dead to that kind of treatment.

He heard the door unlatch behind him and the man's voice, "OK, have it your way. I'll get the truck. You stay downwind of me." It was obvious to York that this influenza thing was really starting to reshape people.

A couple of minutes later they were following the tow truck toward the wrecked car. As they rounded Coburn's Curve, a plume of black smoke could be seen in the air and then the blazing car was fully apparent. York looked past the tow truck, past the blaze and through the smoke. He thought he saw the tailgate of a white pickup rounding the curve in front of them. He swung the Jeep around the tow truck; but the tow truck driver chose that instant to wheel into the middle of the road. York skidded to a halt, his pursuit blocked.

The driver climbed down from the cab and walked to the back of the truck to look at the fire. York could hear the woman sobbing beside him. He got out and approached the tow truck.

"Stay back!" said the driver. "I don't want no flu!"

"Did you see a vehicle in front of you when we arrived here?"

"Maybe I did and maybe I didn't," the driver said. He rubbed his right thumb and forefinger together, obviously expecting to be paid for information.

York peeled off a twenty and tossed it on the ground.

"It was a white pickup, a lot of rust on the tailgate," said the driver. Then "Stay back!" as York approached the back of the truck.

"Go pick up your money," said York as he walked toward the edge of the ditch.

The tow truck driver scurried after the bill and York carefully examined the snow around the edge of the ditch. There were several types of boot prints; some he recognised as his own. There was one very distinctive print, however, a running shoe print that had the NIKE logo in the midst of the grips. It was that set of footprints that led down into the ditch toward the burning car.

York marched back toward the tow truck and Jeep. The driver again scuttled out of his way as he went by.

"Do you know who owns that white pickup?" York asked.

Again the reply, "Maybe I do, and maybe I don't."

York threw another bill on the ground. This time the driver quickly snatched it up. He smirked with his answer, "Sorry, I don't know."

York feinted a move toward the man just to watch him recoil, and then he climbed into the Jeep.

"Hey, you owe me three hundred dollars," shouted the driver.

"You're right," York said. "Just as soon as you have that car at the garage and the hood pounded out, I'll be in to pay you for it."

York ignored the one-fingered salute that he received in return. He swung around the truck and sped down the road. It was an empty road in all directions when he got to the T-junction.

The woman slumped in the seat beside him. He looked at her; and her red rimmed eyes stared back. "Let's go back to my place and you can decide what you want to do," he said. Without waiting for a reply he slipped the clutch and drove steadily and quietly back toward his cabin.

Shamus MacGregor was checking his mailbox at the side of the road. York pulled to a halt and rolled down the window.

"Shamus, did you say something about a white pickup a couple of days ago?"

Shamus bent over and looked at the woman in the car. "Aye, it's been seen several times when there have been break-ins. They say two or three men in it."

"Well this lady's car was in the ditch by Coburn's Corner. When we brought the tow truck to pull it out, it was on fire and there was a white pickup leaving the area. It had a rusty tailgate."

"That would be it then. Did you say in the ditch at Coburn's Corner?"

"Yes, in the ditch." York knew what was coming.

"Were you driving, young lady?" Shamus asked.

"Yes sir. Yes I was."

"That's too bad," Shamus said. "I'm sorry you lost your car. And what would your name be? Just for the record I mean."

"Cat Stevens," she said, visibly bracing herself for the usual stock replies.

"I see," Shamus said.

Obviously his taste in music doesn't tend to 60's and 70's rock, thought York. "Well, we'll be going," said York aloud.

"I'll let you know if I see that truck, York," Shamus said. "Nice to meet you, young lady, Cat." Then he added, "Take care of this young fellow."

She didn't say anything as York rolled up the window and accelerated down the road and up his lane. He paused at the mailbox to remove the few pieces of mail, and then continued up the lane.

"It really is a beautiful spot," she said as they pulled into the yard at the cabin.

York parked the Jeep and let the two of them through the front door. It was noon and he was no farther ahead than when he left.

"That man was nice," Cat said. "Why was he so interested in my name? Just nosy?"

York told her about the naming of the corner where her car was, concealing a grin as he did so. Then he realised that, along with the new name, Shamus would also be spreading the rumour of a female companion. He scowled.

"Well let's sit down and talk about your predicament," he said walking into the main room and throwing a log in the fireplace.

The sun was streaming through the south facing windows adding a fair measure of solar gain. He just needed sufficient fuel to keep the fire from going out. Cat sat on the leather couch and pulled her jacket closed around her.

"What are your options? Where can you go? What can you do?" York asked.

"Well I was on my way to my fiancé's house in St Andrews," she began. Her voice trailed off as she finished the sentence then she resumed in a normal tone, "May I use your phone for a long distance call, please?"

"Sure, do you want some privacy?" he asked. "I can go outside."

"No, that's fine. I'll call and see if he'll come and pick me up."

She walked to the phone and York counted off as she dialled eleven digits. There was a short pause then the one sided conversation.

"Hi, it's me. I've been sick. No, Aunt Martha died. A week ago. No, I'm fine now but my car is burnt. Yeah burnt, I went into the ditch when I was sick and when I went back to get it, it was burning. I don't know how. Look Ron, can we talk about it later? Can you come and pick me up?"

There was a long pause then she continued, "Ron, I'm not sick anymore and you can be here in about two or three hours to pick me up. We don't have to stop anywhere. You won't have any chance to catch the flu."

Another pause then, "Ron, I don't have anywhere else to go. That's where my home is. Are you saying that you won't come to get me?"

York had a feeling that his life was about to get more complicated. He looked out the windows to the south. The sky was clear with a few small wisps of high cloud that signalled a slowly approaching weather change. He went to the woodshed to gather wood for the stove.

"You don't have to leave the house!" he heard her shout into the phone as he came back into the kitchen with an armload of small sticks.

She slapped the phone into its cradle. York avoided eye contact sensing that she must be embarrassed by what he had overheard. She tramped over to the couch and collapsed onto the seat then growled, "Men!"

York continued to work silently, now annoyed that he was being tarred and feathered along with the rest of his gender, just because she had a fight with her boyfriend. The guy sounded like a bit of a wimp from the one sided conversation he had heard, and York took it personally to be compared to him.

"I need to find a way to St Andrews," she said at last. "Can I call the car rental places to arrange a car?"

"Sure, go ahead." York got up and went into the kitchen to make a batch of bread. He always made bread if he was annoyed. The mixing and kneading had a way of settling his mind. He gathered bowls and ingredients and was measuring water and yeast when she came into the kitchen.

"They have nothing anywhere today, but Enterprise said they'll have a car tomorrow," she stated. "May I stay another night and then ask you to drive me to Fredericton tomorrow? Or if there is any sort of cab company, I'll take that."

"There's no cab company, and I'll drive you to Fredericton tomorrow."

"Thank you, again," she said. "It seems that all I do is thank you."

"No problem."

"What are you doing?"

"I'm making bread."

"You're kidding."

"No," he said bracing for another slight.

"That's wonderful," she said. "Can you show me how?"

Somewhat taken aback by the unexpected enthusiasm, York started to explain the procedure, at first a simple description, but then a more elaborate disclosure as Cat asked more and more questions. He showed the technique for blending the ingredients then the kneading. The dough got a bit more of a workout than usual as she insisted on practising until she got it right.

He then showed her how to light a fire in the woodstove, another artistry that she had never before seen. A couple of hours later, after the dough had raised, the two worked together to form loaves of bread and a pan of rolls. Cat showed an eager interest in the knowledge and skills that he was also happy to talk about. She fed the fire in the woodstove and later watched as he tapped on the loaves of bread to determine if they were baked.

"Why do you call those small sticks rabbit wood?" she asked pointing to the pieces of maple branches and small saplings that he had used with kindling to get the fire started.

"I'm not sure. That's just what it's called," he replied. "I guess maybe that's the size of wood that you often see growing in the bush where you set up rabbit snares and such."

"Uuugh! You don't really trap and kill wild animals do you?" She curled her upper lip slightly.

York explained his reasons for hunting.

"That's barbaric! Those are innocent animals. Nature will never hurt you, so why do you have to go around killing it?"

"Look, I hunt for food. It's more honest than deluding yourself that meat comes on a plastic tray. The roast that you had for supper last night was venison. You seemed to think it was OK then."

"How could you! You made me eat deer meat?" Cat fled toward the bathroom. "I feel sick."

York heard the shower running. After a couple of minutes he got out his harmonica and was about to spend some time practising, then he thought better of it. No sense setting himself up for more ridicule. There weren't many people who liked harmonica and he doubted that anyone would like the way he played Twinkle Twinkle Little Star.

After a half-hour he was on the verge of reminding the woman that the well was not bottomless, when the water stopped. He busied himself washing up the baking utensils, and then he heard a sound that he had not heard for a couple of years, a hair dryer.

York stopped in his tracks, a wet bread pan dripping a small pool of soapy water onto the floor. Sadness engulfed him. So much anguish came washing back, so many losses.

He heard the door to the bathroom open and Cat came into the kitchen. He covered his emotions by stooping to wipe up the water spilled on the floor. When he arose, Cat was standing by the counter.

"York, I'm sorry I acted that way. I just can't eat deer or bunnies or anything like that. It's not in me to do that." She reached out to put her hand on the counter close to him. "But I shouldn't have insulted you the way I did. You have the right to act as you wish and I'm sorry."

"No problem," he said as he turned back to the sink and resumed washing the pots and pans.

"I hope you don't mind. I borrowed the hair dryer that was under the sink. Does it belong to the pretty lady who's in the little picture on the bookcase?"

York didn't answer for a few seconds. "Yes."

"Is that your girlfriend?"

"The hair dryer was Victoria's. She died two years ago. We were together for a while then she developed leukaemia." York took a deep breath and gazed out the window at the snow in the evergreens. "I looked after her here in the cabin because she didn't want to die in a hospital. She hated to have dirty hair."

"Oh, God. I'm sorry, York. I do have a way of making things worse."

York looked back at Cat. There were tears in her eyes.

"No problem. I'm over it. Why don't we just forget it?" He grabbed a couple of plates from the cupboard and a knife from the block on the counter. "Let's try your first loaf of bread and see how it turned out. Why don't you get the butter from the fridge?"

He slept in his own room that night. Cat insisted on sleeping on the couch and had York explain the details for keeping the fire efficiently fed and burning overnight. She reminded him of a child introduced to a new game.

He was a while falling asleep and he thought about going out and asking Cat if she wanted to share the bed. There was plenty of room for two people to sleep alone together. He decided not to, afraid that she might think he was making a pass at her, and also perhaps afraid that she might accept.

CHAPTER 8

13 January, morning

The next day dawned cloudy, and he made meticulous preparations for the trip to St Andrews, as if he was heading all the way across the country. He checked the Jeep's tires and fluid levels and rechecked his usual winter emergency kit. He packed bread and cheese and a few energy bars and tea bags. The years of military training were transferable to much of civilian life, although there didn't seem to be a big demand for Special Forces officers on civvy street.

Cat came out to the Jeep as he was finishing his equipment check. "How come you're taking all those things?" she asked. "It's only a short drive."

He sighed. "It's always the short drives that get people into trouble in the winter time," he said. "That's how people get stuck in snow drifts, freeze to death going for help, or die in their car trying to keep warm."

"Do you take this stuff every time you go somewhere?"

"This stuff, as you call it, goes in the Jeep the first of November and comes out the first of May. The only thing extra is some food and a pair of mittens and a toque for you since you don't have any. I don't have any boots to fit you or I'd put those in too."

She looked at the sneakers on her feet and flashed a sheepish grin. “OK, OK, I’ve learned my lesson.”

“Climb in.” He slipped behind the wheel and they started for Fredericton. Cat waved at Shamus as they passed his farm.

York switched on the radio and listened to the ten o’clock news. The announcer gave the rising death toll from the flu and he was shocked at the figures. Estimates in the United States were as high as five million dead already and in Canada about a tenth of that. Millions more were ill and there was no end in sight. All air travel around the world was suspended, as was shipping. In North America, interprovincial and interstate travel was prohibited. In countries throughout the world there were as many as a million dead in each large city and governments seemed incapable of providing a solution of any sort.

The local news was of particular interest to him. There was talk of an impending ban on travel within the province to try to slow the spread of the influenza. Apparently the army was on standby to provide aid to the civil power, although there was no move in that direction yet. The other news of note that he heard was that the road maintenance crews were unable to keep roads clear even with small snowfalls. Side roads were still blocked but were gradually being reopened as further snow held off.

He discussed with Cat the route that she should follow to St Andrews, in light of the news broadcast. There was no traffic on the road and they were soon in Fredericton. He guided the Jeep across the bridge and through the city centre toward the southern outskirts.

At the Enterprise Car Rental location they found the lot empty and the storefront deserted. The front door was smashed and the floor was covered with a mixture of glass and blown snow. The key rack on the wall was empty and hanging from one corner. There had obviously been a few expedient rentals since Cat’s call yesterday.

Not wanting to be long in the area of a break-in, they left the lot and drove toward the nearby shopping centre. York noted a gas station that had a NO GAS sign out front. At the next station that was open, he stopped in and topped up. Every drop could be important in the next few hours.

The traffic lights were out at one large intersection and drivers were easing through the junction while two others were arguing beside their damaged cars. He pulled into the shopping centre parking lot. There were pay phones by the main doors. Calls to all of the other car rental companies were fruitless, and no cab company would consider a fare out of town. Buses were not running.

They sat silent in the Jeep. York knew what was expected of him and he was angry that he should be in this position. He fought the next step, not wanting to be tasked with another day of baby-sitting. Then he realised that his delay only marked him as no better than the faceless Ron that Cat had spoken to yesterday.

He looked Cat straight in the eye. "I guess we're going to St Andrews together."

She exhaled. "One more time I say thank you. I don't know how in my life I can ever pay this debt." She had tears in her eyes.

Now York felt bad that he had waited so long to speak up. "No problem," he stammered. Then to cover his embarrassment he added, "I'll say the same thing I say when I help someone whose car is stuck. No charge. Just do the same for someone else some day."

She smiled. "I promise."

York headed farther out of town. There was almost no traffic on the highway and they made good time. It was noon when they emerged onto the coastal highway just about a mile and a half from St Andrews. There was a restaurant at the junction and Cat suggested a quick lunch before completing the trip.

"Are you sure you want to stop this close to home?" he asked.

"My treat," she said. "I'd like to contribute a little." Her eyes urged him to accept.

"No problem," he said swinging the Jeep into the parking lot in front of the restaurant.

The door was locked but there were two men and a woman inside. There followed the same through-the-window conversation that had occurred in Spencer, with the same predictable results. York rebelled against the prices and ushered Cat back to the Jeep.

"You're right, I guess. I couldn't have afforded it," said Cat. "But I was hoping to talk some more."

"These are weird times, Cat." York started the Jeep and swung out onto the road turning right to head into St Andrews.

"Oh no, not this way," she said. "The other way."

"What? I thought you said St Andrews."

"Well St Andrews is the nearest big town. Ron's place is about thirty minutes the other way."

York braked hard and pulled to the side of the road. He turned in his seat to face Cat. "Please tell me that you're kidding me!"

"No, I'm not kidding. What difference does it make?"

York slammed the Jeep into gear again and pulled a U-turn in the middle of the highway. "The difference is gasoline. There was a shorter route we could have taken if I had known where we were heading."

"Look I'll pay you for the extra gas, all right."

He slowed and pulled around a car that was stopped on the highway, a driverless car that was stopped right in the middle of the road. "It's got nothing to do with the money," he said. "Didn't you see the out of gas signs in Fredericton? There may not be any gas available, period. Every drop that we have may be irreplaceable."

"I'm sorry. I didn't understand."

"You need to tell me when we get to the turn-off," he said.

There was no further conversation.

"The road is just ahead," she said after a half-hour. "It turns off to the right just past the speed limit sign; and yes, I see the 'Welcome to Pocologan' sign. I know this isn't St Andrews."

York swung the Jeep into the lane and immediately saw the debris in the road ahead, a couple of downed trees and a dozen bails of straw. He slowed the vehicle to a crawl.

"Were you expecting this?" he asked.

"No. This isn't usually like this. Can we get around it?"

"Probably, or we can move it. But it looks like a roadblock of sorts."

He eased the vehicle forward and the house beyond the roadblock came into view. There was a light showing from one of the front windows of the bungalow. The terrain around was strewn with old rusted out cars.

"Your Toyota will fit right in," said York, and then regretted it immediately.

He gave a short blast on the horn to attract attention. After a few seconds there was movement at the window then the door opened halfway. York continued to scan the house and the area around it. There was movement at one of the smaller windows to the left and he detected a glint of metal that looked like a rifle barrel.

A man shouted from the doorway "What do you want?"

"That's Ron," said Cat. "Ron! It's me, Cat."

"Cat, what are you doing here?" said the partially seen figure.

She swung herself fully out of the car carrying her handbag. "I got a drive and I've come back to wait this out with you." She headed for the roadblock and started to walk around it.

York stepped out of the Jeep and stood with the door in front of him.

"Stay right there!" shouted Ron. "Don't come no farther."

She halted. "Why not?"

"Just wait right there. We don't want no flu. The radio says the flu is everywhere and you could have it!"

"Ron, it's OK. I've already had the flu. I'm over it. This man saved my life and I'm OK." She started forward again.

"Don't come no closer!" Ron shouted.

Cat stopped again. York saw movement at the small window and the gun barrel poked farther out, now more easily seen. York tensed and then he considered, processed, and evaluated a flood of options.

"Cat, don't move," he half whispered. "There is a gun in the small window to the right."

"A gun? Where? Why?" She looked at the house after a double take at York.

Not exactly subtle, thought York. It's going to take me a while to teach her the tricks. He caught himself. He could not believe that he had actually speculated that way. "Are you sure that this is the right place?" he asked her.

"Ron, why are you pointing a gun at us? It's me, and this man is a friend. He saved my life. He cared for me when I was unconscious and couldn't do anything."

"Yeah, I bet he did," said Ron. "Had a real good time playin' house did you, buddy?"

York bristled but said nothing. This guy was obviously an asshole, and besides there was still another person in the house, someone with a gun.

"Ron, stop that. Don't get jealous with me again. He is a friend. Now let me come in and talk to you."

Suddenly there was a movement at the door and a woman appeared. "We don't need you here, honey. We don't have no flu, and we have just enough food to get along for quite a while."

York glanced back at the window and the gun was still there moving a little. So there were at least three in the house.

"Who are you?" shouted Cat.

"I'm Linda, and me and Diane are all that Ron needs. Ain't that right, Ron?"

"Shut up, Linda. Cat, I just can't take no chances with the flu and all; and we're all clean in here. Why don't you just head off where you came from with your little nurse and give me a call when the flu is all over."

Cat did not move. York held his counsel. The gun moved a little farther into the open. Then Cat turned without a word and returned to the Jeep. York slipped behind the wheel. The engine was still running and he released the parking brake and shifted into reverse. Cat stood by the side of the Jeep staring at her feet.

"May I get in?" She sounded whipped.

"Yes, get in and buckle up."

York released the clutch and backed up quickly until they were out of view of the house, and more importantly out of sight of the gun. He turned the Jeep and headed back to the highway, stopping at the end of the lane.

"I'm sorry it worked out that way, Cat. Do you want to find a phone and call him?"

"No, I don't want to ever see him again. I just want to get out of here."

York turned to the right up the coast highway. He glanced sideways and saw that she was crying, staring straight ahead, unmoving.

After a few minutes he pulled off the road at a picnic site and got out to sit on a table. When Cat got out he looked at her carefully. The tears had stopped. Was it strength, or a cover up, or was she just angry now?

"Cat, we need to talk about what we're going to do. Where do you want to go now? The main problem is going to be gasoline if we're not careful."

"I don't have anywhere to go," she whispered. "That was to be my home. I moved out of my apartment in Saint John. He was my fiancé and I was supposed to live in his house. I went to Miramichi to see my aunt when she called to say that she was sick and now I don't know what to do."

"Couldn't you move back to your apartment?"

"There was someone moving in the day after I moved out. And I'm afraid to go back to the city after everything that they said on the radio."

York said nothing.

"I could go back to my aunt's place. She said the house was going to be mine but that's also a city and I don't know anybody there."

York heard himself saying, "You can stay at my place if you want, until this mess is over. That way you have a chance to think it over."

We might have enough gas to get there, as long as we don't find any more roadblocks, he thought, but refrained from saying it aloud.

Cat searched his face. "Would that really be OK? I will gladly sleep on the couch and I can cook some things really well. And I'll leave as soon as possible."

York was embarrassed by her enthusiasm and he dug out the map to cover his discomfort. He scanned the map and selected a route. Because of his concern about gasoline he chose a different itinerary back toward the capital. One of the drawbacks of the Jeep was its small fuel tank and somewhat limited range. There was more chance of finding fuel along this other route. They continued toward the east and the pall of smoke that rose in front of them marked the city of

Saint John.

They reached the road heading north and left, the smoke disappearing to the rear. This road was not as well cleared as the coastal road. It was colder inland and they were soon travelling on packed snow instead of pavement. Suddenly the road disappeared into a ledge of snow in front of them. The green provincial plow truck was in the ditch; and there had been no further effort to clear the road.

He stopped the Jeep and checked the odometer, then the map. He found their position on the map. They were about four kilometres from the town of Kings Crossing and York knew that there were three gas stations where their present route met Highway 99 in the centre of town.

"Cat we're going to continue down this road. If we go back we have no choice but to go into Saint John to find gas. We don't have enough to go back the way we came."

"Can we go through this snow?" she asked. "It looks kind of deep."

"No problem. She'll take deeper than this as long as we don't go too fast and push snow up onto the belts."

He shifted into four wheel drive, high range, and pushed forward into the small drifts. They travelled slowly but steadily, passing several cars and one pickup abandoned in the ditch. York shook his head; he knew that a pickup without four-wheel drive was practically useless in snow. The Jeep, however, had excellent ground clearance and great traction. The snow thrown up by the heavily lugged tires rattled against the fenders and beat against the floorboards at their feet.

They arrived in Kings Crossing about fifteen minutes later. Two of the gas stations had OUT OF GAS signs on their pumps. The third was doing a roaring business with six cars lined up at the single pump. York pulled into line and gradually moved forward waiting his turn. As he got to the pumps and opened the gas cap the attendant came out of the station.

"Say there, you're not from around here, are you?"

"No, I'm not," York said. "We're on our way to Spencer."

"Well gas is pretty expensive these days," said the attendant.

York knew what was coming. “I need to see your money before you fuel up.”

“How much is it for the gas?” York sighed.

“Depends on how much you want.”

York did a quick calculation. “About fifty litres. That should about fill it.”

“Well that will be three hundred dollars cash in advance,” said the attendant.

York fished out his wallet and counted a hundred and change. He opened the door and asked Cat if she had any money. She had thirty dollars.

“All we have is one hundred and thirty,” he said. What can we get for that?”

“About ten litres,” said the attendant.

Ten litres was not enough to get them even to Fredericton. York could see the other man inside the station. He held a shotgun in his hand. “How about a debit card or a credit card?” York asked.

“Are you kidding? Our system has been down for three days and nobody will come out to fix it. It’s cash or nothing.”

“Well I’ve got something better than cash,” York said.

He stuffed the cash back into his wallet and reached into his shirt pocket to bring out a single yellow coin. “This is a gold Maple Leaf. It is one ounce of the purest gold on earth. Gold is selling for a thousand dollars an ounce today and will probably go higher.” York turned the coin over in his hand, making the most of its seductive shine. “This ounce of gold should be able to buy us a complete fill up and one of those red cans full as well.” York reached into his wallet and brought out the five twenties. ”There’s also the hundred bucks that will satisfy your friend in there. He doesn’t even have to see the gold change hands.”

The attendant licked his lips and held out his hand. York held out the coin and the hundred, and then stopped just short of the hand.

“No funny stuff,” he said. “You weren’t expecting gold and there will be other surprises if you try to cross me.” He looked the attendant in the eye and handed over the money.

The attendant nodded, took the payment and raised a hand to

the man inside. The man reached behind the counter and the power came on at the pump. The attendant walked to the rack beside the door, took down a twenty-litre gas can and opened the cap.

York topped up the Jeep and the gas can, and then he stowed the can in back. He got into the Jeep and drove away as quickly as was practical on the unplowed road.

Cat was silent for about three minutes then she apparently succumbed to curiosity. “York, you never cease to amaze me. Do you always carry thousands of dollars worth of gold in your pocket?”

“Well not always, but these are unusual times. There are five more in little compartments sewn into the usual pockets in my pants and shirt. And I lied a little. The price of gold is only about five hundred dollars today although I wouldn’t be surprised to see it much higher soon.”

“That’s an awful lot of money for a little gas.”

“Cost is relative, Cat. Getting back home is precious the way things are going right now.”

“You’re right, I guess.” Cat looked down at her hands then began to play with the radio.

“Hang on,” said York as he braked and steered into a deep rut. “It’s going to get a little rough ahead.”

CHAPTER 9

13 January, afternoon

The sky was overcast and foreboding as they entered Fredericton from the south. They passed the Department of Transport compound, now marked with a hand-lettered sign that proclaimed VEHICLE DETENTION CENTRE. The chain link fence was wide open. Inside the compound four men were jumping on the roofs of cars, and close by another was swinging a large sledgehammer at the windshield of a bright red Mustang convertible. The long slippery slope, thought York.

He drove all the way into the city and swung the Jeep onto Queen Street noticing two things very quickly. There was almost no traffic on the main street of the city centre, and even downtown the side streets were plugged with snow. There was a narrow lane down the middle of some of the streets as if the plow had made one pass several days ago.

He had a goal in mind and that was the bridge to the north side of the river. Suddenly, however, he swung a quick left onto Marble then right again onto Prince. He jerked to a halt in front of a Victorian house made over into an office building.

He ran up the walk, leaving Cat shouting questions behind

him. He had a plan half formulated and it was beginning to gel as he went through the front doorway. If only the office was open.

He slipped through the office door. There, behind the counter in front of him, was a face that he had nightmares about. Alexander Sloat looked up startled; and then slowly recognition washed over his face.

"Mr. Lancaster, isn't it?"

"Yes it is, Mr. Sloat."

"What can I do for you today, Mr. Lancaster? Property to sell?" The man got up from the desk and sidled up to the counter.

There's a day you'll come to regret that, asshole, York thought. Then out loud, "No, Mr. Sloat, nothing to sell."

The man stood motionless behind the counter. York leaned forward, invading his space.

"I came to see if YOU have any property to sell, Mr Sloat."

"We always have properties for sale, Mr. Lancaster. Although I doubt that you are in the class of buyer that would be purchasing such properties." The sneer curled the thin moustache upward in the centre of his lip.

"Mr. Sloat, have you noticed all the people who are dying of the flu?"

Sloat stirred a little uneasily. He glanced at the phone.

"Have you had the flu yet, Mr. Sloat?"

"No, no I have not."

"Mr. Sloat, I have seen people dying of the flu; puking their guts out, gasping for breath, all of it happening in a couple of days."

"So...so what does that have to do with me, Mr. Lancaster?"

"Well they're saying now that everyone will get the flu and that only ten percent will survive," York lied.

Sloat visibly trembled.

"I've come to see if you would like to save your life," York continued. "I don't have all day and you have one chance. Otherwise I'll just make a squatter's claim when the time comes."

"What are you talking about? I'll notify the authorities if you try anything unsavory."

"This is your opportunity, Mr. Sloat. You can sell me back

my property for the same price you paid for it, and maybe a little bit extra."

"Now, why would I do that?"

"Because I have the flu, Mr. Sloat." York hissed the man's name making sure that his exhaled words carried into Sloat's face. "And we have been in close contact and I've been making sure that I breathe heavily in your direction the whole time that I am here."

The man recoiled.

"And Mr. Sloat, I have the cure in my pocket. I have a full course of Flugone right here and I am willing to trade it, and the original selling price of my house, for the property that is rightfully mine."

There was silence.

"Make the decision now, Sloat," York snapped.

Sloat jolted alert. "The property does not belong to me and it is not rightfully mine to sell. You know that it was purchased for a company. I only had the power of attorney to carry out the company's business."

"You still have the power of attorney," York declared, hoping that he was right.

"Yes, but it could mean the end of my employment."

"It could mean the end of your life," said York tapping the package of Flugone on the counter.

York paused for a few seconds then turned and started quickly for the door.

"Wait," Sloat shouted. "I'll do it. Let me have the medication."

"When the paperwork is done."

"That will take some time, Mr. Lancaster."

"You have five minutes. Fire up that word processor. Churn out the standard form, a simple form that gives me full title to my land. If there is a lot of fine print or any clause that makes me even suspicious, then there will be no further discussion and I will be gone through that door." York leaned toward him, holding the package of pills to one side. "And you will also produce another letter that says you were not under duress or threatened in any way; because this is not duress or a threat. It is a simple offer to purchase and if you refuse I won't harm you in any way. I'll just march out the door."

Sloat scurried to the workstation and started to work at the computer, complaining that there was no secretarial staff there to help. York lifted the phone from its cradle and heard a dial tone. He noted that the instabank machine had power. No doubt he would need to pay. He glanced quickly out the window, saw Cat looking his way, and beckoned her inside.

"Hurry up, Mr. Sloat," he said as Cat came through the door.

"What's happening, York?" she asked.

"I'm buying some real estate. Mr. Sloat is just finishing the paperwork and we need a witness."

York saw him sag at the workstation. An unwitnessed transaction could more easily be overturned in court.

"Give him your name and address please, Cat," said York, then added, "Make sure that there is a place for witness details on the non-coercion letter as well, Sloat."

The paperwork was soon completed and York read it carefully but quickly. He was not a lawyer but it appeared straightforward. He was about to sign when Cat grabbed his arm.

"Don't sign it, York. He's trying to cheat you."

"What? What's wrong?"

"This is a standard 'Offer to Purchase' form that he has just changed the heading on. This is not a bill of sale."

"That's nonsense, young lady," snarled Sloat. "This is a legal document that you know nothing about. Now, Mr. Lancaster, if you would just sign here, you will once again be the owner of your fine home."

"Don't do it, York."

"How do you know that it's not the right form, Cat?" York stared at her.

"I'm a realtor, York. That's my job. I've handled these types of transactions for eleven years. He's trying to cheat you. I know the wording on the forms even if the heading is changed."

York looked from Cat to Sloat to the papers then back to Cat.

"Trust me on this, York," she said. "I don't know much about fires and winter safety gear and such, but I do know real estate sales."

York reached for the papers, pen in hand. He paused, and

then tore the paper into shreds.

He looked up at the other man. “You had your chance.” He turned to the door. “Come on, Cat. Have a nice death, Sloat.”

“Wait, Wait! I am truly sorry. I still want the medication. Your friend can fill out the papers.” He looked beaten. “I accept your offer.”

“The offer just changed,” said Cat before York could speak. “You had the purchase price of one hundred thousand dollars entered on the paperwork.”

“That is the agreement to which Mr Lancaster ascribed; the original price for which the house was purchased by us.”

“Well the offer just changed because you bargained in poor faith. The offer is now twenty five thousand dollars.”

“That’s ridiculous. I won’t agree to it.”

Cat plucked the box of pills from York’s hand and tapped it on Sloat’s nose. “Twenty five thousand dollars and your life, you little weasel, and if you stall any farther it will go to twenty thousand.”

“That’s outrageous,” he blustered.

Cat grabbed York by the hand and turned him to the door. York felt himself being manhandled to the exit even as he felt that his house was slipping from his grasp.

“All right, you win. It will be done,” Sloat whined.

Cat wheeled York back to the counter. “So we’re agreed then, twenty thousand dollars.”

Sloat started to sputter and Cat waved the Flugone in his face and moved as if to leave again. Sloat clamped his jaws shut, obviously fighting back a retort.

“The two of you stay over there,” Cat ordered. She sat at the computer and in five minutes the papers were completed, signed, and Sloat reached for the Flugone.

“Not so fast, Mr. Sloat. Haven’t you forgotten something?” Cat needled. “This is not a robbery, no matter what you may try to tell the police or a judge later. We need to transfer funds to finalise the deal.”

“But the financial establishments are closed,” Sloat protested.

“But the electronic bank is open,” York replied smiling at Cat, “and here is my bank card.”

Sloat initialised the instabank terminal and York swiped the card. This was a card linked to his line of credit and he had a $100,000 limit. The purchase would now only take a fraction of that. He would have paid more if he had to, and had actually expected that Sloat would pressure for more. Fear had obviously placed an enormous value on the Flugone. Not a bad return on his insurance policy. He keyed in his Personal Identification Number and approved the electronic purchase. He held out his hand for the receipt and placed all of the paperwork in his shirt pocket.

"It has been a pleasure doing business with you, Mr. Sloat," said Cat.

York headed for the door. "Sloat, don't try to welch on this deal or cause me trouble over this. At property prices the way they're going to be, your overseers are going to be quite happy that you got the return on your dollar that you did. The pills will be our little secret. If you cross me again I'll be less patient."

York closed the door behind him and headed for the street. "Come on, Cat. Let's get out of here."

They piled into the Jeep like Bonnie and Clyde leaving a bank job. York spun the wheels as he pulled away from the curb.

"Jeez, you were something in there, Cat. You're hell on wheels on your own turf. And the twenty thousand dollars bit. I thought that he was going to bust a gasket."

She laughed out loud along with York. "And it was all entirely legal. He was probably just getting back what he's given out to others in the past."

"Next stop, Spencer," said York.

"No, we have one more stop to make," she said. "Where is the court house?"

York drove to Queen Street and stopped by the courthouse. They quickly went to the office of the Registrar of Title just as a young woman was closing the door.

"Please can you help me? I need to register a property purchase," said Cat.

"We're closed at five."

"Please, it's my parents' house," said York, "and I really need to do it today. You know with the flu and all."

She sighed and unlocked the door. "All right, if the paperwork is all here. If not then you'll have to come back tomorrow."

York handed her the paperwork except for the duress letter. She looked it over and made notations on the forms, had him sign two other forms, and stamped everything several times. York paid her the required fee by cheque and thanked her profusely.

As they were about to leave the office the phone began to ring. "Don't touch it," the young woman said. "I want to get home today."

York glanced at the phone and saw Sloat's name appear on the caller ID. They left the office as the phone continued to ring.

As York wheeled away from the Registry Office, Cat played with the radio attempting to find a local station still operating. She found a station broadcasting a repetitive announcement that all travel in and out of Fredericton was prohibited and that all of the bridges were closed. York pulled to the side of the road to think.

There were two bridges that spanned the St. John River within the city. One of those two was his intended route to the north side of the river and thence to Spencer. These were obvious choke points and there was little benefit in trying those routes at this time. There was another bridge in Oromocto to the south, and the dam over the river north of the city. Those were the more likely sources of escape.

York decided that the northerly route was the farthest out of the built up area and was the best bet for clear passage. With the decision made, he swung the Jeep back into the road and headed for one of the three routes that led in that direction. This was the old Trans Canada Highway, now little used except for local traffic since the new four lane highway had opened. They made good time since the road was deserted. As they crested the hill just before the turn off to the dam road they came face to face with the second roadblock of the day. This one had flashing yellow lights and came fully equipped with a military vehicle and soldiers in combat clothing. York was forced to stand on the brakes to avoid the trees that had been dragged onto the road.

York pulled to a halt at the roadblock. He eyed the soldier approaching the Jeep and also the soldier who remained by the obstruction. He then ignored the obvious and let his eyes travel from right to left across the trees and bushes in the background. There, to the left of centre, he saw the slight glint of metal, and a camouflaged helmet outline nestled below a half blown down tree. From that location the hidden soldier could engage a vehicle from either direction. York again scanned the area but saw no other threat. Strange that I should be considering my own army a threat, he thought. These were, however, strange times.

The soldier approached the driver's side of the car. "Where are you going, sir?" he asked.

"We're on our way to Spencer, just coming out of Fredericton."

"Are you aware that travel has been suspended because of the flu?" he asked.

"No, I wasn't. I live in Spencer and we're just returning home," said York.

"Well I'm afraid that you have to go back. All travel in and out of Fredericton has been closed," said the soldier.

"We can't go back," York argued. "My home is in Spencer. We have no place to stay here."

"I'm sorry, sir, but those are the rules right now. Please turn around and go back. You can turn over there," he said, pointing to a flat area criss-crossed by the tracks of previous vehicles.

York thought of running the roadblock, thought about it for an instant, then remembered the firing position in the woods and dismissed it. It was not fear for himself that made the decision; he had been in more dangerous positions. Cat, however, had not.

York jerked the Jeep into a three point turn and headed back toward Fredericton. He glanced in the mirror and saw the soldier by the roadblock talking on the radio.

"What do we do now?" asked Cat.

"We try an alternate route," he replied. "Let's try Route 6. We can then go north and farther up stream we can cross over the river in a smaller community. We have enough gas."

As they rounded a sharp corner on Route 6 they came face to face with another roadblock. This time there was an armoured personnel carrier in the middle of the road and the machine gun in the cupola was pointed right at them. A soldier on the side of the road approached the Jeep on the passenger side.

"I'm sorry, sir," he started, telling the same story as the previous soldier.

Again York tried to argue, to explain, to perhaps find a way to carry on their way. It was to no avail and he again was forced to head back into Fredericton.

He returned to the outskirts of the city and was about to turn toward the south when a police car swung around after passing them and pulled in behind them, lights flashing. York pulled onto the shoulder and waited for the policeman to approach.

"Good afternoon, sir," the constable began. "May I see your licence and registration?"

They went through the usual formalities then the policeman said, "Sir, you can't keep trying all the roadblocks. The travel restrictions are there to keep the flu from spreading and there are no exceptions."

"But I'm from Spencer, not Fredericton. We have nowhere to go in Fredericton. I can be home in an hour, no stops, just straight home."

"Park your vehicle downtown and walk to city hall from there. They will tell you where the reception centres are. There is shelter and food available."

"Yeah I saw what those reception centres were like a few days ago," York retorted. "People crammed together, dying everywhere, vomit and dead bodies all over the place."

"I'm sorry, sir, but that's all that there is. If you don't take advantage of it, there are detention centres. The conditions are worse and you are not free to move about the city." He handed the licence and registration back to York. "There are a lot worse places to be than the reception centres, believe me."

York put away the identification papers, and the policeman returned to his cruiser. York accelerated onto the highway and pulled off into the city as the police car carried on down the highway. If only they were on the other side of the river they could find a way out of the city. You could not cordon off a whole city without a lot more personnel than York knew were available.

The river was not frozen except in patches. Even travel on foot on the ice would be suicide. But maybe there was a ploy here. If he could convince someone that he didn't want to leave the city, just get to the other side of the river, maybe that could be the first step to getting out of the city.

York turned onto Westmoreland Street and headed up the approach ramp to the bridge. The roadblock was obvious and well manned. Beyond it in the centre of the bridge was a sandbag bunker and another armoured personnel carrier. York pulled to a halt at the roadblock.

As the soldier approached the Jeep, York got the first word in, "Hi there. We're just trying to get across the river. We live on Riverside Drive, right over there. We were just released from hospital and told that we could go home."

"I'm sorry, sir, but travel across the river is prohibited," was the stock reply.

"Can I talk to your officer?" York asked.

"I'll get the section commander," the soldier replied.

He walked back to the roadblock, where another soldier waited, spoke to him briefly then carried on toward the bunker. York could see him talking to another figure that then picked up his helmet and walked with the soldier back to the roadblock. The soldier waited at the roadblock and the section commander approached the vehicle.

York saw him glance at the license plate of the Jeep as he walked to the driver's side. The man was quite a bit older than the first soldier and wore sergeant's stripes on the sleeves of his combat jacket. "Good day, sir. Can I help you?" he asked.

York retold his story and the sergeant listened closely.

"Come on, sir, we've heard all about you from other positions and from the city police. How many silver jeeps with a man and a woman in them do you think there are on the roads today?"

York restarted the Jeep and began to shift into gear. The sergeant placed a hand on his arm.

"I wouldn't do that if I were you, sir," the sergeant said. "Look behind you beside the small shed over there."

There was another firing position beyond the sergeant's pointing finger and two soldiers manned it with a shoulder-fired anti tank weapon. "I have authority to use deadly force, sir," the sergeant stated simply.

York believed him. The sergeant had the look of experience about him. He had probably been in the army for quite a while and was unlikely to be just bluffing. "We'll go to the reception centre," said York.

"I'm sorry, sir, but that's not possible. There is now an order to detain you."

"Why?" asked York.

"Apparently the city police have a complaint that you robbed some real estate agent earlier today and we have orders to detain you."

"That's ridiculous." York bristled. "I bought that property. I have the deed in my pocket."

"May I see your ID, sir?" the sergeant requested. "And yours too, ma'am?"

York and Cat produced driver's licences and handed them to the sergeant. York also tried to show him the bill of sale and the deed for the house. The sergeant told him to hold onto those papers, as there would be an opportunity to use them later.

The sergeant signalled the soldier at the roadblock who approached at the double. The sergeant examined the ID and then looked quickly up at York. York thought of the buck and its double take manoeuvre. The sergeant looked back at the ID.

"Were you ever in the army, sir?"

"Yes, I was, sergeant," York replied, wondering if there was an opening here.

"Are you Captain Lancaster that I would know about from Afghanistan?" he asked.

"That would probably be me," York replied. He glanced at Cat and saw her looking at him strangely.

"Well you'll understand, sir, that I must follow the orders that I've been given."

"I understand," York answered. He realised that there was little chance now of any help at this location.

The soldier from the roadblock arrived and the sergeant turned to him. “Call platoon HQ and have them send the northside vehicle down here to pick up two detainees,” he said.

“The northside vehicle?” asked the soldier. His question was logical since they were on the south side of the river.

“Yes, you heard me correctly,” the sergeant replied softly. No bluster here, just the quiet expectation that he would be obeyed. And he was. This man definitely had time in.

The soldier headed back to the roadblock and the sergeant turned back to the vehicle. “I was in JTF-2 after you left, sir. I know who you are, where you’ve been, and what you’ve done. Everybody who’s been in the army more than five years knows that. Most of these kids barely know how to keep their weapons clean. I’ll get you to the north side of the river if that’s where you want to go, but you have to leave the vehicle here. I’ll drive it to the compound myself when my shift is over.”

York thought back to the vehicles they had seen being destroyed in the vehicle lock-up earlier in the day.

“I appreciate that sergeant. I’d appreciate it more if you’d use the Jeep and hang onto it until all this is over. I think that I’d have more chance of seeing it again if you had it.”

“If somebody saw me driving this I’d be accused of looting,” said the sergeant.

“Can I have the registration back for a minute,” York asked. He took the registration, signed the transfer of ownership form attached and handed it back to the sergeant. “Fill your name in there,” said York. “Maybe you’ll sell it back to me for a dollar when all of this is over.”

“OK, sir, if that’s what you’d like,” he said. “I’ll take care of it for you.”

The approach of a truck from the other side of the river hurried them. York took his survival kit from the back of the Jeep and he and Cat climbed into the back of the military transport. A soldier climbed in also and the driver raised the tailgate. The soldier in the back pulled down the canvas tarp and the truck headed across the bridge. They would now be on foot but they were across the river and only sixty miles from home. To many that would be a daunting situation; but to York it was only a fact. In warm weather, travelling light, that was a twenty-hour walk, or perhaps two days with lots of sleep and rest. Of course this was not warm weather and travelling light was out of the question.

CHAPTER 10

13 January, evening

As the truck sped down the roads, York planned his next moves. Oh how he wished he were alone. The young soldier next to him was too close to defend himself if York were to attack. He could easily disable and disarm the soldier, and it would then be simple to jump from the truck as it slowed to make a corner. Cat could not know how to make that jump and would likely be injured in the attempt even if she could be coerced into trying the jump at short notice. No, he would have to await their destination before making his break.

And what about the sixty miles to Spencer? She was not equipped physically for that kind of trek and she had no warm clothing. Even if he found a quick way out of confinement then what was he to do about Cat?

The answer was actually quite simple. Nothing. Cat was not his problem. He had done his best to help her out. She was not his responsibility. She was someone else's fiancée, even if the guy was an asshole. York had rescued her from her car, had saved her life from a deadly illness, and had gone out of his way to try to get her home. What more could anybody ask? True she had helped him with Sloat. But, she was probably safer and better off staying here than trying to make it home with him. And if she were separated from him, then there was less likely to be trouble for her over the Sloat affair. It was settled. He would make a break for it when the chance presented itself.

The truck slowed almost to a crawl as it made a sharp turn to the right. Tree branches scraped along the canvas cover. The soldier by the tailgate stirred and glanced out beside the back tarpaulin cover, then thrust it up onto the roof as the truck jerked to a stop. York glanced at his watch. It was 5:35 and already starting to get dark. It was only a couple of weeks past the winter solstice and the long nights came early.

Two other soldiers appeared at the back of the truck, unlatched the tailgate, and lowered it. Then all three soldiers, with weapons drawn, stood back and called for York and Cat to climb down. York jumped easily to the ground then helped Cat to climb down. He grabbed his survival pack and followed the soldier who led the way to the front of the truck.

He saw several military vehicles parked amongst the trees. The trail they were on continued ahead through the woods. Three modular tents were visible as well as some small lean-to structures that appeared to shelter supplies. To York's experienced eye it looked well organised and efficient. The commander on the ground was not letting a little epidemic get in the way of military discipline and function. The soldiers were largely young and inexperienced but obviously well led.

"Turn around and place your hands on the truck, sir," said a sergeant who emerged from the nearest modular tent.

York did as he was told, dropping the survival bag at his feet. He was searched, as was his bag. With no warning, his hands were seized behind his back and bound with electrical ties. He felt a momentary twinge of panic as he recalled the years of captivity in Afghanistan, then he regained control and began to get angry. He was seething and getting ready to lash out when he heard the sergeant speaking softly at his ear.

"Easy, Captain Lancaster. This is not Afghanistan. We'll find an excuse to get you out of here."

Then York heard him say to Cat, "Pardon me, miss, but I have no choice but to search you to make sure that you are not armed. Although if Captain Lancaster will vouch for you, and you swear that you are carrying no weapons, then I will break the rules and not physically search you. We are not the enemy here. It is the damned flu, but there are precautions we must take."

"Sergeant, she is not a danger to you and I do not believe she is armed," York asserted.

"I am not carrying anything more dangerous than a set of nail clippers," Cat stated.

"That's good enough for me," the sergeant said. "Any friend of Captain Lancaster is a friend of mine. I have no choice about securing your hands though.

"These will not be tight," he said as he slipped the electrical ties about Cat's wrists.

She began to weep softly.

"Take Captain Lancaster to the Administration tent, Smith," the sergeant said motioning to the soldier who had sat in the back of the truck on the ride from the bridge. "It's warmer in the OPS tent and the lady can wait there until the company commander gets back."

As they started to move in separate directions Cat sobbed and shouted, "Don't leave me, York! Don't leave me!"

To relieve her fear he called back, "It's OK, I won't leave you." He regretted it as soon as he had said it, although it quieted her crying.

Inside the tent, the soldier motioned York to a folding metal chair. The Coleman lantern provided a little warmth. It all had an "all too familiar" feel for York.

"That's pretty special treatment for you and the lady from the Sarge," the young soldier said. "He usually does everything right by the book. When were you in the Forces?"

"JTF-2, during Afghanistan," York answered.

A low whistle escaped the soldier's lips. "You're THAT Captain Lancaster? That explains a lot. Is it true that you led the attack back to the camp where they held you for the two years?"

"Yeah, it's true. I had a score to settle."

"I feel really embarrassed with you sitting here with your hands tied and all, but I have to follow orders."

"That's OK, you follow orders. That's the right thing to do. This will all work out." He did not add that it didn't really matter if he had his hands tied or not. He didn't plan on being tied for long.

The sergeant came into the tent and had York's bindings removed then reapplied with his hands in front. "You know, if you would give me your word that you wouldn't try to escape, then I could leave these off, Captain."

"And you know that it's always a soldier's duty to try to escape," York replied. His word would bind him more tightly than ten electrical ties and he didn't want that kind of constraint.

"I kind of thought that might be your feeling." The sergeant grinned, then without smiling added, "Please remember that my soldiers are not the enemy, Captain."

"I will remember that, Sergeant," York answered looking him straight in the eye.

The sergeant left the tent, and York and the young soldier traded war stories although York did most of the story telling. About an hour later another soldier appeared in the tent door relieving the first soldier of guard duty.

The newcomer had only been in the tent for about a minute when he spoke his first words to York. "So you're the famous York Lancaster. If you ask me you're not so hot sitting here tied up," he taunted. "If it was up to me I'd have treated you just like any one of the other looting, stealing bastards that are roaming the streets." He looked at York for a minute then continued, "I don't believe a word of that shit about being captured. I think you chickened out and ran to the enemy. That's why they kept you alive for two years." He stubbed his toe hard into the packed snow that formed the floor of the tent, and drove a spray of icy particles into York's face. "And I think that you're a traitor and probably waiting for the right time to stick a knife in our back again."

York said, "You don't know what the hell you're talking about, kid, and you wouldn't be saying that if my hands were free."

"Well your hands aren't free. They're tied like any traitor should be and if you try anything I'll shoot you like a traitor should be too."

York started to boil. The young soldier was stupid, arrogant, and inexperienced, but that did not excuse in York's mind the fact that he had been called a traitor. Two years lost, a career lost, a fiancée lost, a home lost; and this whelp had called him a traitor! York controlled the anger, giving no outward sign of his emotion. There was danger here if the soldier took it in his mind to cause him harm. York had initially planned on escape, but as the sympathetic treatment prevailed, had planned on pleading his case to the company commander when he returned. Now he began to plan escape again as his captivity took on a more dangerous tone. He had been lulled into relying on others. Now he must once again focus on being self-reliant.

The soldier busied himself at the propane stove that was sitting on the folding table. York worked at the long electrical ties binding his hands together but there was no give. At least his hands were in front of him. He remembered the pain and stiffness he had suffered when his hands were bound behind his back in Afghanistan. As the soldier turned away from the stove and toward York with a cup of coffee in his hand, York ceased his efforts and sat still head lowered.

At least the tent was warm. The wind rattled the sides intermittently. The lantern hissed. York stiffened as he realised that he was in danger of falling asleep.

"Any chance of a cup of that for me?" he asked.

The soldier glanced his way. "When the major comes back to talk to you, maybe he'll exchange it for a little information."

"What kind of information are you looking for?" York asked.

"What were you doing sneaking around? Why were you out when there is a curfew? What group do you belong to? Things like that," replied the soldier.

"What do you mean a curfew?"

"The curfew, dummy. You know, stay in your houses to keep from spreading the flu and to prevent looting," replied the soldier.

"I never heard of any curfew. When did that start?"

"Sure, that's what they all say," the soldier sneered.

"No, really, we've been isolated for the last couple of days. When did that start?"

"Three days ago. The government said that everyone had to stay in their houses except to go out to purchase food during daylight. No public gatherings. They're trying to stop the flu spreading. Some goons tried to raid the grocery stores to hoard food, burned the big one down on William Street."

"Why did you ask what group I belonged to?" York continued his own interrogation.

"There's been two or three groups that have started robbing stores and other peoples' houses, armed, stealing food and anything else that they can find." The soldier sipped his coffee. "At first they just said that they were trying to get food but then they started forcing people to give them money and stuff not to hurt them or burn their houses down."

"Then how come you are out here on the outskirts of the city and not in the middle of it?" asked York.

"We are here to keep people from coming to the city looking for food and also to keep people from leaving the city, spreading the flu."

"You look pretty thin on the ground," York said, slipping into the military vernacular.

"Yeah, we've got a company spread out around the city. We can only cover the largest routes."

"Many flu casualties?" York slipped in.

"A lot of the company is sick. I think the sergeant major said this morning that eleven had died. I haven't had it." He eyed York. "Have you got the flu?"

"No, I guess I'm immune. I've been around people that have had it but I've never got it. Where is the major now?"

"In the tent next door, probably interrogating your girlfriend. Nice looking babe."

The soldier grinned. "Maybe I'll do a little personal interrogating myself later on. If you know what I mean." He made an obscene gesture.

York processed the information that he had acquired. A company of maybe a hundred men; no, the soldier was wearing the insignia of the Royal New Brunswick Regiment, understrength reserve forces, so the company was maybe eighty men. Probably twenty ill and he said eleven dead. Covering main routes only. There were ten that he could think of. That meant about an understrength section of men per route. If they were covering twenty-four hours a day they would do well to have two or three men at a time at each location. And only the largest most obvious routes would be covered, and little in the way of a rapid response force. If he could get his hands free they could get out of this. He felt the press of his boot knife against his right ankle.

CHAPTER 11

13 January, night

York started a little psychological warfare. He had gathered enough information for the moment and it was time to make some moves. "How about taking me out to have a leak?" he said.

"You can wait until sentry change, when there are two of us," the soldier replied. "Maybe the great York Lancaster will piss his pants."

York hoped that the suggestion that he had just made, as well as the three cups of coffee that the sentry had drunk, and combined with the cold weather, had sowed the seeds of urinary pressure. He had not been given the coffee that he had requested from the soldier and he had no need to urinate.

Sure enough, a couple of minutes later, the sentry started to check his watch, pace the floor and repeatedly glance at the door of the tent.

After ten minutes of increasing movement on the part of the sentry, York decided to turn up the heat. "Man, my bladder is going to burst," he said softly.

The soldier stormed over to York and kicked the chair from under him. York sprawled in the snow and curled up as he absorbed a kick to the stomach.

"Shut the fuck up, traitor."

York rolled out of the way to dodge another kick that just missed his head. The soldier stalked to the other side of the tent and sat on another chair. About two minutes later the sentry got up again and walked to the tent door and glanced out into the night, as if he could will his replacement to appear sooner. He looked at York, then back outside, then at York again.

"You behave yourself for thirty seconds. I'm going to take a piss. If you behave yourself, then I'll take you out to drain your lizard when I come back." He flaunted his submachine gun at York. "If you screw around you'll regret it."

"OK, just hurry."

The soldier slipped through the door. At least he took his rifle with him, so he's not completely stupid, York thought. He knew that the right answer to the problem facing the soldier would have been to void on the ground and accept the derisive comments of his fellow soldiers. Instead he had chosen the solution that York hoped that he would. He had given York a few seconds of freedom from observation.

York twisted on the ground and bent forward swinging his bound hands to his right boot. He retrieved the boot knife and wedged it, cutting side up, between his knees. In seconds the razor sharp edge had parted the electrical tie and he thrust the knife back into the sheath in his boot. He repositioned the electrical tie over his wrists concealing the cut ends below the wrists. He sat up and slumped forward partially hiding his wrists and adopting a position that would not alarm the sentry. While awaiting the soldier's return he worked the muscles in his wrists and hands.

York did not have long to wait. The soldier burst through the door and stared at him, and then smiled. Probably pleased with himself for beating the system and not getting caught, thought York.

"Can I go for a piss now?" York asked.

"When the sentry changes."

"Come on, man, I'm going to piss myself. You said that you'd take me after you came back if I behaved myself."

"Well I lied, traitor," snorted the soldier as he stalked over to York and stood above him.

"So did I," whispered York. He slashed his right leg behind the sentry's knee and the man went down like scythed corn. He scrambled on top of the soldier in an instant and slapped a chokehold on him.

There was no sound as he applied pressure to the hold and at the same time immobilised the soldier with his legs. He wrestled him to submission with pure brute force and pinned him until he stopped struggling. He waited a few more seconds then released the pressure.

He checked to see that the soldier was breathing, then trussed his hands behind him and taped his mouth with a roll of gun tape that was sitting on the table. He unrolled a sleeping bag from the pile in the corner and dragged the unconscious soldier onto the fabric. He then threw another sleeping bag over the soldier, remembering his promise to the sergeant not to hurt his men. Not that this guy deserved any consideration.

York searched inside the tent for items that might be required as he continued his escape. He kept his right eye, his dominant eye, closed. By shutting out the glaring light of the lantern, the right eye at least would be quicker to adjust to the darkness when he left the tent. That could give him an advantage if he was discovered or chased.

He gathered up a pair of gloves and a few packs of tea and sugar. He stuffed the items into his survival bag and attached the shoulder straps that turned the bag into a backpack. He took his belt knife from the pack and secured it at his waist.

He moved to the doorway to leave, then returned to the table. He scribbled a note explaining how the sentry had treated him, and then placed the man's weapon on the note. As an afterthought, using the indelible marker from the map board, he wrote STUPID on the man's forehead. That would take a week or more to wear off. His buddies would make some hay out of that and maybe it would teach him a little humility.

He slipped out the door of the tent. He moved a few steps away from the door, closed his left eye and opened the eye that he had kept from the light for the last few minutes.

He made note of the other tent alongside his temporary cell. That would be where Cat was being questioned. Well, she was safe and warm where she was. They might hold her for a bit, and perhaps place her in some sort of detention facility for a while until the flu was over and the usual civilian government structure was re-established. She would be safe and warm where she was, he assured himself.

He felt the tang of a snowflake on his lips and raised his face to the sky. There was a faint glow of moon through fleeing clouds and more flakes fell on his face, cheeks and eyes. The wind was increasing to match the march of the clouds and was beginning to raise a low whistle in the spruce trees that surrounded the camp.

York slipped farther into the shadows of the tree line and continued to look around. He saw a tracked vehicle with camouflage net in place parked among the trees. Unusual. Vehicles were usually stripped of nets at last light in case they needed to move suddenly after dark. He knew that nets were a pain in the butt after dark, catching on every clip and tie-down point when you were in a hurry. Probably another indicator of reduced manpower.

He considered stealing the tracked armoured personnel carrier, then rejected the idea. The starting process would alert any troops nearby and the noise would preclude a quiet escape. The camouflage nets would interfere and he would likely be rapidly chased, with his vehicle tracks easily followed.

He rejected stealing one of the wheeled vehicles for similar reasons. And heaven knew the condition of the roads outside the city. Likely impassable to wheeled vehicles in spots. He could try to disable all of the soldiers then leave at his own will but there was no telling where all the soldiers were at this time. It made more sense to slip out of camp and melt into the woods.

There was a small trail alongside the vehicle and he quickly made his way along it, ending a few feet later at a hole-and-pole latrine. He lifted the roll of toilet paper from the stick by the latrine and slipped the paper into his pocket. He then returned to the camp area and investigated two small lean-tos set to one side.

He froze, wondering if soldiers were sleeping inside. He slipped his belt knife into his right hand. Even the threat of the knife might quiet a groggy man. He had no desire to kill anyone and least of all not a soldier of his own country.

With knife in right hand he grasped the edge of the lean-to with his left and snapped it open. He reacted instantly to what he found. Bringing his right hand to the throat, and left hand to the sleeping soldier's mouth he came face to face with a dead man. Cold, stiff, dead.

York held his position listening to see if anyone had alerted to the small amount of noise that he had made. The wind grew stronger and now flapped the tentage, providing cover for a lot of noisy sins.

He had seen death before. He had done his own killing when necessary. The discovery of death did not shock him. He remained motionless. No movement anywhere. The light seeping around the tent doorways reflected off the snow. No one moved.

He arose and circled the camp searching for anything else that would hinder or aid in his escape. He then made a decision and slipped into the treeline avoiding the open track that could seduce him into recapture. He moved like a ghost through the woods heading roughly in the direction of the road to more accurately determine his present location. You cannot get to where you are going if you don't know where you are to start with. A hundred yards later he stopped. Damn!

"Don't leave me alone," she had said.

But what can I offer her? She was warm where she was now. She would be fed. She would be taken to a place where she had a roof over her head. He could only offer cold, starvation, and very possibly death. If he were a sensible man himself then he would stay where he was also, even if he had to live in detention. But I cannot be caged again!

York turned back to the campsite, unsure of why he did so. Step by step, he approached the operations tent, listening for any sound above the rising wind. He closed his right eye again, eased to the ground and peered into the tent with his left eye, moving the flap just an inch.

Cat was seated on a bench. She clutched a military small pack on her lap and drank from a plastic mug. York scanned the tent looking for another person. There was nobody else in the tent. He leaped to his feet, drew back the flap and slipped into the tent. Cat started and spilled some of her drink on the ground, then smiled at York. "I knew you'd come for me."

"Come quickly," he whispered as he sliced the electrical tie from her wrist. She came off the bench and headed for the door and he realised that she had only her light windbreaker for outer clothing. They exited the tent and York led her toward the makeshift morgue that he had discovered earlier.

As quickly as he could, he stripped parka and gloves from the stiff corpse. He could hear the horror in Cat's voice. "What are you doing?"

"He doesn't need these anymore. And you'll freeze to death without them." He passed the parka to Cat. "Take this," he whispered to her. "Put it on over your own jacket. It's plenty big enough."

"Absolutely not!" Her voice was beginning to rise. "That man is dead. I'm not going to wear his clothes."

"Get them on quickly. And keep your voice down."

"I said no," she hissed. "There is no way that I am putting that on."

"It's time to make a decision and you have ten seconds," York said. "Put these on and you come with me. Leave the gear here and I leave you here. It's that simple."

She hesitated, and then donned the clothing. York tugged off the man's boots and stuffed them in the pack he carried. As an afterthought he tore down the lean to, quickly wrapped it into a ball, and then took the lead and they melted into the forest.

The snow was heavier now and the moon was no longer visible. The ambient light reflected by the snow cover made it possible to move rapidly, with the black towers of the trees silhouetted against the white blanket on the ground.

The whine of a snowmobile engine rose above the sound of the wind. York stopped and glanced back toward the camp. The glow of a single headlight lanced through the snow like the light sabre from a Star Wars sequel. The headlight then disappeared and the engine stopped. There was little chance of the snow machine following them through the woods but the thicker the trees, the safer they were from that threat.

"Come on, Cat." York touched her arm. "We need to get out of the immediate area."

He led the way through the woods. As they walked he reached into the side pocket of his survival pack and found the compass that he had put there so many months ago. He selected north and kept to that heading for thirty minutes.

The wind was now driving the snow into their faces, coming slightly from the right. This was a "nor-easter" and could bring lots of accumulation. The air was still mild, probably no less than minus 10C.

CHAPTER 12

13 January, late night

York led the way through the trees, covering a kilometre in about fifteen minutes. Then he stopped to take stock of their situation. He knew that they were on the north side of the river. That was a blessing at least. But where exactly were they and now that they were free, what next?

"Cat, we are not so far away that we can't go back. You said not to leave you so I didn't; but you don't really know what you're getting into." York almost had to shout to make himself heard above the wind in the trees. "We have dozens of miles to go to find shelter and we may die trying. We can go back and you will be safe and warm. They'll feed you and you will survive."

"I don't want to go back," Cat shouted at him. "The officer told me what the detention facilities are like. There are people dying like rats in a box. There is no medicine. The flu is killing them all anyway; and If I'm going to die I'd rather not die in a sewer."

"Are you sure?" York asked again, "because I can't go back to a cage and if we start on this together there's no turning back later. We're burning bridges."

"I'm sure," she said.

"OK," he said. "Let's take stock of where we are and what we have." He steered Cat into the lee of a large spruce tree. "What do you have in the pack you're carrying? Where did you get it?"

"The officer gave it to me. He told me to keep it in my hands and not to put it down for any reason."

"What? Quick, let me see."

He took the flashlight from his pocket and had the contents of the small pack exposed in a few seconds. There were some granola bars, a couple of glow sticks, a military pocket-knife, a dry pair of socks and a folded map.

"Tell me about what the officer said inside the tent."

"He asked me about us and why we were driving around. He was actually very nice. After the first few minutes I didn't feel afraid. I was more afraid of the detention centres."

"What else?" York prompted.

"He asked about you. He seemed to know you quite well. He said that you had soldiered together, whatever that means. He said that you were the best soldier that he had ever known; that I was lucky to know you and that if I was with you I had the best chance of surviving this mess."

York encouraged her to continue not sure what to make of what he was hearing.

"That's part of the reason that I said now that I wanted to keep going."

"OK, but what else did he say?"

"Well, he asked how I came to be with you and whether I was your girlfriend." She glanced at York then paused. "I told him that I liked you but I was still not sure what had happened with my fiancée and that whole thing."

"Anything else?" York hurried her along.

"Nothing else. He just said that he was taking his Jeep to bring back a vehicle to take us out of there. And then he left.

"Oh," she added, "I kind of felt sorry for him. He said his wife died of the flu a week ago."

York felt a chill, more than just the dropping temperature.

"Did he tell you his name or did he have a name tag on?"

"He didn't have a name tag that I could see. He said that his name was Russell. Do you know him?"

"Yeah, I think I might," York said. He was quiet for a moment then turned back to the items in the pack.

"You know, I think he might have known that you were coming for me," Cat said. "He wished me luck as he left."

He spread the topographical map out full size. It had been covered with self-stick clear plastic to make it waterproof. The snow pattered on the map and he had to brush it away as he scanned for the information that he needed. He immediately saw the small circle that was the only extra mark on an obviously new map. The circle was at a small track junction just off Route 12 leading into Fredericton. That had to be where the camp was. The company commander had provided a start point. He took out the compass, made a quick estimate of where they had travelled and searched the map for a likely route to continue.

He refilled the small pack and distributed some of the burden amongst their pockets. Better not to have all your eggs in one basket. He handed gloves and toque to Cat, the ones that he had packed in his survival kit. Then he produced the boots from the dead man and insisted that Cat put them on. The extra pair of socks made them fit a little better. When he felt that all of the immediate preparations had been completed he gave a few instructions.

"We need to travel steadily but not too quickly. If we sweat we will freeze. On the other hand, if we don't make progress and find some shelter then we will also die." He unzipped his parka. "Once we start to move, start to unbutton layers to ventilate heat."

Cat also unzipped her parka. "OK." Her voice sounded frightened.

"It's going to be rough going in spots," he said, "especially when the ground gets uneven and when we get into drifts. We have to get far enough away from here by daylight to avoid recapture if they start to look for us. "That trooper that was watching me is going to have a headache and after he looks in the mirror we may not get the same easy treatment the next time." He shrugged into the backpack. "Are you still sure that you want to come along?"

Cat slung the small pack over her head and one shoulder. "Yes,

I'm sure. It can't be any worse than the detention centres."

* * *

They headed north and east toward the closest collection of buildings enroute to Spencer. They were losing heat rapidly with the wind blowing in their faces. At each brief pause they closed their parkas to conserve heat. As they resumed the forced march they opened layers to avoid sweating. It was becoming darker in the thicker woods and any pretence of a moon was long gone. Cat was beginning to stumble more frequently. They were far enough from the camp to avoid recapture and it would make more sense to wait until daylight to continue. A branch in the eye or a sprained ankle could be disastrous.

York saw a downed tree at the edge of a thicket and investigated. This could be just big enough for two. The thicket had held the snow and the tree had altered the wind flow to create a drift.

He took off the pack and laid it to one side. He helped Cat out of hers. She collapsed on the ground beside it.

"Don't do that!" he shouted jerking her to her feet. "You'll melt the snow under you and it will soak through your clothing. Stay up for now."

He got down on his knees and started to burrow in the drift with his gloved hands. Cat knelt down to start digging as well. He stopped her. The doorway had to be the right size or the wall would collapse.

"Get the ground sheet out of the pack." He pointed at his load. "It's the large green plastic rectangle that was the lean-to where you got your new wardrobe. And give me the metal cup that's in there too." He continued to dig.

Cat returned with the ground sheet and cup. He took it from her and lay on the plastic and started to dig with the cup. Gradually he cleared out the inside of the snowdrift and, lying on one side then the other, created a cave big enough for two.

"Cat, try to make a large snowball the size of this opening. The snow is packy enough." She looked puzzled so he added, "Just pretend that you're starting a snow man."

She started to make a snowball then roll it on the ground. By the time the snow cave was ready, so was the snowball.

York pulled a collapsible saw out of the pack and quickly cut fir boughs from the far side of the thicket. Cat carried them to the opening. He spread the ground sheet on the floor of the cave then a thick layer of boughs.

"Crawl inside. Try not to get too much snow in there so it won't melt and get you wet. I'll pass the packs in."

He handed her the flashlight and stood back as Cat crawled into the cave. Her back and butt began to scrape against the top of the cave opening and threatened to collapse the doorway. He put his hand on her rump and pushed down to force her to crawl on her belly into the cave. He could hear her protests through the snow. Damn! It would be so easy if he were by himself.

After Cat and the pack were inside he rolled the snowball to the doorway and trimmed it a little. He then backed into the cave and with a bit of effort coaxed the ball against the opening.

There was an orange glow inside the cave with the flashlight turned on. The snow was barely thick enough to provide insulation but it already felt warmer out of the wind. He lit one of the candles that was in the pack and wedged it between a pair of fir boughs, then switched off the flashlight to conserve battery power.

Cat looked a little uncomfortable.

"What's the matter? Are you claustrophobic?"

"No, it's not that."

"It won't collapse and it will get a lot warmer."

"No, it's not that either," she said.

"Well, what is it?"

"I have to go to the bathroom," she said. "I've had to go for the last hour!"

York laughed out loud like he had not laughed in years. The more he laughed the angrier Cat became. Then she started laughing as well.

"Stop it," she said. "If you don't stop making me laugh, I'll pee myself."

York did stop as quickly as he could. Wet clothes in the winter were nothing to laugh about, even if Cat did not know the significance of what she had just said. "You know, when you're out of school you don't need to ask permission to go." He pushed the snowball from the door and squeezed to one side to let her past. He dug into his jacket pocket.

"Now listen carefully, Cat. Go around to the left alongside the thicket. When you're done, don't come back. Call out to me and home in on my voice and the light. In the dark and the snow you can easily become disoriented and you could wander into the night, never to be seen again."

She acknowledged the instructions and he reached out his hand to her. "Here, take this, but it may be all that we have for years."

"Oh my God, where did you get that?" she said as she took the roll of army issue toilet paper.

"It's a secret," he joked.

About five minutes later he heard her call and then she quickly vectored in on his voice and the splash of light from the flickering candle. She handed back the roll of paper. Not many sheets gone, York noted. He would not have been surprised if half the roll was missing.

"The secret papers, sir" she said as she crawled back into the cave.

York arranged the door again and they found reasonably comfortable positions, as best they could in the cramped surroundings.

"If you have to go again in the middle of the night, the same rule applies. Always go to the left to use the toilet. We'll go to the right if we need clean snow for water. Make sure you wake me up, although I imagine I would be awake anyway. You'd have to crawl over me to get out."

He saw Cat glance at him and then jerk her gaze away. Surely she knew by now that he was not going to attack her. It was so much easier by yourself, he thought. Nobody else to worry about, and nobody else to have to rely on.

York extinguished the candle and returned it to the pack. He worked in the dark, by feel alone, wanting to conserve the battery power of the flashlight. When all was as he wanted it, he settled back to try to sleep. He shifted the sharp end of a bough out of the small of his back, and then relaxed in the aroma of the fresh cut balsam that surrounded them. He was feeling the first fingers of sleep pulling on him when she spoke.

"York?" a tentative word.

"Yup."

"This is almost like a bad dream. I can't believe that this is happening. That I'm doing these things."

"Well it's no dream. You can pinch yourself if you're not sure."

"I'm wearing a dead man's clothing."

"That's called survival, Cat."

The wind shrieked outside and blew spicules of snow through the crack in the ill-fitting door onto York's face.

"I don't know if I can survive, York."

He could feel it coming now, the plea to return. After the trek that they had been through, they were going to have to go back tomorrow. He'd get her within sight of the camp then leave her to return the rest of the way. Hopefully he could make his escape the second time.

"But I don't want to go back. I just wanted you to know that," she said.

York raised his eyebrows in the pitch black. "OK, get some sleep, Cat."

CHAPTER 13

14 January, morning

When York opened his eyes the roof of the snow cave glowed with a blue translucent light. Cat was still asleep beside him squeezed tight against his back. He reached out and pushed on the snowball door and bright light stabbed into the snow cave. Along with the light came a shot of cold air that instantly cleared his thoughts. He was stiff from the cold; and the boughs, once soft and inviting, now dug into his right hip. It was daylight and they had to be on the move. He rolled to his knees and Cat stirred and whimpered a little.

York jostled her shoulder. "Wake up. It's daylight."

She opened her eyes then started and sat bolt upright. "What's happening? Where are we? I'm cold."

"Time to get a move on. It's daylight. We have a long way to go."

York pushed the snowball the rest of the way out of the doorway and crawled out. He scanned the woods around, then searched the sky and listened for a full minute.

"We have to make headway while we have the weather. There's an awful lot of red in the east and we'll soon get snow again," he called to Cat inside the shelter.

Cat followed him out of the snow cave and headed off to the left where she had made her way in the snow last night. York reached into his pocket. “Cat, do you want the secret papers again?”

She didn’t turn but kept walking. “No thanks, I saved a few sheets last night.”

York smiled to himself. Smart lady. He crawled back into the cave and brought out the pack and the parkas, collected the ground sheet then searched carefully for anything that shouldn’t be left behind. He was knocking the snow off the ground sheet as Cat reappeared. He dug out a small metal stove and heating tablets, as well as the metal cup, and then replaced the ground sheet in the pack. He lit the heating tablets, filled the cup with snow and put it over the fire. He dug out the map to plan their route.

“Cat, will you please keep adding snow to that cup after the first bit melts? Don’t pack it too full initially. The snow will scorch if you don’t give it a chance to melt slowly at first. It’s the only way you can actually burn water.” He turned away to the map. “There’s hot chocolate mix in the pack that we can use when you have a cup of hot water.”

The map told the full story of their travel situation. He measured sixty-five kilometres direct route to his cabin. Of course the direct route was practically impossible. It made a lot more sense to avoid the uphill struggle over some of the large wooded hills and to travel through the valleys and saddles. It also made a lot of sense that they follow some of the trails that were marked on the map. After all this was not war.

He looked up from the map to see how Cat was doing and he instantly became angry. She was stirring the cup over the heating stove. The contents of the backpack were all spread out on the ground sheet, which was laid out fully on the snow, like this was a picnic outing.

“What the hell are you doing?” he hissed.

She jerked and stopped stirring the cup. “Making hot chocolate like you asked.”

“Sorry,” he said. “You just don’t know.” He walked over to the equipment that she had arrayed on the ground sheet. “You have to remember that we are hunted at the moment. You can’t have everything all spread out. We have to be ready to move at a moment's notice and we have to take all of our kit with us when we move." He started to refill the pack.

"There's nobody around here," she argued. "Look, we're the only living creatures for miles. Why don't you dump this soldier crap."

"This soldier crap is the reason that you're alive right now," York threw back at her. "This soldier crap is what will give you at least some chance of living to see the spring. Look around you. How far can you see? Almost a hundred metres at best. How do you know that there isn't someone a hundred and fifty metres away, or a hundred and two metres away, or over there where that thicket is, thirty metres away." He continued filling the pack. "I intend to survive this foolishness. I intend to get back to my cabin, to continue my life. If you want to come along then you have to learn some of this soldier crap." He pulled the straps closed on the pack and stood up. "If you want to learn some new rules, follow those new rules, and put up with a lot of that soldier crap, then you can walk the trail with me. If you don't want it that way then I'll lead you back to the camp where we were and then I'll carry on."

"Well that's just exactly what I want," she retorted. "If I had wanted to be walked all over, then I could have stayed with Ron. He was better at it than you are."

"Fine," York said, lowering his voice so that it was barely audible, "now drink up the hot chocolate and we'll start back." Just what he needed, he thought. A bitchy woman who couldn't make up her mind what she wanted. He was much better off by himself. He could make better time with fewer hassles and less grief if he didn't have to worry about her. He just wanted to be left alone. He looked over at the woman, where she was sitting looking into the cup.

"You have to drink up," said York. He softened his voice, "I have a long way to go and we have to start right away."

"I can't. It's too hot. You drink it." She pouted.

York strode to where she stood. He looked in the cup, walked to an area of fresh snow, scooped up a handful and carefully dropped it in the cup. "It won't be quite as creamy but all of the nutrition is still there and it's still warm but now drinkable." He handed the cup back to her.

He walked over to a downed tree, wiped off some snow and sat down to plot a route back to the camp. A couple of minutes later, her shadow fell on the map and he looked up.

"I never thought of the snow thing even though the snow is what we used to make the hot chocolate. I'd like to learn some more of the soldier crap. It's not really crap at all. It's actually very smart. It's just also very new to me." She held out the half empty cup. "Your half is still here, and I'd like to go with you, not back to the camp. If you'd rather go alone then I understand and I won't argue, but I know I can learn this stuff. I'm sorry I said what I did. It's a long story, why I acted that way, but it was still wrong."

York accepted the cup with a shrug and took a drink. "We all have our long stories," he said. "Are you sure that you don't want to go back? This has been a walk in the park so far compared to what is coming."

"I'm sure," she said without hesitation. She paused and stared at him while he collected his thoughts.

"All right then, sit here and let's look at the map. Maybe if you know what's happening, then it will make more sense and not look so much like crap." He brushed the snow off the limb beside him.

"Just a minute," she said and walked over to the stove. She upended the fuel tablets into the snow, extinguished the fire and carried all of the items to the pack and set them down. She then returned to York. "I thought that we should conserve the fuel. They're too hot to pack right yet."

York smiled and nodded his head. "Now that's good soldier crap."

She grinned back at him. For some reason he felt that the day was brighter. He shook off the feeling and returned to the map.

For the next half-hour he explained the most obvious features of map reading and decided on the route to follow. He would have preferred to just head off on the first leg of the day, but he was enough of a leader to know that information was important to the followers as well as to the leader. This could mean the difference between life and death, and if he kept her content then it would be fewer hassles for him in the long run. Why did life have to be so complicated?

It was almost eight when they headed out. The weather was cold, likely minus 20C. There was no wind but the sky was very grey, threatening snow.

They headed first for a road junction where a bridge crossed a small stream. The stream needed to be crossed somewhere and it was better to avoid wet feet if possible. Probably the stream was frozen but the junction provided several additional benefits. They could perhaps find help or even a ride. There were several houses close by. They could also assess the condition of the roads. Were they plowed? The route to the bridge added about a mile to their total trip but more than made up for it with information. Perhaps if there was no transportation available then he could buy some snowshoes or even skis. He fingered the gold coins sewn into the jacket.

It was shortly before noon when they came to the stream. It was covered by snow but there were open areas visible a little downstream so York did not trust the ice to cross. His compass bearing had been deliberately west of the direction to the bridge, so that when they reached the stream he knew that the bridge lay to the right. They followed the bank of the stream until the bridge came in view.

York led them back well into the trees and they closed in on the bridge. It was not plowed and there was only a snowmobile track breaking the snow. There was a house close by on the right after the road crossed the bridge.

"Wait here, Cat, while I cross first. When I call you to follow, walk exactly in my footprints. By doing that there's no easy way to tell how many in our party."

While Cat remained in the trees, he walked to the bridge. He scrutinized the area from that new vantage point, and then waved her forward. As she reached the bridge, he started forward again, motioning her to follow. He had taken small footsteps so she should have no problem in his tracks.

They re-entered the trees on the other side of the bridge, on the right side of the road. They headed in the direction of the house, keeping within the woodline. The distant moan of a snowmobile came from behind them and they crouched in the cover of an old spruce as the snowmobile got closer.

The machine advanced around the hillside curve from the direction of the city. A second machine followed about fifty metres behind. Each had one only rider, obviously military, with rifles slung on their backs. One sled stopped on the high ground overlooking the bridge while the other slowly crossed and turned left down the intersecting road. When the driver reached a point about a hundred meters down the road he stopped and scanned the surrounding territory. After a minute he raised his hand and returned to scanning. The first machine then made its way across the bridge and stopped briefly to examine the footprints. York and Cat remained motionless and fully hidden in the woodline.

The second machine started again and turned onto the intersecting road. It passed the first sled and continued down the road. After another couple of minutes the stationary snowmobile followed the new leader out of sight around the bend of the road.

"That was some more of that good soldier crap, wasn't it?" said Cat. She was grinning beside him.

"Sure was." York grinned back. "But you notice that they never saw us. Our crap was better." He got to his feet and they started toward the house staying in the trees.

They circled behind the house. York wanted to be past it, enroute to his destination if they were discovered. He had no wish to have to pass the house later if there was a threat from that location. He also had no wish to be trapped between the stream and the road.

They stopped and examined the dwelling for a while. There was no movement, no sign of life.

"Wait here, Cat. I'm going to approach the house. If there's trouble, I'm going to my left out of sight of the door and then back here. There may be a bit of a detour but you wait here and I'll come for you. He headed for the house, wading through a waist high drift that had formed where the trees formed a windbreak.

He stopped short of the door, looked around, and then went onto the front doorstep. The doorbell was one of those that had a little light in it. He shaded it from the daylight but still could detect no light. Perhaps the power was out, or perhaps the switch was not working. He rapped on the door and stepped back off the stoop. The curtain in the front picture window moved and then stilled. He remained where he was. He wanted no armed confrontation such as had occurred with Ron at Pocologan. After a couple of minutes the front window beside the door opened a crack.

"Stay back! What do you want?"

"I'm on foot, have been for two days. I'm trying to get to my home in Spencer, and I was looking for help. Food, warmth, transportation, snowmobile, snowshoes, anything." York stood still, not wanting to appear a threat in any way.

"Mister, I'd like to help you but I'm barely staying alive as it is. There's no power, hasn't been any for two days. All I have is electric heat so it's freezing in here. There's no food in the house. I haven't had anything to eat in four days. All of the grocery stores were cleared out." There was a pause, then he said, "My car is in the garage but it won't go anywhere in this snow. The radio says there are no drivers for most of the plows. I don't have a snowmobile." The door opened part way to reveal an elderly man with a cane. "I can't let you in, mister. You might have the flu. The flu killed my wife."

"You don't have any snowshoes or skis, do you?" York asked.

"Mister, I'm seventy five years old. I haven't been on skis in my life."

"York reached into his pocket and pulled out a granola bar. He tossed it to the man in the doorway. "Here's something that might help a little. Thanks anyway." He turned to go.

"Wait a minute, mister," said the old man. "Go out to my garage. There's a set of snowshoes there. One of them is broken, has been for twenty years, but there's also tools and you can probably mend it if you're handy."

"Thanks," York said. He turned away as the door closed. He moved to where he knew Cat could see him and flashed ten fingers at her twice, hoping she would understand. He saw a flash of white in return. He then headed toward the garage.

The small side door was unlocked. Inside was a Volvo S80. The man obviously believed in quality, he thought. The garage was immaculate. The snowshoes were hanging on the wall beside the door and in front of the car was a neat workbench. With the snowshoes laid out on the bench, he examined the damage. These were bear-paw snowshoes, an almost round platform. One was in perfect shape. The other had a split in the perimeter but all of the lashing and the bootstraps were fine.

York selected a couple of pieces of hardwood from a scrap pile and made splints for the frame. Finding a couple of small hinges and screws in the hardware cabinet, he was able to secure the frame. It wasn't pretty, but it would work for a while at least. He surveyed the garage searching for anything else that might make their task easier. No such luck. He left the garage and carrying the snowshoes made his way back to Cat.

He showed her how to wear the shoes and to walk in them without getting 'mal de raquet'. He also told her what the old man had said about the general conditions. They headed roughly north through the woods again, toward the next house that was marked on the map. Because she was inexperienced on snowshoes Cat still had difficulty keeping up with him but that would correct itself with time.

The next house was about a kilometre farther down the road and on the other side of the highway, although the highway looked more like a long narrow curved snowfield in its present condition. It was early afternoon before they got there. York led them to the other side of the road, the same side as the house, before they came in sight of it. They again moved through the woods past the house before attempting an approach. There were several out buildings, sheds that were chicken coops, tool storage, and such in previous times. There might be shelter here for the night, and perhaps more.

As York and Cat discussed the next move, he noticed that the temperature had moderated, and that heralded the snow. What they really needed was another pair of snowshoes. Unless there was a blizzard, they were OK to get to his cabin as long as they could make time on the road. He took the snowshoes from Cat so he would struggle less going to and from the house.

"Same drill as before," he said as he headed for the side of the house.

He approached the house and rounded to the front to knock on the door. No sense even trying the doorbell if there was no power. He stepped off the step and waited until the door opened; and a young man carrying a shotgun appeared in the doorway.

"What do you want?" he asked, his eyes drifting to York's feet and the snowshoes that he was sporting.

York saw that the man's finger was inside the trigger guard. He held both hands out to his side, palms forward in a gesture to show that he was unarmed. "We're looking for a bit of help," he said, purposefully using the plural we. That might give the man second thought if he was considering a quick kill.

"Who's we?"

"My friends and I," York replied then continued, "We're not meaning to cause you any trouble." He thought that he'd come straight to the point since he didn't like the way the meeting had gone so far. The way the man came onto the step, finger on trigger, implied an aggressive not just fearful attitude. "We're trying to get to Spencer. Do you have any transportation that would help, snowmobile, skis, snowshoes?"

The man with the shotgun again glanced at York's feet. "No, but I'll buy those ones that you're wearing. I'll give you good money."

York now knew that he had to buy some time. "Yeah, how much?"

The man paused. "How about two hundred and fifty dollars?"

"I don't think so," York said, "but one of the other guys might. I just wanted to replace this one because it's broken," he said pointing to the broken shoe. He then turned and was walking away as he shouted, "Hey Buster, do you want to sell your snowshoes to this gentleman?" He also waved his hand in the air, anything to distract the shotgunner and buy a few steps.

"Hey, wait!" He heard the man behind him shout but he had reached the corner of the house. He stepped sideways into the shelter of the wall and then started to run as fast as he could for the woodline. He was halfway there when he heard another shout and a shotgun blast sprayed the snow to his left.

He looked back as he ran. The man had moved to the back

step now, gun raised. York veered right and again a blast peppered the snow to his left. By now the pattern of shot was quite spread out. He had reached the limit of the effective range of the shotgun, and he powered straight ahead. The shotgun roared a third time and York felt a sting on his ear and heard other pellets whistling close by. Then he was in the woods. He moved left and when he knew he was close he called for Cat.

Her eyes were wide like a deer caught in the headlights of an approaching car. "He shot you. He shot you. You're bleeding."

He put his hand up to his ear. It came away bloody but everything was intact. "It's OK, no problem." Then because he could see worry on her face, he added in a fake British accent, "Merely a flesh wound, my dear."

"Why did he shoot you?" She picked up some snow and applied it to the side of his face.

York stood still while his ear stung with the cold. "Apparently he wanted the snowshoes."

"Well why didn't you just give them to him?"

"There are at least two reasons," York said. "First of all these are life and death tools right now. Look at the sky. It's going to snow again and from the feel of it, snow hard. It hasn't been too bad moving through the woods on foot so far but that's all going to change soon." He moved Cat's hand away from his ear and started unbuckling the snowshoes. "Without snowshoes we will die of starvation and the cold before we can get to my cabin. Even one pair could make a difference. So when it became apparent that he was determined to have the snowshoes I decided to leave. More of that soldier crap."

Cat looked at him for a moment. "Touché. And what is the second reason?"

"Well," he grinned at her, "he didn't seem to be in the mood to negotiate." He kicked off the snowshoes and passed them to Cat.

"How can you joke about that? Someone was shooting at you! Someone was trying to kill you!"

"Cat, look, I've been in worse situations than that, much worse. If I got depressed every time I was in a bad situation, I'd have packed it in long ago. I'll tell you about it sometime. For now we need to make some tracks." York bent over again and helped her to strap on the snowshoe. "Even though he's a lousy shot, he might have more firepower in there and I have no wish to find out at this point. If things become desperate then I'll take on the guys with the guns. Until then I'll stick to obeying the law as much as I can."

She finished buckling the snowshoes and stood up. "Lead on."

He checked the map and compass and headed to the north, paralleling the road, but in the woods where there were fewer drifts. He could hear Cat muttering something about "desperate" behind him.

By the time the snow started they were only half way to the next house that was shown on the map. Daylight was disappearing as they came to a track through the woods. It was perpendicular to the route that they were following. York took out the map. There was a trail on the map that probably corresponded to the trail in front of them; to the right there was a small black square on the map about a kilometre away. That small black square meant a building of some sort. The highway was by now about two kilometres to the right as it took a long loop to the east.

They needed shelter for the night. Straight north through the woods there was nothing. To the left down the track there was a large white square on the map. That was probably a clear cut, logged bare of timber. Behind them was nothing. That made the building a kilometre away look awfully attractive. Remembering his resolution this morning to teach Cat, he spent some time explaining the situation to her and answering questions. Then they turned right and headed down the trail.

CHAPTER 14

14 January, evening

They were struggling through a full blown snow storm by the time they arrived at the building. The structure was not much to lift their spirits. The ramshackle hut had four walls and a roof, but that was the best of it. There was an ancient, not too sturdy, wood stove in the shack; but one of the walls of the shack had a large gap in the middle, the size of a quarter sheet of plywood. The boards had been broken and splintered. The rest of the structure was far from airtight as well, although there was a large pile of firewood to feed the stove. A table and benches and an old car bench seat rounded out the comforts.

York found a couple of old saw blades hanging on the wall along with some rusty snare wire. He set about making a fire. He showed Cat how to get dried branches still attached to a live spruce tree, Squaw wood as it was locally called, and probably the best kindling that you could find. He showed her how to prepare a fire, a fire that would start with one match not a dozen; but he did not use one of the few matches that they had. He took his metal match out of his pocket, a small bar of magnesium alloy that could be shaved off with a knife. The metal filings that it produced would burn rapidly and with great heat when sparked. The backside of the metal match had a bar of flint set into it and could be sparked with the knife to ignite the filings.

With a bed of finely shredded birch bark, he soon had a fire started in the kindling and in about a half-hour the cabin was much warmer although very draughty. York left Cat in charge of preparing something warm to drink, grabbed the snare wire off the wall and headed outside.

He put on the snowshoes and went looking for food. He searched the woods around the cabin, gradually expanding his circle. In a small grove of maple saplings, he found what he was looking for. Almost obscured by snow was a rabbit run. He prepared a snare at a likely spot and a second snare on the opposite side of the copse.

York returned to the cabin and, working from the outside, was able to partially close the hole in the back wall of the cabin, using discarded wood from around the building. He glanced up at the roof. The smoke streamed from the rusty chimney. He took off the snowshoes, hung them on a hook on the wall outside the door and went into the cabin.

Cat had used snow to wash down the table and benches. There was a mug of water warming on the stove. The pack was sitting closed and sealed by the door, and she was perched on the old car seat with boots off and her feet resting on a bench by the open oven door.

"Where did you go?" she asked. "To use the secret papers?" She smiled up at him. "I did a bit of house work while you were at the office."

"I can see that," he replied. "Yes, I did use the secret papers if you must know, but mainly I went to the grocery store."

"The grocery store?" She was intrigued.

"Now don't get your hopes up. I set a couple of snares. If we're lucky we'll have a rabbit tomorrow. You can't live on rabbit alone. There's not enough fat, but it will help to keep us going."

"Uuggh! You don't mean a live rabbit?"

"Well, it won't be live when I'm finished with it."

She shuddered. "There's no way that I can eat a live animal. I told you I don't believe in hunting." She got up and walked over to the stove. "There's hot water for a warm drink. I'll just wait for food until we get to where we're going."

"Where we're going has mainly deer steaks and moose meat and partridge; and it's a few days away. You might want to reconsider."

"Hunting is barbaric; those poor defenceless animals. How can you kill them?"

He had heard it all before and he was tired of arguing with others about hunting. He sighed and one more time explained why he was not murdering Bambi, Thumper, and Bullwinkle. Life was so much simpler when you didn't have to explain everything to someone else. When he got back to his cabin and the world got back to an even keel he vowed to spend a month enjoying his own company before venturing out for human contact again.

It was dark outside but they did not light any of the emergency candles. There was a faint glow from the flames in the old stove. Like the walls, it too was less than airtight. They drank hot chocolate and each had a granola bar and finished the bread that York had packed from home. He thought of the old man at the house where he had obtained the snowshoes, and he wondered to himself if the old fellow would survive.

It was quite warm in the cabin and they could remove their outdoor clothes. They had been gone three days from his cabin and their clothing was beginning to look and smell the part. York went to the door and stepped out. His eyes slowly adjusted and he could tell from the hiss of the snow in the trees and the caress on his cheek that it was snowing hard. As he dark-adapted, his eyes picked up a flash of light behind the veil of snow. About fifteen seconds later there was a dull rumble that could only be thunder. As confirmation, a second flash came brighter followed by a louder crack of thunder. The time from flash to bang was only ten seconds, so he knew that the lightning was only three kilometres away. Thunder snow was rare but not unheard of in this part of the country. It was an eerie sensation with the brilliant flashes diffused by the snow, and the thunder echoing for miles.

The snow turned to rain as the lightning bayoneted the sky around them. It rained for a half-hour and then, as the lightning moved away to the south, the rain turned back to snow again. Thank God they were not in the open. That storm spelled death for anyone unprotected in its path. Wet clothing followed by the cold was the ultimate sentence.

After the storm passed he and Cat talked for hours. They drank a lot of water, replenishing the fluids that they had voided, sweated and exhaled as they had trekked cross-country. They discussed the flu and speculated on its aftermath. York found himself talking about his family's homestead, and how his sister sold it while he was away at war. He felt a little guilty when he worded it as such, but he pushed those guilty thoughts aside.

"Have you always lived alone, except for the lady in the picture?" Cat eventually asked.

He did not want to go down that highway so he made light of it. "Nobody else would be able to stand living with me."

He got up and put some wood in the stove, and went outside to gather another can of snow to melt. When he came back to sit down he saw that Cat was still in a chatty mood and was afraid where the conversation would reopen. Why do other people always have to pry into your business, he thought?

"Well I'm a little tired," he said making a pre-emptive strike to avoid further conversation. "I think I'll try to get some sleep. Tomorrow is sure to be one long day." He grabbed his parka for a blanket and curled up on one of the benches with his head lying on his arm. "First one who wakes up feeds the fire."

Cat selected the car seat where she had been sitting and made the same preparations for sleep. After a few minutes of silence she whispered, "York?"

He was awake but in no mood for conversation. There was no apparent danger so he remained silent. Eventually he could hear her breathing deepen. It was a couple of hours before he fell asleep.

When he awoke it was cold in the cabin. The wind had picked up, and the stove had burned the fuel rapidly because of the extra draw on the chimney. He walked to the window but could not see out. It was daylight but there was a heavy frost that had coated the pane with a half-inch of semi-opaque ice. He filled the firebox of the stove; there were plenty of coals so he did not have to relight it. He put water on to heat and went to the door. The snowfall continued and there was a lot of it. He estimated a forty-centimetre fall overnight already.

He put on his parka. It was a lot colder outside than last evening and the wind was gusting as well. With the temperature dropping the snow should stop soon; but the wind was worrisome, as it seemed to be gaining strength even since he had woken. He grabbed the snowshoes and headed for the snares. Each of the snares had caught a rabbit and there would be meat in the pot tonight, if only they had a pot.

He reset the snares, then cleaned and skinned the rabbits halfway between the snares and the cabin. No point in offending the sensibilities of the lady of the house any more than necessary, he thought. With luck they would get more game and would be able to rebuild some of their energy stores. He hung the snowshoes and the carcasses on the hook outside the door, then went to a nearby maple and cut a couple of small branches. He went in to find Cat awake and drinking water.

"I'm so hungry I could eat a horse," she said.

"You mean that you'd eat a horse, but not a moose?" he taunted. He slipped off his parka and had some water to drink also.

"Using the secret papers again?" she asked.

"No, I've been to the grocery store for breakfast." He glanced over at her and saw that she was not happy about this turn of events. "We have fresh rabbit. I'm going to barbecue some over the coals. You don't have to eat it if you don't want but I strongly encourage you to do so. There's one granola bar left if you want it."

"I'll have the granola bar then," she said. "I don't even want to watch you eat anything furry."

"I usually take the fur off before I eat it," he shot back and went outside to bring in one of the rabbits. He fed the two green maple sticks through the carcass, opened the door to the stove and began to roast it. The meat spattered a little and he would occasionally flip the sticks to ensure that it was cooked on both sides. When the meat first started to show signs of dragging off the bone he declared it done. He knew that there was always a tiny risk of getting infected with Tularaemia by eating wild rabbit, but the risk of starvation was infinitely higher.

He set the meat on the table and broke off pieces. The smell of cooked meat filled the cabin and he glanced over at Cat. "Just think of it as chicken," he said as he offered a piece.

She looked hungry and yet frightened at the same time. He refrained from teasing her about her feelings and went back to eating. After a couple of minutes, he offered again and this time she approached the table. The carcass was now just several pieces of meat that did look remarkably like poultry.

She took a small piece and tentatively put it in her mouth and started to chew. "It's kind of tough," she said.

"Pardon me, milady," York replied, "but I don't have a lot to work with here."

"No, it tastes good. I'm not complaining. That was just the first thought that came into my mind. It does sort of taste like chicken."

York felt that it tasted distinctly like rabbit and nothing like chicken, but who was he to interfere with her defence mechanism. He was just happy to have her eating. The last thing that he needed was someone on the trail who couldn't pull her own weight because she didn't eat what was available.

He scrubbed down the table again after scraping it well with his belt knife. It was hard to keep clean and safe with food in these conditions but he would do the best that he could. He went to the door and stepped outside to assess the weather. He had been aware of the rising wail of the wind as he was cooking and eating; and the scene outside confirmed the change of plans that had been forming in his mind.

He had been hoping to get on the trail again right after eating but the conditions were not good for travel. It was still snowing but the snowfall was diminishing. As the intensity of the snow dropped so did the temperature; and the wind chill would soon be deadly. With the clothing and equipment that they had, travel would he out of the question. Frostbite would quickly become a peril, and with the snow stopping there was nothing to urge them on to travel. The damage had been done.

He went back inside to tell Cat about the change in plans. She did not express displeasure and she seemed to want to get chatty again, so he searched for some way to head that off. He had no wish for a starring role in Cat's personal chick flick. By himself, he would have slept and been ready to hit the trail as soon as the wind dropped, day or night. With Cat along he really did not feel comfortable travelling after dark. It was too easy to trip on uneven ground or to stab an eye with a low hanging branch.

To head off her conversation he chose that time for a little navigation training. He first of all reviewed map reading and concentrated on trying to teach her to see the two dimensional map as a representation of a three dimensional view on the ground. He knew that was perhaps the most difficult concept of navigation by map and compass. He also taught her how to plot a bearing and then set the compass to read that bearing. The compass was a Canadian military compass graduated in 6400 mils to a complete circle rather than the 360 degrees that most civilian compasses use. This change in measurement gave her a lot of trouble for a while, then she seemed to get the hang of it. She still had some difficulty at the end of the session though. She often confused the bearing with the back bearing and he would often find her facing in the opposite direction from what she should. They chewed up several hours in navigation school.

Mid afternoon came upon them and he went out to check the snares before nightfall. The wind and blowing snow stung his face and he had to search to locate the snares. They were buried under the snow that had been whipped up by the wind. Both snares were again full, and this time he took down the snares when he had recovered the rabbits. He wanted no animal killed or entangled by the snares if he was not going to require the meat. He rolled up the wire and put it in his pocket for use later.

He went to the same expedient abattoir that he had used yesterday. The snow was disturbed and the offal had been consumed. Nothing went to waste in the wild. The snow had concealed the footprints of whatever animal had been here but he had the distinct impression that it was something big, not just a fox or coyote. He was not aware of any wolves in the area. He cleaned the catch and returned to the hut.

He hung the new rabbits outside with the snowshoes and took the remaining carcass from yesterday inside the cabin to thaw. Even with a single day hanging, the rabbit would be more tender than yesterday. They would have fresh meat to carry with them tomorrow. It was a relief to be out of the wind, however it was still very cold in the hut. The walls admitted the wind like a sieve. He again broiled the meat over the coals in the stove and both he and Cat wolfed down the food. There was no hesitation on her part this time.

There was also no escape for York on this occasion when Cat wanted to talk. Predictable, he thought to himself as she asked again about him always living alone. This time though he told her about his fiancée, and her marrying his brother. On this occasion he did say however that they thought he was killed in Afghanistan. He told her about Victoria who had lived with him at his cabin for two years.

Cat reciprocated with a not too pretty tale of life with Ron, who she said was very nice on the outside but had submitted her to physical and emotional abuse.

York thought of a different description from what he had seen so far. Asshole.

After a while it began to be difficult to hold a conversation. The wind had been growing in intensity all evening and it howled as it came through the cabin walls. They were filling the stove every hour. They agreed that the best idea was to sleep if they could and be on the move at first light if the wind dropped. Cat wanted the candle lit for a while. For some reason tonight she did not want the dark to be wrapped so closely around her.

York awoke when she was feeding the ravenous glowing stove. He had been asleep for about two hours and he got up to give Cat the car seat to sleep on. He extinguished the candle when she was asleep and relit it two hours later when he awoke her to do stove watch. To let the fire go out tonight would not be a wise thing.

CHAPTER 15

16 January, the wee hours

The old wood stove glowed cherry red in the dark. The wind screamed around the ramshackle hut and sucked on the stovepipe like a child sucks on a straw in a milkshake. The draw on the flu could not be controlled, as there was no damper. To keep warm they had to keep the fire going but York did not like to overheat the stove so badly.

The wind detoured around the hut but a large measure of it found its way through the chinks in the wall and through the poorly blocked off hole. Despite the colour of the stove the temperature in the hut was barely above freezing. The candle guttered so badly in the draft that they decided to extinguish it.

The wind proclaimed a blizzard but there was no falling snow. There were dark clouds scudding across the face of the moon and a small amount of snow was still kicked up and forced before the wind.

Even when unlatched, the stove door remained closed, held by the draw on the flue. York used a stick to open it and tossed in a couple of sticks from the vanishing woodpile in the corner. At least there was another large pile outside. If need be, they could stay here for several days until better weather. He looked at Cat, who leaned over the small table close to the stove. In her borrowed parka she would be warm enough. They had shelter, a measure of warmth and, with the snow down, little chance of being found.

He slipped a couple of loose items into her pack and did up the latches. It would probably be less confrontational not to broach the topic again but she had to learn to be ready at a moment's notice. Tomorrow in the light of day he would provide some additional gentle tutoring.

This really was more than he had bargained for; having to look after someone else complicated the problem. If he were alone, it would be tough but not complicated. He knew the drills, knew the techniques and it was actually exhilarating to be challenged like this again. York lay down on the bench along the wall. The cold would wake him before the fire was out.

* * *

It was the ripping of the stovepipe and the splintering of wood that actually woke him. The hut was filling with smoke and the wall behind the stove was already in flames.

He shouted for Cat as he rolled to the floor. He pulled her to the floor and she came awake flailing her arms.

"Fire, follow me!" he shouted, crawling to the door. He reached up unlatched it and tugged it open.

He pushed Cat past him out the door then scrambled on his knees back to the table. He snatched the pack onto the floor and scrabbled to the door. He threw the small pack to Cat, who was revealed in the light of the fire. He grabbed his rucsac and followed her into the night.

One wall of the hut was already engulfed in flames and the flames stretched horizontally downwind like a blowtorch. There would be no extinguishing this fire until it had consumed the whole hut. Although there was only a small chance, a forest fire was also possible.

He moved upwind to a relative position of safety. He had hoped for a couple of days here to allow Cat to recover.

They needed some food to make it to the safety of his own cabin. He turned back to retrieve the two rabbits hanging in a tree, and the snowshoes from the hook on the side of the shack. He stopped in his tracks. A huge black shadow had moved in front of the blazing hut and was pawing at a tree.

Then the shadow was gone. Was it just a shadow after all? Suddenly chilled, he abandoned the snowshoes that were now engulfed in flames and continued to lead through the woods although now at an angle to the wind. He checked his equipment as he walked and fingered his belt knife.

After they had gone a couple of kilometres Cat pulled on his arm. "What do we do now?"

"We need to keep moving to keep warm," he said. "If we find shelter we'll stop again but until we do, we need to move toward our objective."

He now took out the map and his compass. "We are just about here." The two of them struggled to keep the map from blowing away. The moonlight was now unobstructed and gave plenty of light for reading.

"We need to keep going this way," he pointed on the map. "See these open fields? See this little black dot at the corner? That's another building of some sort. At least there was one there when the map was surveyed fifteen years ago."

"What kind of building?"

"There's no way to tell. It could be a house or an open lean-to for feeding cattle, or a collapsed shack. There isn't much of a trail leading to it, so it's not likely a house."

"How far is it?"

He counted grid squares and added a little. "About ten kilometres as the crow flies. More with ups and downs. It's 2:15 now and it will be at least noon before we can hope to get there, even with the easy going in these woods."

"Can't we go out to the road, York? It would be easier going, wouldn't it?"

"The road won't be plowed and would probably be drifted worse than in the woods. And the nearest shelter is that house there." He pointed to another building on the map alongside the main highway. "If we go that way, who knows what kind of a reception that we'll get there? And it would probably take us an extra six hours to get there."

"York, I'm sorry but I don't know if I can walk that long or that far."

"Yes you can, Cat. We can make it if we want to." He didn't voice his thoughts about what they would do if there were no shelter when they arrived.

He led the way compass in hand, pausing occasionally to consult the dial. He kept the pace slow but steady. The moon provided background illumination so they could make their way through the trees. Initially to their right and overhead, it made its way to their left and low in the sky. The wind was dropping but it felt like the temperature was also.

At one of their hourly ten-minute halts, in a small clearing he thought that he could detect a faint glow in the southeast. Sunrise? Or a forest fire? Or the glow of lights from Fredericton? No, the glow was increasing and a first linear hint of gold was in the sky.

The snow crunched underfoot. It was definitely getting colder.

Cat looked at him with a brave smile but he could tell that she was exhausted. They still had five more hours to go. He rechecked the map and his bearing, and led off again. He felt chilled right through. It must be getting a lot colder.

An hour later they stopped again in front of a field that was not expected. He rechecked the map, their route and his watch. He was sure of their position but there was no field on the map; although it was fifteen years out of date.

He headed into the field happy to take any opportunity that would help their slog. The snow was drifted almost chest high along the wood line but he surged ahead.

"Come on, Cat," he called encouragement. "Once we're through the deep stuff it should be easier going, and we'll be an hour ahead of schedule."

She was barely able to move in the drift despite him breaking trail ahead of her. Oh for some snowshoes, he thought. If they got more snow before they got to the cabin then they would die, unable to make headway in the woods or in the open.

He was just about through the drift and looked back at Cat

struggling. He pushed ahead, caught his foot, and tripped landing face first in the snow. His chest hurt where he had landed on something, a stump.

He got up, shouted to Cat to be careful and moved ahead again. This time his shin scraped against a limb buried in the snow and his other foot became entangled in some branches intertwined and hidden from view. Now he recognised the field for what it was.

This was a clear cut where loggers had removed the standing trees leaving a maze of slash and cast aside timber. No, a maze implied some route available. There was no route here, just a million dead ends. Even in the summer this would be barely passable, with a broken leg risked at every step. Only a fool would cross this field until Mother Nature had taken a few years to soften it up. Hidden under the snow, this was now a death trap.

He turned to Cat. “We can’t go this way. It’s too dangerous. We have to go around.”

Her disappointment was obvious but she did not complain. “OK.” She turned to go back.

“Wait till I go by you so I can break trail again,” York said. He felt out of breath from the exertions in the deep snow and his chest hurt where he had fallen on the stump.

They fought their way to the woodline again and started through the woods to circumnavigate the clear cut. An hour later they were on the other side of the opening, now almost two hours behind the original estimate.

“Let’s stop for a breather,” he said. The extra exertion had left him quite winded. He was used to this kind of travel with a hundred-pound pack on his back. Of course that was a few years ago and with snowshoes. But still it shouldn’t be this tough on him.

“You haven’t been ventilating, York. Your parka is still done up. How come?”

“I feel cold,” he said, “and I didn’t notice.”

She stared at him until he looked away. He gathered his breath over the next five minutes, and then led the way through the woods and up a steep incline. The snow was deeper here and it took almost an hour to reach the top of the ridge. At the end York was pulling himself from tree to tree using every bit of strength in arms and legs to make it to the top.

He collapsed in the snow, panting. He would wait for Cat to arrive using the extra minutes to recover. His chest hurt. Surprised, he saw Cat's boots in front of his face. She had arrived at the top right along with him. She was tired, he could see, but he could also tell that something was wrong with this picture.

"York, are you all right? You're going to get wet on the ground you told me."

He struggled to get to his feet. Cat helped to tug him erect. He felt light-headed as he dug out the map.

"York, you're sick, aren't you?"

"I think so. I'm really weak. I can't get my breath. I'm cold, really cold."

"That's how I felt when I was getting the flu," said Cat.

"That's the situation," he said trying to sound matter of fact. I'm going to show you the map again and the compass bearing to those fields so you can go on."

"We've got to get you to a hospital."

"Cat, there is no help here. This is a come-as-you-are party. There are no ambulances or doctors or any other help. We were heading for these fields because that was the best way to survive." He stopped to catch his breath. "Nothing has changed except that you have to get there on your own."

"We can both get there. I'll help you. You've broken trail all the way. I'll go first and it'll be easier for you."

"Cat, you can make it on your own. There's not as much snow on this ridge." He bent over and braced his hands against his knees. "The wind blew it all off and it's easy walking between these pines. I'll keep coming but I've seen the way this flu acts." Again a pause. "It's fast. I won't be walking long then it will be all over." He bent over and gasped for breath.

"No, I'm not leaving you here alone."

"Cat, this is what I've always wanted, to be left alone and to spend my time in the woods." He was getting tired just arguing with her. "You get to the fields and the building; and then when you can, you need to continue north to this village and hope you can get help to survive the winter." He pointed out the route on the map. "Just travel along this ridge until it makes a sharp curve to the east, to the right, and then follow the north arrow on the compass to the fields." He paused again and shook his head to clear the cobwebs. "The building will be to the right. You're only about two hours away."

"Give me the map and the compass."

He watched her fold the map into the pocket and tie the compass thong to her parka pocket. She had obviously been watching. She would have made a good student. Never complained. She took the pack from his back. Then she heaved on him, to help him to his feet.

He protested. "Leave me be, I'll be fine."

"Look, York, I'm not leaving you. Now either you walk with me or we both die here together."

He didn't have the strength to protest and every step that he took would take her a step closer to the fields so that when he died she might make it to safety. Thank God he had planned the route with this ridge in mind. The ridgeline and the north face were scoured almost bare of snow. Pity help them when they got to the bottom of the ridge though. The snow would be like a wall.

He shut out everything except making his feet move. He struggled to breathe. Maybe he was a fool to have traded his medicine for the old house. The hell with Sloat, the bastard. They stopped and Cat spread the ground sheet on the hardened ground. He collapsed. A little while later he was awakened; he didn't want to move. He thought he heard a droning sound and he was dreaming of driving his Jeep.

"York, I think we are at the place where we have to go down the hill. I went farther along the ridge to make sure it was the big turn. Can you set the compass for me?"

"OK." He could barely hear the weak whisper of his own voice. He reached for the compass then remembered. "You don't have to set it this time. Just follow the small red arrow. Down the hill, one kilometre to the fields. I'll stay here."

"No you won't. We've come this far together. We can go the last kilometre."

"You don't understand," he gasped, "The snow. Will be deep. At the bottom. Of the ridge."

"Tough! You die we all die."

He struggled onto his knees, and then with help to his feet, and then started down the slope behind Cat. The day was darker than he last remembered it. Probably more snow coming.

He fell headlong down the hill fetching up against an old tree. The branch in front of his face had five long needles, one for every letter in the word WHITE. A white pine. A bed of white pine needles would be a soft place to die. Odd that he couldn't smell the pine. He felt Cat tugging at his arm. He struggled up again and followed. What was that old marching song? "...pick 'em up and put 'em down and follow me."

He felt himself fall, over and over again. Each time it was more difficult to get to his feet. His breath was shallow and rasping and he found himself walking in time to his breathing, then a step every three breaths.

It was difficult to move. The snow was around his waist. He was holding onto the soldier in front of him as they made their way upstream. The water held them back. But why was it so cold?

He felt the cold on his face again and then a voice shouting at him. He was dragged to firmer footing and then he began to stumble forward again. It was dark. Maybe this was the end.

He looked up at the moon and realised that he was on his back. A woman was shouting at him.

"York, get up! If you die here then you'll never get back to your cabin or your house. Your sister will sell your house again, and Mr Sloat will have it all again."

He tried to speak but couldn't. He moved his arms.

"York, get up. The building is just a hundred meters away. I've been there. But I can't drag you or carry you."

He was still wrestling with her previous statement. Sloat and his house again. He rolled over and tried to push up. Hands helped to support him as he half took a step. His chest burned and he could hear a terrible gurgling in the breathing that he knew must be his own. He opened his mouth to speak but nothing came out. He took another step, then another. He leaned to the left on the support that was there and heard himself whisper, “Fuck Sloat!”

Then he felt himself falling for the last time.

CHAPTER 16

19 January

York saw the room shimmering at the end of a tunnel. The tunnel widened as details became clear but then the temperature plummeted and he began to shudder under the blanket. The fog shrouding his vision waxed and waned as he breathed in and out.

A grating noise drew his eyes toward his feet; and he moved his head to better see the source. His vision began to swim again and nausea pushed curiosity from his mind. Holding motionless he forced the nausea into the background. Again he tried to move his head, only this time with more care, inching to the field of view that he sought.

A hooded figure was stirring a metal container that sat on a rusty wood stove. The grating sound corresponded exactly to the circular arm movements. A shaft of light entered the room from somewhere behind York's head. The smell of wood smoke was mixed with a mouldy odour that he could not place.

He sat up, or at least he tried. What he managed to do was lift his head off the cot and restart the waves of nausea. He moaned as he sank back, and when he opened his eyes again his field of vision was filled with a face in a hood. The face looked vaguely familiar; then his memories began to pile one on top of the other.

"York, are you awake?"

He snapped out a macho reply, but even to his own ears it was only a moan. The face disappeared from view and moments later he felt coolness on his forehead and cheek as a cloth was wiped over his face.

"Where are we?" he managed to whisper.

"You were right, York. The cabin at the edge of the field was where you said it was. We're in that cabin."

"How did we get here?"

"We walked, but we'll talk about it later. I'll get you some soup."

He awoke again to feel a gentle hand on his right shoulder. He opened his eyes to see Cat's face; and then with her help he struggled into a half-sitting position, as she pushed something behind him to keep him upright. He felt heat at his lips and he opened them to admit a warm liquid. He did not know the taste, only that it tasted good. He had several mouthfuls then fatigue forced him to sag back against the prop behind him. A strong arm helped to ease him back and he slipped into the darkness.

* * *

As his eyes opened he found himself lying on his side on the edge of the cot. The cabin was very cold. He saw Cat pushing a piece of wood into the stove. It must have been the noise of her activities that had awakened him. In the glow of the open door he could see frost on the walls, frost that extended from the floor almost all the way to the ceiling. She closed the stove door. He watched her walk, no he watched her limp, to the chair that sat a few feet from the stove. She slumped into the chair and huddled into a ball pulling her feet onto the rungs of the chair.

* * *

He awoke to see sunlight again streaming into the room. The frost line on the wall had retreated downward to waist height. The light dimmed as he heard the door close and saw Cat come into his field of view. She was carrying a large bucket of snow that she placed on the stove.

"You actually can burn water," he squeaked.

Cat started. "Oh you're awake again." She came toward him and placed her hand on his forehead. "How do you feel?"

"I'm OK," he whispered.

Cat moved over to the stove and poured some water from a kettle into a bowl on the table. She carried the bowl to him and he gobbled down the food as she fed him.

"What is this?" he asked.

"There was some flour in a can on the shelf. I mixed it with the last of the sugar that we had and added some water."

"Well it's delicious," he croaked. "Thank you."

"I think your fever broke. Your breathing is so much better. How do you feel?"

"Great," he started to lie, and then added, "No, not really great. I'm very weak. How long have I been asleep?"

"Three days. I've been very scared and I'm glad that you're awake." She managed a weak smile. "Now you need to rest a bit longer."

"What I need is to have a leak," he blurted out, aware of an urgent call from his bladder. He started to sit up.

"Wait a minute, you'll need these," she said, picking a stack of clothing off the table.

He lifted the blanket and gazed down his body. "Tit for tat I see."

Cat grinned at him and winked. "I'll go out for some more snow," she said lifting the bucket from the stove and heading out the door. "Latrine is to the left and clean snow to the right," she cast over her shoulder as she closed the door.

He dragged himself out of bed, cold and naked. He struggled into his pants, shirt, and boots. That was all that he could see of his clothing. His legs quivered as he baby stepped to the door and inched out into the daylight.

The sun was low in the sky. He had no reference for direction at first then remembering the map, realised that he was facing west. It must be late afternoon he thought to himself. He stumbled along a trail to the left, snow crunching beneath his boots. After relieving the pressure of his bladder he took another look at the terrain.

The cabin was at the corner of a field probably 20 hectares in area. It was butt against the woodline, a stand of fir with some hardwood mixed in. It was probably minus 20 Celsius, and with no wind the forest was silent as a tomb.

York walked back to the cabin entrance feeling chilled again. There was a bucket of snow melting by the door. The snow was melting in the water that Cat had already produced with the first load. She came around the corner of the cabin with several articles of clothing in her arm, clothing that in their frozen state resembled lumber more than textiles.

He opened the door so she could enter, then he walked around the back of the cabin noting the clothesline strung between two trees. There was a small woodpile beside the cabin and this was obviously well depleted. He re-entered the cabin, his eyes adapting to the relative darkness inside.

Cat was hanging the clothing, some of it his, on another line inside. The cabin was probably six metres by six metres with a low ceiling, no more than two metres high. The few pots and utensils rested on the table and beside them sat the two packs, filled and buckled shut. There was a small bench and a chair and a woodbin filled to the brim. The bed he had just left was a rude metal cot and he saw that the only visible blankets were the ones on the bed.

He felt ashamed that he had occupied the only bedspace and blankets for the last three days. “Cat, I can imagine what you’ve been through. Thank you for looking after me.”

“No problem,” she said, and then began to sob, hiding her face in her hands.

He approached her, unsure of what to do, afraid to touch her, settling for words. “OK, OK, tell me about the last few days. It’ll make it a little easier. Tell me first of all how we got here. The last I remember is deep snow.”

“Well we got to the bottom of the ridge. Do you remember

that?"

"Vaguely."

"You were barely moving, falling all the time. Your breathing was terrible. When we got to the deep snow at the bottom of the ridge we were half crawling and half walking barely able to move. Then we came upon some snowmobile tracks and we were able to walk down the tracks. You fell a lot but I was always able to get you up. Then we came to the fields."

She wiped her eyes with the heel of her hand. "It was just dark and the snowmobile tracks went to the left across the fields. I couldn't see anything to the right but you had said turn right. The snow was deep and I left you in the snow and walked to the right. It wasn't until I was almost upon it that I saw the cabin, right where you said it would be."

Cat sat on the bed and York perched on the chair.

"I opened the door, saw that we could stay here and I went back for you. You were very sleepy and very weak. It took almost three hours more to get to the cabin. I helped you onto the bed and lit a fire. There was paper and wood and stuff in the woodbin. I found matches on the shelf.

"Your breathing was terrible and you threw up all over the place. You can still smell it actually. I got you under the covers and found some flour and stuff. There are a few cans of food on the shelf still but I've been trying to conserve them. I gave you water as best I could and then a bit of soup. That took the next day. It got really cold at night and then a bit warmer in the daytime. Then you woke up that next night for a while."

"You must be exhausted," he said.

"I'm really tired."

"Cat, why don't you take over the bed for a while? I'll take stove watch. When you're awake we can plan our next moves."

She nodded, took off her parka and crawled under the blankets. York helped himself to some warm water and some of the porridge that Cat had made. He quenched his thirst slowly over the next few hours, but took little of the food, wanting to make sure that the vomiting had fully cleared.

It was two in the morning when Cat awoke. She didn't look rested but the cold was likely more pressing than the sleepiness. York stacked as much firewood into the stove as he dared as Cat went outside to the latrine. He crawled into the bed after Cat had returned. They would sleep turn about in the bed from now on.

He awoke an unknown period of time later. He could see Cat in the moonlight from the window. She was washing beside the stove. For the first time he noticed that she was a very beautiful woman. The moonlight accentuated the curve of her breasts, her waist, and her thighs. He closed his eyes and slipped back to sleep.

At 6 a.m. they were both awake. They catalogued the supplies in the cabin. There was enough firewood to last another two days in the penetrating cold that had settled over the countryside. There was enough food to have a couple of good meals. Water would last as long as they could melt snow.

A map study showed them to be still thirty kilometres from York's cabin. Without snowshoes they would most certainly be unable to travel very far cross-country. The terrain was more rugged than that which they had already covered.

They could not stay where they were. That meant that they had to find their way to an intermediate destination, or they had to travel to the highway and hope that it was passable.

About five miles away, the highway wound through the hills. There were two houses marked on the map alongside the highway, and he knew which houses they were. Both were inhabited, at least they had been until the Flu. There might be assistance there, and if nothing else the highway would be smooth travel, even if snowbound. The situation had changed in the last five days and this new route was really their only chance at this point.

They were both still tired from the exertions of the last few days and he was still very weak. They spent the next two days resting, eating, and drying clothes. He set snares, showing Cat how it was done. Unfortunately they remained empty. He used the last of the flour and sugar to make some bannock that both agreed tasted better than the finest French pastry. Along with the last can of Spaghetti-O's it made a fine meal, fine for starvation appetites.

They also spent hours talking. York talked about his time in Afghanistan, something that he had resisted since his return. He passed on more survival tips and Cat was a rapid learner. She talked about her failed engagement and her aunt in Mirimichi. Most of all, he sensed that they enjoyed each other's company. He did not mention that they could both die tomorrow leaving no trace after the coyotes had finished with them.

CHAPTER 17

23 January

York retrieved the snare wire before they departed. He had left the snares in place as long as possible hoping they could catch something to carry on their journey. He packed the snares into his pack and shrugged his shoulders in reply to Cat's unasked question.

They headed out travelling on a direct compass bearing toward the nearest house. The path they were to follow avoided the biggest hills in the area and there was no advantage to a more elaborate route. The greatest obstacle at this time was the snow. They struggled ahead at no more than a kilometre and a half an hour, and most of the time it was a lot less. By the time they reached the highway they were desperate for rest and wet to the thighs because of wading through the deep snow.

The snowbound road was pristine. There were no vehicle tracks, no snowmobile tracks, not even animal tracks. He knew that they were south of their destination and turned to the left heading north. Travel was a little easier on the road since they could walk around the worst of the drifts. Because the right of way in this area was graded up above the surrounding terrain, the wind had blown a lot of the snow off the road. York knew that they were in greater danger of freezing than they were of recapture. There were more houses and more chances for shelter along the road for this part of the journey so he knew that the highway was the solution for travel at this time.

It was almost two p.m. when they came in sight of the first of the two houses they had previously identified on the map. He led into the woods before they came to the house. He approached the house under cover remembering the meeting with Ron, and the later meeting with the shotgunner. Lights were on. There was power in this area of the grid, or perhaps now the power was on everywhere.

The driveway was not plowed, he saw, and the steps were not shovelled. Nobody had been in or out of this house for at least a few hours. There was no smoke from the chimney. Electric heat probably, although there was a large woodpile alongside the house. No vehicle was in sight. It was likely in the garage.

"Cat, you wait here. I'm going to walk around the area before we make ourselves known."

York crept through the woods, pausing every once in a while to scrutinize the windows. When he was downwind of the house he caught a strange odour. Maybe they'd be careful about what they ate here. If that was meat cooking it might be suspicious for its freshness. His thoughts flashed to the bear that had alerted the buck. Was that only three months ago?

He returned to Cat. "Why don't you try hailing the house? A woman's voice may be less threatening."

"Oh, right," she scoffed. "The last time I tried that, my fiancé told me to get lost."

"Yeah, but he knew you really well," York said with a smile, instantly wondering if he had gone too far, if he had touched a nerve.

Cat didn't say anything for a couple of seconds, her face like a mask. Then she chuckled. "Guess I didn't know him too well. What a loser. Him, not me." Then she shouted, "Hello in the house."

No answer. "Hello in the house."

Together. "Hello in the house!"

"I'll go to the door," York said. "If you see anything, call out and let me know."

He crept toward the house every sense on edge. He stepped

onto the porch and pushed the doorbell that was lit beside the door. He heard the bell inside. After a couple of minutes and several tries he banged on the door with his fist.

Well, he and Cat had to find some sort of shelter so he tried the doorknob. The door opened and the odour struck him in the face. The house was no warmer than outdoors. If it had been, the stench would have been worse. He stepped into the foyer and peered into the living room to the left. A Christmas tree sat in the corner with multi-coloured lights twinkling, and under the tree were rows of neatly displayed gifts.

A woman in a dress and sweater was sprawled on the floor alongside a couch. A child, probably seven or eight, was on the couch covered to the chin with a blanket. Both were obviously dead; the woman especially so, as a rat looked up from her bloated arm, barely pausing in its meal.

There was no sanctuary in this house. York heard footsteps behind him and he wheeled to intercept Cat and hustle her out the door.

"You don't want to go in there, Cat."

"Why, what's there?"

"Disease," he said. "Let's check the garage."

There was no car in the garage, just tire tread marks frozen into some snow and ice on the floor. Who knows, he thought, what the story was that led to the pitiful scene in the house.

He poked through the usual garage junk on the jury-rigged shelves, a flashlight that didn't work, a few pitted hand tools. There was one treasure however, a pair of hunting boots, fur lined and lace up calf high. They would fit Cat better than the military boots that she had been wearing. He found some old newspapers and fashioned insoles to make them fit better.

"They're cold," she said, putting her first foot in.

"They'll warm up. Try the second one."

She put her military boots on the shelf where the others had stood. "I'll leave these here."

"No, bring them with you. You don't want to leave anything behind that may be needed," said York. "We don't know when there will be shoes in a shoe store next."

He packed the boots into the small pack that she still carried, and then started out the driveway. He led to the road and they started to the north again. There was still time to get to the next house before nightfall.

As they approached the next house they moved into the woods on the left side of the road to be on the same side as the structure. Behind the house was an expanse of open field, several hundred acres spread out along the road. They would avoid that field where they could be seen, with no place to run and hide. He turned his attention back to the house and its garage standing on the north side and set a little farther back than the house.

The house was a single story with a front door facing the highway, set about fifty metres off the road. The garage was actually more of a Quonset hut, like a long half cylinder lying with its open face down. A large sliding door occupied most of the end that was visible to them, and there was a small doorway to the right of the large door. A flicker of light sparked from the house and a clashing of metal on metal echoed from the garage.

This felt bad. He could not explain exactly why, but it felt bad.

The wind had picked up again coming from the northwest. A glow of sunlight suddenly appeared beneath the clouds in the west and he noted that he and Cat would be perfectly illuminated at the edge of the tree line. He led Cat farther back into the woods and explained the situation to her. He decided that they would wait until dark to approach the house. It was last light at that point and there was just time to formulate a plan of reconnaissance.

As the last vestiges of daylight dropped behind the horizon, the temperature seemed to drop another ten degrees. Or perhaps that was just his apprehension coming to the forefront.

They moved together to the edge of the woodline. The plan was for him to approach the house from the south, the side of the house closest to them. There was only one small window on that side and it likely marked a bathroom. He should be unseen as he approached the house and he could then work his way around the house and try to observe the occupants without being detected.

He easily gained the position that he wanted against the south wall. To the left the terrain dropped off at the back of the building and the windows would be less accessible on that side. He moved to the right, to the front of the house. A couple of small windows higher up likely marked bedrooms. He scurried under them and past the front doorstep to the picture window that came next. With an ear cocked to detect approaching footsteps, or voices inside the house, he eased his head and eyes up to the lower corner of the window.

Dull yellow light flickered from another room at the back of the house. That would be the kitchen and there was either candle or lantern light. There was no electricity here, or it had been cut off again. As he raised his head above the window sill a bit more and peered into the house, he saw a living room in a shambles of clothing, cans, bottles, refuse, and piles of wood. Obviously not a cover home from Architectural Digest. It also said something about the inhabitants and confirmed his concern about approaching this dwelling.

He saw a man inside walk toward the kitchen on the far side of the house. There would be a driveway on that side that would lead to the garage and there was also likely a side entry to the house. That meant that he was now trapped between two doorways although it was unlikely that anyone knew that he was there. The man that he saw was tall with a beard, and dressed in military fatigues. That much he could determine in the moments that the man was visible.

York tensed as he heard an aluminum storm door clang open on the north side of the house. He prepared to beat a hasty retreat to the tree line.

"Come and get it," bellowed a voice that could only belong to the cook of the day. That was the man that he had seen in the house. "Hey, Jerk offs!"

After a pause, "What do you want?" a second voice came from farther away, from the garage.

"If you want anything to eat, come now," shouted the first voice again. "I've been bustin' my butt while you three have been fartin' around with them snowmobiles."

"All right. Don't get your shorts in a knot, Pierce. I'll get the rest of them. Those snowmobiles are what keep us in food right now, and the red one is running rough." The voice trailed off followed by a bang of a metal door.

"I'll be damn glad when this snow is gone and I can get my truck out again," Pierce, the cook, hollered. A door slammed shut, probably the garage door.

York moved away from the picture window and back past the front steps. There was shadow there and he would be out of view as he hunched against the house. He soon heard the sound of voices from the north side. Obviously the others were trooping in to eat.

One figure, a short box-like man, appeared at the far corner of the house. York peeked over the front step and watched as he gazed up and down the road, then urinated in the snow, grunted, and turned out of sight. The side door banged closed, and then there was an undercurrent of conversation from inside the house.

York crept back to the picture window and continued his reconnaissance. He now knew that there were four men here, one named Pierce. They had at least two snowmobiles and probably a truck.

Light slashed from the picture window across the snow in front of the house. York looked through the window again and right into the glare of a propane camp lantern. The lantern had been set on the windowsill and the glare blocked his view of the room.

There was no better time, he thought, as he crawled under the window and toward the north side of the house. They would probably be inside for a half-hour and his footprints would blend with those of the men who had come in from the garage. He got to the corner of the house and after a quick look dashed to the Quonset hut. He was about to enter by the small door when the glow of light on the far side caught his eye and he veered around the building. A glance in the window might give him almost as much information as entering the building, and it was infinitely safer.

Through the window he saw first the two snowmobiles, illuminated by a lantern hanging from the ceiling. The red machine had its cowling raised, and there were several major assemblies removed from the engine. That was no source of transportation for them; not that the men in the house appeared to be the sort of persons to rush to offer their aid. The other machine was a yellow Bombardier that was parked closest to the door. The next thing that caught his eye, however, changed his whole approach to seeking any assistance from this household. Parked farther up in the shed was a pickup, a white pickup, a white pickup with a rusty tailgate.

York continued his search for information, scanning the walls and floor with his eyes. There were three sets of snowshoes hanging on the far wall. The keys were in the ignitions of the snowmobiles. A workbench was littered with tools and rags. There were several gas cans scattered around the shop. Some garden tools were hanging on the wall. There was another window on the far side and a third at the far end of the Quonset in front of the pickup.

The survey had taken about two minutes. He edged to the corner of the hut and then dashed to the front of the house and quickly retraced his steps to the woods. He found Cat easily. She gave a low whistle that guided him to her position.

"A girl that can whistle. Aren't you full of surprises."

"I keep telling you, I'm not just a pretty face."

He discussed his findings with Cat. He was tired of running from one event to another, always reacting to disaster or someone else's plans. He was about to take back some of the initiative. He outlined the plan to Cat and they spent the next three hours reviewing and memorising their actions and moving around to keep warm.

The banging and crashing and occasional shouts restarted from the direction of the garage. York made a silent wish that the men would not tear apart the yellow snowmobile.

It started to snow about nine o'clock. That was also about the last time they heard any noise from the area of the house.

The lights went out at about ten thirty, and a half-hour later York and Cat moved out of the woodline.

He led the way to the house and across the front of the building, crawling the last twenty feet under the picture window. At the corner of the house they separated. Cat, carrying the snare wire, headed for the side door to the house. Her first mission was to string the wire between the handrails of the steps, at the top step, just about a foot above the platform. In case they were discovered that would give them a few extra moments to make a getaway.

York went to the small doorway of the Quonset hut and was thankful to find it unlocked. Men such as those that lived here had no respect for locks on others' houses and couldn't be bothered with their own. He inched the door open; there was little sound. He propped it with a cinder block that he found inside. With his flashlight he located the snowshoes and placed two pair on the ground by the yellow snowmobile. He flashed the light on the red snowmobile and saw that it was all reassembled. As far as he could tell it was ready to go, as was the yellow machine. This called for a change of plan.

He gathered three of the gas cans and carried them to the sleds. The yellow was full of gas already and so was the red. He siphoned off some of the gas from the red one and poured in some varsol and then as much snow as he could gather off the floor. There were two half full mugs of coffee on the workbench and he added their contents to the fuel tank as well. He pulled the key out of the ignition of the red machine and threw it out the door.

Next he turned his attention to the rusty pickup. It was a Ford F150 about ten years old. He took a rag from the workbench and stuffed it in the gas tank opening and soaked the rag with some of the remaining varsol. He took a dozen boxes of matches off the workbench, placed all but one in his pocket and laid the other one on the side of the truck box.

Cat came through the doorway and whistled. Together they manhandled the yellow snowmobile 180 degrees so that it was facing out the door, unlike the other vehicles in the hut. He took the gas cans to the front of the house and set them on the front step, one with a rag wicking into the gasoline. The snowfall was picking up now, but at least there was no wind so matches should be reliable.

On return to the garage he stepped over the second snare wire entanglement that Cat had just completed. This time she had worked at the small door opening into the Quonset. He emptied another gas can onto the snow in front of the large sliding door. Cat picked up the two pair of snowshoes, and they conferred once more to finalise the last few steps of the attack, steps that had to happen simultaneously. Together they worked the large door open enough to let the snowmobile out.

She then headed for the front door to light the gas can there. If the snowmobile started then they would flee mounted. If the machine did not start then they would cross the road and flee on snowshoes. There was only a brief window of opportunity once he tried the snowmobile. The noise would be heard in the house and within seconds the alert would be on. He dared not leave the snowmobile once it had started as he would have to feed the throttle to keep it going in the bitter cold.

He needed to light the wick at the truck first, and that meant he then had limited time to leave the hut. Cat was poised to light the front gas cans when she heard the snowmobile start, or when the truck blew up, whichever came first. He walked to the side of the truck checking to make sure that his return route was clear. He fastened all his pockets, picked up the box of matches off the truck and lit a match.

He touched the match flame to the wick in the truck gas tank. It flamed immediately and he ran to the snowmobile and turned the key. It turned over but didn't start. The light in the hut increased to a yellow glow. He didn't look over his shoulder; he knew the source of the light. He turned the key again, still no joy. He had one more try before he must leave the hut either on the sled or on foot. Must remember to step over the wire at the small door. He twisted the throttle and turned the key again and the engine coughed a few times then stopped. The light was bright yellow in the Quonset hut.

He turned the key and the engine roared to life. He dared not throttle back too far for fear the engine would quit. He threw it into forward gear and it lunged toward the main doorway.

He went through cleanly and stopped the sled just outside the door. He lit another match and threw it into the gas soaked snow behind him. At that moment he saw the wick fall from the fuel opening of the truck. Better luck next time.

Cat was coming on the run, snowshoes in each hand. He jerked the sled forward to meet her and stopped while she climbed on. He looked behind. The wall of fire obscured the large door opening but the small door stood open, beckoning, illuminated by the fire without and a glow within.

As Cat climbed aboard he saw the side door of the house open and a tall bearded figure start for the steps, roaring at them while he ran. As if struck from behind, the man suddenly pivoted forward at the ankles and fell like a chopped tree, face first onto the steps. He bounced. He actually bounced but he didn't get up.

Other voices could now be heard in the house and York gunned the snowmobile out onto the road and north toward Spencer. The front step was aglow and one of the gas cans exploded. Then there was another sharper explosion and a whistling around their heads. He looked back to see a man with a rifle or shotgun on the back step. He was raising it again and York swerved the sled back and forth. The weapon spat a large bloom of fire. It was a shotgun and York relaxed. It couldn't reach them. He saw a figure heading for the hut and then he concentrated on the road. He hit the lights and twisted the throttle.

After about five minutes there was a low rumble from behind them, and then as they both looked back a yellow glow lit the sky. At the same time they saw the flash of a white light, a headlight waving across the sky like a chastising finger. The red snowmobile was in pursuit.

"Second set of keys," muttered York.

He faced forward. The snow was heavy now and would cover their tracks but not soon enough to hide them from the snowmobile coming behind. He looked for a turnoff or some other cover that would hide them but their tracks would give them away. Speed was the only option at this time. He shouted to Cat to hang on and opened the throttle more.

They careened along the highway toward the north, and he kept a lookout behind to try to judge the progress of the other sled. There was no doubt that they were being overtaken. If the other sled got too close he would have to choose a piece of woodland to hide them.

With snowshoes they would be able to go faster through the woods than their pursuers, as long as the woods were thick enough to prevent snowmobiles from entering. On the other hand, if the pursuit was slow enough, they might be able to make it all the way to his cabin. Then, equally armed, he would stand and face any of these people, alone or together. The deep gully of North Trout Brook appeared in front of them. It was twenty kilometres to his cabin.

They were across the bridge and part way up the other side as the second snowmobile roared onto the downward slope. He needed to find that copse of woods, and he needed it now. Maybe he had left it too long. Maybe the pursuers were not armed. Maybe they still had a chance.

At the top of the hill he looked back again. His mood brightened as he saw that the other snowmobile was stopped dead at the bridge in the bottom of the gully. The headlight was still on. Two men were beside the machine and they had the engine cowling up. The expedient fuel additives that he had provided had worked their way into the fuel line and at last had done their job.

The air cracked by York and Cat, followed by a thump from the bottom of the hill. He had been shot at enough to recognise the crack-thump of a supersonic bullet. The crack was the bullet going by, breaking the sound barrier. The thump was the sound of the gun being fired, arriving after the bullet since it only travelled at the speed of sound. He reached for the throttle but there was a clang of metal and a rap that he felt through the snowmobile. He could smell gas, and as the snowmobile leapt ahead he wanted only to get as much distance as he could toward the north. They managed about five kilometres before the engine began to cough, and then it abruptly died.

CHAPTER 18

24 January, early morning

York and Cat manhandled the snowmobile to the side of the road and rolled it down the bank. He wanted nobody to accidentally run into it concealed by snow. It was only a few weeks ago that he had taken the same care with his Jeep when he went to investigate Cat's wreck. He looked toward her in the darkness, and could not suppress a grin. What a change in her life.

They had just pulled off a hit and run mission that, considering what they had to work with, any special forces team could be proud of. They had captured the most valuable equipment, the snowshoes. Two of the four enemy were now stranded in a blizzard miles from their shelter. One other was badly injured from the fall on the steps; York winced when he remembered that fall. Both snowmobiles were badly damaged and, possibly the truck and the Quonset were destroyed. The house would probably be fine. He had not intended to destroy the house just create a diversion and deny the enemy the use of the front door. After all, they were not at war. They were trying to survive and incidentally mete out a little justice, but this was not war.

"Come on, Cat, we're not out of the woods yet," he said as he started putting on his snowshoes.

There had been no time to adjust the straps before they fled the Quonset and it took a bit of time now. It was far better, he knew, to spend a couple of extra minutes at this point than to struggle with the shoes over the next few hours. They still had about fifteen kilometres to go to reach his cabin. For the first time, though, that was his primary goal; not the distant goal, but an attainable goal that could be realised in the next twenty-four hours if they were lucky.

"You know, York, that was amazing the way it all happened. What a rush! I didn't have time to be scared." She tugged at her straps and stood up adjusting the pack on her back. "I've got to admit, though, that it was nice to ride for a while."

"Yeah, that rush as you call it can kind of grow on you," he replied. "The trick is to not let it control you. Some people end up feasting on the rush and then getting killed because they forgot to think." He checked his pockets to make sure all were secure. They were now missing some snare wire but he had lots at the cabin. "Let's get going," he said. "I want to be well away from here by daylight and I won't feel comfortable unless we're close to woods. You never can tell what else those guys will come up with."

He led the way down the road. Travel was a cake walk compared to the last couple of days when they had struggled through the snow. Now walking across the packed snowscape they could make a couple of kilometres an hour easily. Cat was not an experienced snowshoe walker and they had to stop once in a while when a misstep landed her face down on the snow. On the last occasion she was not as quick to get up as the previous times.

"I'm sorry, York, but I just need to rest a few minutes. This is so much better than the deep snow but I just can't keep up."

He glanced at his watch. It was almost four in the morning. "No problem. We've made good time." He pulled her to her feet. "We'll take ten minutes right here. See those woods to the right?" He pointed to a dark wood line that was visible through the falling snow. "If anything comes down the road in either direction we head for those woods. It's not likely to happen, though, so we'll stay here rather than waste the energy going there to rest."

After a couple of minutes Cat zipped her parka part way up

and he followed suit. "How much farther is it, York?" Then she added, "I'm not complaining. I just like to know what we're doing."

"It's about another seven or eight kilometres to the corner where this road meets the Old Connector Road. You know, the road that I live on." He studied the view to the north and then behind them to the south. "At that point we're likely going to leave the road and head through the woods." He heard her groan a little bit. "Don't worry, you're on good snowshoes now and it's actually a lot shorter through the woods. The road takes a long loop around."

"Won't we be slow, pushing through the woods?" she asked.

"Yes, but it will be about equal effort and we'll have the added benefit of not being seen. We can stop when we want and not have to worry about those guys catching up with us."

"How would they know where we've gone?"

As he looked at the snowshoe tracks being obliterated by snow behind them, the wind picked up a little. "They may not," he answered "but I didn't survive this long by ignoring possibilities."

"More of that army crap, eh." There was no scorn in her voice. "I can buy that." She reopened her parka and headed north up the road. "Follow me," she shouted over her shoulder. "We stop for ten minutes every hour."

He grinned, and then laughed out loud and followed behind her, checking their back trail one more time. The snow was easing a little and the wind was from the northwest. This would soon break and he wanted no telltale snowshoe trail to lead the hounds to the foxes.

Three hours passed uneventfully, until in the southeast the first seam of daylight was visible in the fabric of the night. The snow was noticeably less intense then, but even with regular stops to rest, Cat was looking fatigued.

There was still a good two kilometres to the turnoff when he made the decision.

"Cat, we need to leave the road. I'm sorry but the snow is easing and daylight will soon be upon us." He pointed to a drift that led from the road to the left. "We can turn left along the north side of that drift and our tracks will not likely be noticed. If we go now, there is still enough snow to erase everything."

"OK, you're the boss." She heaved in a deep breath and bent over resting her palms on her knees. "Just give me our ten minute break and we can set off."

"I'll make you a deal," he said. "Let's go now so we get ten extra minutes of snow cover, and then in the woods we can rest for twenty."

Cat said nothing, just nodded her head and stood up.

He led the way forward and along the north edge of the drift where there was already blowing snow to wipe out their tracks. They reached the woods where the wind on his face dropped to almost nothing. He dug out the compass and headed on a bearing due west until he estimated they were one hundred yards into the woods. He then found a downed tree that could be a seat for a while. Together they dropped their packs and brushed snow off the tree to make a dry place to sit.

He dug out the map and examined their route in minute detail. The rest of the trip, until they reached the woodlot in which his cabin rested, would be by day. They were afoot, albeit with snowshoes, and hunted by armed men. They had no arms themselves and only concealment could keep them out of trouble. In return for their hunted status, they had made more than two thirds of the way to his cabin in short order. He felt that it was a fair trade.

The snowshoes were their saviours in the snow conditions that they faced. Without last night's escapades they would be more than twenty kilometres to the south and likely at death's door from exhaustion. They might have just taken the snowshoes but then the snowmobiles might have been able to catch them. Besides, he thought, the people who burned Cat's car, and several houses in the area, deserved a little lesson. Pierce, whoever he was, would never look at a doorstep the same way again for the rest of his life!

The woodlot where they rested was teardrop shaped with the narrow end where they had entered from the road. Cleared fields stretched beyond and to the next piece of wooded land that would take them almost all the way to the Old Connector Road. Then there was a small gap close to the corner and after that the woods that were so familiar to him, a forest that would cover them all the way to his cabin.

He took various bearings from the map and committed them to memory. At one point he toyed with changing sides of the road along the route. Doc Simpson had a house about a mile or so up a side road and he would not turn them away. He might, however, be dead and that would be a several mile detour if there was no help there. York knew the terrain around his cabin and knew the supply and shelter situation at his own place. There was little benefit to be gained by deviating from the present plan.

They had not eaten for eighteen hours and what they had then was almost nothing. Of greater concern to him was that they had had little to drink. He could get a fire going without effort but he was still very concerned about the possible reappearance of those chasing them. He discussed the route with Cat and she agreed to forego any cooking fires until they were at least out of the teardrop woods.

He led the way deeper into the woods and after about a thousand metres he changed course a few degrees to the right, and a half-hour after that they arrived at the back edge of the woods. He took several bearings on woodline features and a distant tall round hill that was an obvious landmark on the map. They stayed in the treeline and moved to the right another hundred yards.

"Cat, this is where we'll cross to those woods over there. See, there's a little low ground here," he pointed to the field. "So we'll not be as visible from the road."

"I don't see much difference but I believe you," she said.

"If we hear anything or see anything we only have two choices while we're in the open," he explained. "We can either make a run for it to the nearest woods or we can go to ground and hope that we can stay out of sight. We'll decide at the time."

"I understand, as long as you realise just exactly what I'm capable of doing if you decide to make a run for it. I really don't have any reserves left, York."

"I'll keep that in mind."

It was now full morning daylight although it would be an overcast day. There was still a fine snow falling, *la petite neige* as he had heard some call it. It softened the edge of the far treeline and it would also make them harder to see at a distance. The wind was much stronger here at the edge of the woods, and blowing snow added to the indistinct appearance of things.

"We have four hundred metres to go to the far side. Are you OK to go now, or do you need a couple of minutes to rest?" he asked.

Cat reached down and tightened her snowshoe bindings, stood up and smiled at him. "I'm as ready as I'll ever be but you owe me a multi-course breakfast after this."

He led the way into the field. Cat was right that there was not a lot of low ground here, but farther out into the field a small knoll rose up to their right and he fixed his thoughts on making it that far before even slacking the pace. They were about halfway when he heard a drone to the right and behind them.

"Cat, pick up the pace. I can hear something coming."

He knew that she didn't have a lot of reserve but this was the time to use it. They moved at a trot and had made it to the shallow low ground before he dared look over his shoulder. Nothing was in sight so he pushed on, exhorting Cat to keep up. They would be mostly hidden from the road by the knoll, by the lightly falling snow, and by the blowing snow. Even so he did not want to be in the open if someone was looking for them and especially if that someone decided to search the field.

They were just about at the woodline when the noise became more clear and more distinct. A single snowmobile was visible on the road moving north. Its sound had become more prominent when it moved out of the cover of the teardrop woods.

"Down," he barked.

They went to ground and he could no longer see the snowmobile. That also meant that the driver of the snowmobile could not see them. Carefully he rose a little and was able to peer over the small rise. The snowmobile was stopped on the road. There were two men working around it. He could not tell what colour the machine was or any other detail. At the same time, the blowing snow and the trees in the background would make it impossible for the two snowmobilers to spot him. In fact there was really nothing that would prevent him and Cat from continuing forward from this point.

"York," Cat hissed at him. "What's happening?"

"Let's get up, just crouching, and keep going. I'll tell you all about it when we get to the trees."

They walked to the woods, bending forward as much as possible, not an easy task on snowshoes. He occasionally glanced toward the road. There was no sign of pursuit. At the treeline they slipped into the full cover of the woods.

He turned and studied the tableau behind him. The snowmobile was still motionless and the men were standing talking. The snow was almost stopped. Then as he watched, the two climbed onto the snow machine and turned it to face south. The sled seemed to be white or yellow.

"Those boys are more resourceful than I thought. I'm not sure how they got here so fast, unless they had extra gas with them on the red machine and for some reason decided to follow our sled instead of heading back."

The yellow snowmobile started moving back toward the south, its motor barely audible.

"Maybe they came up the hill to where our machine was when it was shot and found the gas that had gushed onto the snow," he said. "That might lead them to think that it was easier to keep coming after us rather than to go back."

He watched as the snowmobile picked up speed. "They must have carried extra gas in cans on the red snowmobile and then repaired the gas tank on the yellow. A screw might plug most of the bullet hole. I guess that's the way I would have called it in that situation."

He led the way a couple of hundred metres into the woods and then found a spruce and fir thicket. He could see that Cat was dragging her snowshoes with every step. He tramped down the snow near a deadfall and dragged over three large partly rotting logs to form a fire platform. He gathered an armful of squaw wood and then some larger dry sticks. The wind could barely penetrate the thicket and he ignited the tinder with ease. The fire was smokeless and would be invisible from a hundred metres away. He opened his pack and got out the metal cup, filling it with snow before standing it next to the fire.

"Keep the fire going and the cup filled with snow, please, Cat. I'll be right back."

He walked to a birch tree, stripped off some of the paper and quickly fashioned two conical cups. He returned to the fire and filled each with snow then set them upright in the snow. The metal cup was full of water and he placed it closer to the fire. He got out the ground sheet and laid it on the packed snow and then started to pile soft fir boughs on top. Cat then joined in to help, taking her cue from what she saw him doing.

"What, no snow cave this time?"

"We're not going to be here that long," he replied. "Besides, have you not heard what bears say about snow caves?"

"No, I haven't, but I bet that I'm about to."

"You'll love these," York growled in his best bear imitation. "They're cool and crusty on the outside but have a warm chewy centre."

"Now that's not funny, York. I'll never be able to sleep in a snow cave again." She threw a snowball at him. "You know I thought I heard something moving around outside, the night we were in the snow cave, but I knew that you would let me know if there was anything to be worried about."

He turned away toward the fire to tend to the water. He had slept like a log that night in the snow cave and hadn't heard a thing. Probably it was all her imagination, or maybe they had just been lucky. He picked up the birch bark cones and handed one to Cat.

"What's this for?" she asked.

"The metal cup would burn your lips. The birch bark is a great insulator. There wasn't any birch around the last time we had to do this. The snow in the bottom of the cone will cool the hot water so you can drink it. Remember the hot drink before." He poured hot water into each of their cups and put more snow in the metal cup to melt and heat.

"How could I forget," she said. "How am I doing these days?"

He paused in mock contemplation. He started to speak then stopped and played the thinker again. A snowball in the side of the head seemed to solidify his thoughts.

"You're doing great. . . for a girl." He ducked the next snowball and then held up his hands in surrender. "All right, all right, I give up. You're doing great, period."

He drank the water in his cup and refilled it with snow. "I couldn't have asked for any more from you," he said. "We even pulled off a search and destroy mission last night." He swirled the water in the metal cup and put it back on the fire and then added fuel. "It'll only be another few hours and we'll be at the cabin. Then you'll be comfortable and warm, lots to drink and lots to eat. We won't have running water if there's no power. The well pump is electric. But you'll be able to have a warm bath. The water jacket on the wood stove in the kitchen will provide all the hot water you'll want. And you'll have a real bed to sleep in." He poured some more hot water into his birchbark cup. "Imagine that, a real bed. How will you like that?"

There was no answer and he looked over to see Cat asleep on the boughs, parka zipped, hood up. "I guess this means that I have first watch," he whispered to himself.

He knew that they were both exhausted and a couple of hours sleep was probably a good idea. Now was the best time for it in the relative warmth of the day, if you could call minus 10C warm. He sipped his water and was content. If only he had a weapon, then he would feel positively happy.

His old MP-5 silenced submachine gun would even the score. Well that was just dreaming. He would rehydrate himself over the next couple of hours and then wake Cat to do the same before they headed out.

He woke Cat two hours later. She was feeling chilled, and was happy for the warm water. He plied her with fluids until she protested and went to the far side of the thicket to relieve herself. He then gave her instructions to wake him in an hour and for her to keep pushing fluids. He lay down on the boughs relishing the feeling of stretching out full length.

He came to, with Cat nudging his shoulder. He listened for anything that was out of place and heard nothing amiss. "Everything OK?" he asked.

"Just fine. It's been an hour. I thought about letting you sleep longer but then decided that you'd had enough."

"Good decision," he said, and winced as he crawled to his feet. "I'm getting too old for this shit." He threw the boughs farther into the thicket and rolled up the ground sheet and packed it away.

They shared another couple of drinks and then prepared to head off. He pointed out their route on the map. It was a straight bearing to the corner and he set the compass a little bit east of the direct route. That meant that they would hit the main road and could then follow it to where the roads met. They had to cross Sturgeon Brook about two thirds of the way there, but they were less than two kilometres to that waypoint.

The first half of the leg was uneventful. At Sturgeon Brook, he searched for a downed tree or some other way of crossing the watercourse. It was likely frozen solid but he was uncomfortable crossing the ice if there was a makeshift bridge available. It was not the depth of water that bothered him although there were some pools that were deep enough to drown in; it was rather the thought of wet boots and feet. Eventually he came to the conclusion that they had no other choice, and he led Cat down to the edge of the frozen stream carrying a twelve foot sapling that he had cut and limbed.

"I'll go first. If it will hold me then it will hold you. Leave your snowshoes on. They'll help to spread the load."

He took off his pack and threw it across to the snow on the other side, then reached for Cat's. "We may as well make ourselves as light as possible."

He threw her pack across then continued, "If you get a soaker then get your wet foot into some powder snow as quickly as possible. That will soak up a lot of the water."

He moved out onto the ice with the pole held crossways in front of him. His footing seemed firm enough although there was a crack under his left foot at one point. He made it to the far side and turned to face Cat.

"I guess that I should tell you that I can't swim," she said, inching out onto the snow-covered ice, as if it would open like a trap door at every step.

"That's OK. There's not enough water to swim. It's the cold

and wet that we're concerned about."

She made her way toward him and he extended the pole in her direction as soon as she was in range. There was one awesome crack as she made her last step onto solid ground. A wet stain appeared in her last snowshoe print and spread over the surrounding snow. They looked at each other then simultaneously shrugged and stooped to pick up their packs.

The next part of the journey was demanding. They had to climb from the level of the stream out of the gully to the higher terrain around. It was tough and slow going as Cat had difficulty climbing in snowshoes and could not keep up with him. They were a full hour covering the one hundred meters out of the depression. It was difficult to see the sky from within the woods but his watch said 16:30.

They stopped to take a breather once they were out of the gully. The temperature was surprisingly cold once they stopped moving. After just a couple of moments he got them marching again.

"We need to get a wiggle on. It's getting dark and I want to get across the Old Connector Road and into my woods before dark." He helped Cat to shrug back into her pack. "We can be there by midnight if it keeps clearing. The moon will help. But it's going to be cold."

CHAPTER 19

24 January, evening

"Midnight? Then how much longer to the cabin?" asked Cat. There was dismay in her voice.

"No, I mean at the cabin by midnight," he said. "We'll be at the corner in an hour or less."

She lost her scowl. He led the way forward through the woods and in forty-five minutes they came to the edge of the woods. Keeping inside the woods they turned to the left and five minutes later arrived at the corner. He led on five minutes to the west up the Old Connector Road, keeping in the woods. Then they crossed where their tracks would not be as easily noticed, especially where they would not be noticed by anyone travelling the main road. Once on the other side he led them into the woods and then stopped to study the map again.

"Do you know where you are now, Cat?"

"Well, if we go down that road that we just crossed then we'll come to where that old farmer lives and then eventually to your place."

"That's right and if we carried on to the north on the other road that we were following, we would come to where you had your car accident and then eventually we would come to Spencer."

"How far are we to your cabin?"

"Straight ahead through the woods," he pointed with the compass, "about five kilometres. It's going to take a lot longer after dark so every step that we can take in the rest of the daylight will be a bonus for us."

"That's a polite way of you once again pushing us to get going, isn't it?"

"You've broken my code," he replied.

"All right, let's go, but you owe me a hot bath when we get to your cabin tonight."

"Agreed."

He turned and, checking the compass, moved off at a brisk pace into the woods. Cat came puffing behind him but not complaining. They continued to stop for ten minutes every hour. It was after the second break that disaster struck. Cat broke a snowshoe.

Fatigue was taking its toll and he had slowed the pace considerably. He helped her to her feet after a tumble and at the very next step she fell forward, her knee landing on the frame of the snowshoe in front of her. He knew what happened when he heard the crack.

After getting Cat back to her feet he examined the snowshoe. It could be mended just as he had mended the bear paw previously, but they were a couple of kilometres from tools and patching material. He dug the ground sheet out of the pack and made a spot for Cat to lie down and rest.

It was full dark and getting much colder as he moved into an evergreen thicket nearby and cut several sturdy boughs. Retrieving some riser cord from his pack, he lashed the boughs to the bottom of the broken snowshoe. After about a half-hour he declared to himself that he had done all that could be done with the materials at hand.

He woke Cat and buckled the ugly mass of boughs and the remains of the snowshoe to her foot. She weighed less than him, and it made sense for her to use the repaired snowshoe. He took her small pack and buckled it to the outside of his rucksack, thereby further lightening the load on the repair job. Cat protested at that move but relented when he explained why.

They headed off in the dark, York leading at a very slow pace and stopping ten minutes every twenty. Cat was having trouble keeping up and he knew that she was close to exhaustion. Because of their footwear it was difficult for him to walk close to Cat to help her. They kept stepping on each other's snowshoes.

A faint orange luminescent strip appeared in the trees to his left. Another was visible just ahead to the right. He knew to the centimetre where they were, walking out from the area of his bow hunting stand.

At last they emerged from the woods into the open field. It was almost pitch black and the snow was drifted ten feet deep along the edge of the woods.

"Cat, we're only a couple of hundred metres from the cabin." He pointed to the south. "It's just over that knoll right there."

Her only reply was a sigh.

They pushed on directly up the centre of the field to the low ridge of high ground then stopped and rested. He knew that he was in the right place; but the view was not exactly as it should be. The cabin roof should be visible even in the present low light. Perhaps the snow and wind had created an artificial horizon line that concealed the cabin.

"Come on, Cat, it's just over the next hill."

They trudged on with ever more wearisome steps, until he stopped with an acrid scent at his nose. No, it couldn't be, not after all this distance.

"Wait here, Cat. I'll be right back."

He surged ahead using much of his reserve strength but driven to know now if it was true.

At this point a curse was an understatement so he said nothing. He just stood staring as the moon slipped from behind a cloud. The rafters of the partially consumed roof pointed skyward like so many ribs of a decomposing animal half buried by snow. The smell of scorched wood hung heavy in the air this close to the wreckage.

He was amazed that the sight did not totally devastate him. It was only a cabin after all. He now had his old house back from Sloat, although that was not the immediate concern. The problem right now was shelter and warmth and that was not possible here at the burnt cabin.

His fall back position was the only hope for them at this point. The closest shelter and warmth available was the old sugar shack. They had passed within a kilometre of it on their route here. If it had also been destroyed then it was unlikely that they would survive to see the daylight.

He returned to where Cat had sunk to her knees in the snow. He wrestled her to her feet and held her head in his hands, mouthing the words close to her face wreathed in the fur of the parka hood.

"Cat, the cabin has been burnt. There is no shelter here. We need to travel a while longer. I know where there is another place that's sure to be OK."

"York, I don't think that I can go any farther. My legs are like jelly and I'm so tired I can hardly breathe."

"Cat, if we stay here we will freeze to death tonight. There is no way here to find shelter and certainly no way to get warm."

"You go ahead. I'll just rest a while."

"Look, Cat, you're going to die here anyway, so why don't you come with me and we'll at least die together."

She turned and faced back the way they had come then to the west and east. "You need to tell me how far it is."

"It's about two kilometres, but it is all in the open or on a good trail. There is no bushwhacking and it is half downhill and half level. I know that you can do it."

"OK, York, we've gone this far together and I trust you. But you have to go slowly. I have nothing left."

"I'm glad to hear you say it, because that means I don't have to show off for you," he said, and then headed in baby steps along their previous route. He wanted to take advantage of anything that would make the next few hours easier.

Seconds turned into minutes, and minutes made the first hour. Cat had fallen several times and it was laborious to raise her. On the last occasion he had cajoled her and tugged at her for five minutes before he was able to get her mobile again. She was in peril of freezing to death in the next hour.

He knew that they were close to the trail into the woods, the trail that led to the sugar shack. From even a short distance away, however, he could not make out the three bull spruces that concealed the entrance. The branches of all the trees were heavily laden with snow and in the dark the trees appeared to form an impenetrable wall of black and white. The moonlight was of little use. Things just looked so different by night and in the winter. He needed to cruise along the wood line to find the opening, but he also didn't want to tire Cat with extra steps. He was also afraid that if he left her alone he would return to find her dead.

Just as he was wrestling with that decision he found the trail opening and led Cat into the pathway. The snow was less deep once they got into the woods and Cat only fell once in the next hour. They plodded forward like some tiny elephant safari in a frigid jungle carpeted by white.

At last the shack loomed in front of them. It was intact. The door opened outward and it was blocked by snow. He took off his snowshoes and used one as a shovel to move snow from the doorway. He hit a layer of ice, probably from the rain during the thunder snow a few days ago. There had been plenty of snow on the ground first though, and it had absorbed the excess moisture, so he was able to break through the crust and clear the mixture away from the opening.

He pulled on the handle and it didn't budge. Using his heel he rapped the door in as many areas as he could, and threw his weight against the door to loosen the ice seal that had formed. He pulled on the handle again and the door opened, fetching up against snow that had yet to be cleared, but there was an opening that was sufficient for entry. He took Cat's hand and then had to catch her and lower her to the ground. She had fallen asleep on her feet.

"We're here, Cat. We're at another cabin. You only have to get up one more time then you'll be warm."

He knew that he did not have the strength to carry her. He was about to start trying to drag her through the doorway when she awoke and with assistance was able to struggle to her feet.

Inside the shack he moved the table against the wall close to the stove, but not too close. There would, in a few minutes, be warmth; but the warmth would be more palpable off the floor. He helped Cat onto the table and laid her down leaned against the wall. She was so tired she would not likely move but there was no sense risking a fall at this point.

He didn't think he had the strength left to do the flint and steel thing right now. He opened the glass jar on the shelf and took out one wooden match. These would be scarce and precious commodities for a while and should be saved for a rainy day, he thought.

"This isn't just a rainy day, it's pouring," he said aloud; and lit the fire materials that he had laid in the stove three months ago.

It took a while for the paper to catch. It had absorbed a little dampness, but the match heat was insistent and the fire spread amongst the paper. There was soon a crackle from the dry cedar and the stove and cabin were revealed in the firelight. All was unchanged from his last visit here. The dirt around the hearth was undisturbed and the cans of provisions were where he had left them.

As usual the radiant heat was instantly apparent, but it took an hour before the full effect of the heat could be felt throughout the hut. Cat slept on the table and he forced himself to remain awake for two hours. By then there was a good bed of coals in the stove. He filled the stove again, to last as long as possible.

He woke Cat, not an easy task. As she climbed down from the table, very unsteady on her feet, she clung to him like a child. He sat her on the bench and moved the table to a safer distance from the fire, then helped her back on top.

She was instantly asleep again. He pulled the two benches together and curled up on them and slept.

* * *

When he awoke there was daylight visible through the tiny window to the left of the door. The cabin was cold, but compared to what they had experienced over the last few days, it was heaven. He looked over at Cat. She was still curled on the table and had not moved since she had gone to sleep.

He swung himself upright to sit on the benches. His shoulders ached and his legs protested as he stood. He opened the door of the stove and stirred up the coals that were still present beneath the ash.

The glow was warm on his face. He selected kindling from the box by the stove and soon had the fire refreshed and roaring. He took the kettle from the shelf above the stove and went to the door.

The morning was frigid. It had snowed again but had now stopped and the sky had cleared to a deep cerulean blue. There was no wind. York surveyed the woods from the doorway. There were no tracks visible, not even their own snowshoe tracks from last night. He smiled. Nobody could know where they were; to any pursuer they had just faded into the woods like ghosts in the shadows.

He tapped dust from the kettle and wiped the inside with snow. He then filled the kettle with fresh snow and slipped back into the sugar shack to put it on the stove.

He selected the pointed spade from the collection of hand tools in the corner and set to work. He dug up the soil in front of the stove, soil that had been warmed by the stove last night. There was still frost in the ground but it was softer there than in more distant parts of the shack. Winter access was the reason that he had chosen this as a burial location last fall.

When he struck resistance he dug more carefully and cleared the soil more gently from the canvas and plastic-wrapped parcel. He lifted the bundle to the benches, paused long enough to add more snow to the kettle, and then opened the package that contained his rifle.

The grease and silica gel packets had done their job of absorbing moisture. There was no rust on the .45-70 lever-action rifle. He wiped off the grease, unwrapped the cleaning kit, pulled an oiled cleaning patch through the bore, and then applied some graphite into the breach mechanism. In this cold weather the graphite had less chance of freezing than oil did.

He loaded the tubular magazine with flat-point cartridges then placed the rifle in the rack above the door. He ran the palm of his hand along the smooth walnut stock. They had shelter, food, water, and now protection. Now they could just wait for the thaw.

He attended to the stove and the kettle and then leaned close to Cat, just to reassure himself that she was still breathing. He shovelled the soil back into the crater in front of the stove. It was going to be a little muddy in here until all the ground had thawed and dried. He cleared away the wrappings for the rifle and climbed into the rafters to recover some of the tins that he had stored there.

"Hi," he heard. He looked down from his perch to see Cat smiling up at him from her bed on the table.

"Good morning, sleepy head," he replied. "I won't say sleeping beauty because you do look a little worse for wear."

"Well thanks a lot. I feel great."

"Wait until you move," he warned.

A long groan rewarded his prediction as Cat sat up on the tabletop. "You promised me a hot bath and a real bed, York Lancaster."

"Beyond the control of the management." He dropped several of the large tins onto the floor. "Now that you're finished sleeping in, we can put the table to its intended use." He swung down and hung from the rafter then dropped to the floor.

Cat arose with more groans and stretches then contemplated the shack. He realised that this was the first time she had seen the place. She was in no condition for the grand tour when they had arrived last night.

"I guess the four piece bath must be in the other building," she said. "Let me guess, latrine left, water right?"

He mounted a sheepish grin and nodded his head. She disappeared out the door, and then came back in again.

"I don't suppose you have any of the secret papers left?" she said.

He walked to the back of the shack and lifted the cover on a five-gallon plastic can, displaying several rolls. She grinned as she caught the roll of toilet paper that he threw to her.

"That's why you get the big bucks," she said, and disappeared again out the door.

He piled the tins on the table and moved the benches back in position. He located the can opener and started on the first tin. It was full of wheat. He snapped the accompanying plastic cover over the grain and he placed the metal top on the shelf above the stove. Even something as simple as a can cover could be priceless in the next few years. With the grinder that he had, they would soon have flour.

The next tin contained beans, and the third held milk powder. He opened a small tin of cheese and one that contained bacon, then a sealed pack that contained vitamins, Tylenol, and Aspirin.

Cat came back through the door and he handed her a gallon bucket to fill with snow. This he placed on the back of the stove and they continued to open tins and packages of lentils, pasta, tea, coffee, fruit juice powder and spices.

He made a pot of tea as they discussed the best way to use the supplies that lay before them. Then Cat prepared a breakfast of cheese and bacon while he set up the mill and ground wheat into flour. He had to change the mill from coarse to fine over three grindings but in an hour he had enough flour to make bread. The rest of the morning was spent on basic domestic chores but by mid afternoon the smell of baking bread filled the shack. That evening they had bread still warm from the oven, lentils, and a pudding made with the milk powder.

He put beans to soak overnight and banked the fire in the stove, and they retired with the sunset. He awoke at first light to see Cat returning from outside. That was the first full night that he had slept in weeks. He glanced above the door at the rifle then sat up on the benches.

"Good morning. How did you sleep?"

Cat jumped at his voice. "I thought that you were still asleep."

"It was a good snooze," he said. "But I can do better than these benches and table. I just need a little time."

"You're right. I think the boughs on the snow are a step up. Then again, this place is a lot warmer than a snow cave."

"Yes, it's nice to have a roof, walls, and a stove."

What's the plan for today?" she asked.

"Well, we're here for the long haul. This is what we have for the next few months. We need to work to make ourselves as comfortable as possible."

He got up and loaded wood into the stove. He poured the beans, which had been soaking overnight, into the crock that was sitting on the wall shelf. He added some of the tinned bacon, then molasses.

Cat came over to watch what he was doing. "That looks disgusting," she said.

"Don't judge too quickly," he said, adding some brown sugar and then some dried mustard from the spice pack. "I don't have maple syrup to finish it off. Won't have any for a month or so, but this will still be delicious. You just mark my words."

"You think that we'll be able to go to a store and buy maple syrup in a month?"

"No, not at all. I think it will be a lot longer than that." He stirred the beans in the crock then opened the oven door and slipped it inside. "See those long cans in the corner? We'll be making our own maple syrup in a few weeks."

Cat shook her head and walked to the back of the shack, peering into boxes and cans, while he set about starting to rearrange the shack for the best use of space. He was happy in these surroundings, spartan as they were. We're probably some of the most comfortable people in the country right now, he thought.

CHAPTER 20

27 January

The next day as he was pawing through the supplies in the cabin he rediscovered his hand-powered radio; it had been stored with the foodstuffs. He cranked it to life and dialled in several of the local stations in succession, receiving only a static return at each frequency. The radio appeared to be in working order but there was nothing to be heard.

He tuned to the local CBC station and was rewarded with music. It was classical music, no songs with lyrics, only music. After a few minutes a voice announced that it was a recording and that the daily news and information broadcast would be made at noon Eastern. York checked his watch, adjusted for the time zone, then set aside the radio and went outside to let Cat know that they would have some news in an hour.

She was gathering fresh snow. They had to go farther afield to find large quantities and York was already thinking of the most labour efficient way to get water from the brook a kilometre away. That would be their only source of water once the snow had gone. It would probably take a while to restore any sort of well-water source.

He helped carry the two buckets of snow back to the shack. It was a bright cloudless day, barely below freezing and they set the radio on a stump outside the shack to get the best possible reception. He cranked the radio for five minutes so they would have an uninterrupted ten minutes of listening.

The broadcast began with the playing of the national anthem. The announcer then stated that the total known Canadian deaths to date numbered seven million. York could only look at Cat and shake his head. There were sixty five million reported dead in the United States.

The announcer reassured the audience that there was a central government functioning in Ottawa, although there were no provincial governments of any effect. Apparently in the United States the opposite had occurred. The states had re-established functional government control but nothing had been heard of the national government since it had gone into a secret bunker at the height of the flu crisis.

The announcer stated that the previously reported nuclear exchange between Pakistan and India had been confirmed. It was unknown at this time the size of the weapon yields or the potential effect on North America.

"Holy shit!" York said, but he was promptly "shushed" by Cat.

The announcer gave a brief and very broad-brush weather report. "Cold and clear for the eastern half of the country. Chance of snow in some areas."

York started to comment on the usefulness of the forecast but was again stilled by Cat.

The announcer completed the broadcast with five minutes of advice about public health issues and survival strategies for those that were listening. Most items were applicable only to city dwellers, things such as designating rooms on the bottom floor of apartment buildings for latrines instead of using rooms on each floor.

This time Cat gasped. "My God, York, imagine a city with no running water. And I was complaining because we had to carry snow fifty metres."

He cranked the radio again for a couple of minutes. The broadcast ended after a brief religious passage and after announcing the next broadcast at noon the following day. He and Cat stood motionless staring at the radio.

After a couple of minutes he picked up the radio and carried it back into the cabin, storing it on the shelf with their medications. There seemed to be no framework upon which to discuss what they had heard. He busied himself collecting snow and carrying firewood into the shack. Cat hung their blankets and parkas on the clothesline out back for airing. Neither seemed able to communicate with the other.

The following day at noon they returned to their posts to listen again to the CBC broadcast. The announcer reiterated the same figures from the day before. When you're dealing in the tens of millions, York thought, you don't expect the numbers to change daily.

They heard a second voice in the broadcast today. In a classic 'interview the reporter' format, the new voice told about a trip to Montreal. There were reports of cannibalism from that city as food supplies were exhausted. There were also rumours of people being kidnapped off the street and from dwellings, and being slaughtered for meat. Locals told of human meat shops springing up in various neighbourhoods all over the city.

"York, I can't listen to this," Cat said, as she went into the shack.

He refrained from a jibe about hunting. This was not the time for that type of humour. The remainder of the broadcast was similar to previous.

A couple of days later, after morning chores, he turned his attention to something that had been gnawing at him since their arrival at the sugar shack. He grabbed his parka and the undamaged pair of snowshoes. It was early in the morning and he felt the bite of the cold on his cheeks as he snowshoed down the path leading to the field below his burnt out cabin. An hour's brisk walk, sometimes a trot, took him to the cabin's remains.

He walked around the cabin twice. Once at a radius of about ten metres, then a second time closer to the debris. The northeast corner and the southeast corner retained their walls. The roof was caved in over the western half of the cabin but was still partially supported on the eastern half. The wind must have been from the east or northeast when this happened. That meant during a storm.

He went to the workshop and garage that stood to the west of the house. The wall of the garage that was closest to the house was scorched but intact. The door was open and snow lay a foot deep on the floor. Tools and equipment were strewn everywhere as if a giant hand had swept it all onto the floor. "That's probably what actually happened," he said to himself. "This is not wind damage." He picked up a pry bar from the corner and headed outdoors.

Careful to avoid weakened floorboards and unstable walls, he headed into the wreckage of the house. He had two goals on this mission. He wanted to see what remained of his possessions, including what he could salvage. He also wanted to look for clues to origin of the fire.

His books were soaked and there was little that would be salvageable in the main room. To be this wet, the fire must have been the night of the thundersnow and rainstorm. There would certainly have been nobody here fighting the fire, pouring water on the flames, so it had to be during that rainstorm. The computer was melted but the wires were normal where they plugged into the wall. The bedroom and the bathroom were burned out hulks with the charred shell of the roof collapsed on top. The small arms cabinet was broken open and the rifles were missing. Only his bow and a half dozen arrows were left on the floor below the cabinet.

The kitchen was almost intact, he saw, with only scorching and smoke damage apparent. The cupboard doors were open however, and the crockery was scattered in shards all over the floor. Fires did not open cupboard doors or throw dishes onto the floor. The broken pieces of plates and bowls had no unsmoked fracture surfaces. Everything was covered with the same smooth coat of soot. Only those surfaces where the pieces touched the floor were clean. The damage had happened before the fire. He began to realise that this was no electrical fire, no mere accident. His cabin had been purposely burnt!

Both of his questions had been partially answered. He moved aside the debris that littered the doorway between the kitchen and the main room and found the trapdoor that led to the basement. The brass foldaway handle was frozen in place but the pry bar quickly broke away the ice. He lifted the door and eased himself down the stairway, pulling his flashlight from his pocket. The basement was untouched except for some ice build-up in the southwest corner where the floor had been damaged, and the water and snow had been admitted.

Most of the preserved vegetables and jams that he could see were intact. A few had burst when the temperature had dropped and they had been allowed to freeze. There had been no entry to this part of the house; this was natural breakage. The arms cabinet here was unbreached, but he had no need to open it at this time. The metal cabinet had moisture proof seals and a desiccant inside. No sense opening the vapour barrier until there was a way to protect the weapons. The small cabinet upstairs held the rifles that he used the most but he never kept all of his weapons in one place.

The hiding places for the gold coins were undisturbed. Only the few that he had hidden in the bedroom area were perhaps lost. He would search for those at another time.

His fifty-pound bags of potatoes were frozen but would be usable if cooked straight from frozen as soup thickening and such. He picked up another pair of snowshoes from the wall rack and headed back upstairs.

He went through the woodshed and stopped at the freezer. Inside everything looked clean, dry and healthy. The north wind had protected his woodpile as well. In fact the wind and the rain had likely kept the fire from totally destroying the contents of the cabin. He and Cat would eat better, even if not live more comfortably, because of that wind and rain.

Leaving the woodshed he stepped on the outside door that had been hacked from its hinges. This was where the arsonists had entered the house. A sledgehammer that used to stand in the shed was lying half-buried in the snow beside the door. Careful to avoid splinters, he lifted the destroyed door out of the way. There beneath it was a more precise answer to his question "What started the fire?" Frozen into the slush that must have been formed during the storm was a footprint. It was a running shoe with a NIKE logo in the centre of the print. He looked around the yard again, half expecting to see a white pickup.

He walked to the shed and pulled his toboggan from the rafters. He took down some rigger's cord, very strong parachute quality cord, and attached a wooden apple box to the toboggan. He went back down into the basement and brought up an armful of preserves. He loaded those, the spare snowshoes, and some meat from the freezer into the apple box. He gathered a few other items that were stored in bulk in the cellar.

He headed back to the south towing the toboggan and feeling somewhat naked without a rifle in his other hand. Now that he was on his own terrain, with shelter and a few supplies, winter was a toothless lion. There was a more dangerous predator in the area, man.

He arrived back at the sugar shack, shouting when he was still fifty meters away to avoid scaring Cat. She opened the door and stepped out shielding her eyes from the sun. He stopped at the door and pulled the toboggan in close.

"What have you got there?"

"A few of life's little comforts," he replied bending over and unlashing the box from the toboggan. Even the box would be of benefit in the sparse cabin.

He trundled the box inside and set it on the table and pulled out one item at a time like Santa unloading his sack. With each item the response from Cat was more gratifying. New snowshoes to replace her broken ones; a smile. A few pots and utensils, and some spices; a grin. Frozen vegetables and venison steaks; "All Right." Towels, soap and shampoo; a squeal of delight.

He had spent years living in holes in the ground, and had never underestimated the joy of being clean. Cat had been uncomplaining through many days of deprivation and she must have found it very hard to have to endure the filth thrust upon her.

"I'm going to scout the area around us," he said. "I'll be gone for at least another hour." That would give her plenty of time to heat water and have a leisurely sponge bath. "It's the heat of the day and it's a good time to have a look around," he continued.

He hoped that she would take the hint that she would be undisturbed for a while. Woe betide me, he thought, should I tell her more directly that she should have a bath. The repercussions could echo for weeks. He grinned to himself and headed into the woods, travelling in a large ellipse with the cabin at one focus.

He took stock of the available firewood, mainly windfalls that were held partially off the ground by trees around them. Those that had fallen in the summer or fall were probably now dry enough to burn if necessary. Although there was plenty of chopped wood at the sugar shack, it was always good to know where your next woodpile was coming from.

He looked for animal tracks, burrows, and game trails. Subconsciously he was searching also for hiding places, ambush locations, and routes to disappear out of sight. That skill of observation and analysis was hard earned and not easily lost.

A Canada Jay followed him for a few minutes then disappeared, searching for a better food source. An old bull raven gave its familiar “CRONK” as it circled overhead. A slight breeze brushed his face as he turned to the west. The snow was probably three feet deep in the woods now, with drifts twice that height. Without snowshoes he would flounder for hours trying to make any progress at all.

As he made the swing back to the south he came upon something that startled him. At eye level an old black spruce was clawed two inches into the bark. This was the mark of a large bear. Then he remembered that he was probably only a kilometre from where he had seen the black bear at his hunting stand. Was it only three months ago?

So much had changed in the world since that morning. Perhaps he should pay even more attention to his changed environment. Thousands, maybe tens of thousands had died in the surrounding counties. Roads were impassable and the usual civil authority was powerless to reach his location let alone provide assistance. Persons unknown, not so far from here, were burning buildings and vehicles, and who knew what other activities; and here was ample evidence of an animal that could outrun and outclimb him.

He never carried a weapon, and certainly not a firearm, unless it was legal hunting season. He did not consider his belt knife or boot knife as weapons. They were tools that had many uses. On the other hand the world had changed.

"Maybe it's time that I modified my usual habits just a bit," he said aloud.

He resumed his loop toward the sugar shack, hailing the building as he approached, and slowing his pace. Cat emerged again, this time towelling her hair and leaning against the doorjamb. The pose was familiar from the day she awoke from the flu in his cabin, although the surroundings were a bit more Spartan on this occasion.

"Did you find anything of interest?" she asked.

"A whole lot of not much," he replied, unstrapping his snowshoes and sticking them tail first into the snow by the door. "You've been busy giving the soap a work-out I see."

"Does that mean that it's my turn to go for an hour long walk now?" she asked grinning.

"Was I that obvious?"

"No, not really. I only realised a few minutes ago why you had decided now was the best time to, how do you say it, 'go for a reconnaissance'."

"I thought that you'd like a little time to yourself."

"I appreciate that, but after what we've been through you don't have to disappear into the bush for an hour."

"Just trying to add a touch of normalcy," he said, taking off gloves and earband, then picking up the apple box, following her into the shack.

"Do you think things will ever be normal again?" she asked, pausing to glance out the door and then closing it.

"Well that's a good question." He placed the apple box in the corner farthest from the stove and covered it with some large sticks of firewood. "I don't think that I can answer that for you. I have a question for you on a less philosophical note."

"Oh, and what's that?"

"Do you remember a somewhat heated discussion that we had concerning deer hunting?"

"Yeeess, but I've managed to get over the rabbits."

"Well, the entrée tonight is roast venison." He continued before she had a chance to respond. “The items I brought were the top layer from the freezer. There are some pork cuts in the freezer as well and I’ll get some for you eventually.”

“York, I am so hungry for anything except bread and beans right now that I would eat the family budgie. I’m just worried that I won’t like it. At this point I can truly see your point of view as far as providing for yourself. I just hope that I’ll like it.”

“Well I can guarantee that you’ll like it. It won’t be a five star meal. We don’t have a lot to work with, but you stand aside and let me work my magic.”

That evening they dined like king and queen on cranberry roast venison, peas, fresh bread and tinned peaches. A true monarch would have sneered at their simple fare but there were probably few people any happier for hundreds of miles around. They took care not to overindulge, not only to conserve their supplies but also to ease their digestive systems back into a wider diet.

They talked in the dark until they were both exhausted, then one on the table and one on the bench they tried to get some sleep. He awoke regularly to feed the fire and on one occasion thought he heard an animal call faintly in the distance. In the glow of the open stove door he glanced at the rifle hanging over the door to the shack then resumed feeding the fire.

CHAPTER 21

15 March

The next few weeks passed quickly. The days were filled with work around the camp to try to improve the living conditions. Together they ferried hundreds of usable items from cabin to shack. York worked with hand tools in his workshop beside the fire-damaged cabin. He fashioned beds, cupboards, benches and tables that he then towed on the toboggan to the sugar shack. Rough planks that had been stored for woodworking were put to use as floor boards in the shack. Cat commented that she had always wanted hardwood floors in her kitchen but had always imagined them in combination with indoor plumbing.

Each day at noon they listened to the CBC broadcast. They heard that the southern United States had formed a Confederacy and had affirmed that slavery was not to be a part of the constitution. Israel had fought off attack from its neighbours and driven the Syrians back to the Golan Heights again. Calgary was plagued by attacks from wild dogs sweeping the streets at night in packs of two hundred or more. Those living in single floor dwellings were the prey of choice. The Hoover Dam had cracked and it was unknown if it could be saved.

The evenings were filled with long talks and discussions of every topic that they could imagine. York found that Cat was an interesting, well read, and thoughtful conversationalist. They usually struck up a conversation at supper that spilled over into the cleanup tasks and then carried on into the evening over coffee or tea. Darkness, fatigue and resolution of the conversation were the signals to sleep; which they did soundly.

One of Cat's favourite things was to tell stories. They each selected a book that had not been read by the other. They took turns telling 'chapters' from the books as best they could remember. York was telling *Battlefield Earth* by L Ron Hubbard. Cat was describing *Outlander* by Diana Gabaldon.

They shared everything except a bed. York was still leery of her previous relationship, expecting that it might rekindle as the present situation stabilised. He had seen a lot of women tied up with some pretty odious characters in the past. He didn't understand it, but assumed that it had something to do with love. He wanted to do nothing that would cause difficulties for her in the future. He also did not know whether he was ready for a long-term relationship and wanted nothing that would forge a bond that he did not feel ready for.

Nevertheless he enjoyed her company, enjoyed the way they had become a team, and found that his desire to be left alone was softening to include Cat as an integral part of his day to day life.

* * *

The nights shortened and the days lengthened. He prepared sap buckets and, as the first melting days appeared, tapped some of the maple trees, and boiled sap for syrup and sugar. They boiled outside. Since they were living in the shack they could not afford to steam and humidify their house and possessions.

He returned to the camp with the first pail of maple sap of the day. He started the outdoor boiling fire and set the stainless steel syrup pan on the metal legs that he had fashioned for it, and dumped the bucket of sap into the pan. He poked his head through the doorway and was greeted by the smell of frying meat.

"Boys that smells good."

"I'll have a breakfast ready in about ten minutes," Cat said.

"That gives me time to gather another bucket from the sap cans. There'll be less chance of burning the syrup if there's more in the pan." He pulled his head outside the doorway and headed into the woods again.

He gathered two more buckets from the pails hanging on the trees, poured them in the pan, and returned inside. Cat was kneading bread at one end of the table. The cabin was very warm to allow the yeast to work.

"Help yourself to what's on the stove. I'm up to my elbows in this at the moment."

"Now you're just showing off," he said as he washed his hands at the sideboard. "You know, I admit that you are the better baker."

Cat laughed. "So you finally admit it."

"Yes, but don't forget who your teacher is. And I still do make the best pot roast."

He took up two plates of meat, opened a jar of rhubarb-strawberry preserves that he had made last summer. It seemed so long ago. Some frozen blueberries and a piece of cheese from one of the large tins would complete the meal along with bread from the last baking day. They were getting low on tea bags and he took down a package of coffee and set a percolator full of water on the stove.

Cat set the dough on the table by the stove to allow it to rise then joined him for breakfast.

"York, what's going to happen in the spring?"

"Well, the sun will get warmer, and the snow will melt, and there will be lots of birds and grass and stuff."

"I know, silly." She punched him on the arm. "That's not what I meant. I mean what is the world going to be like?" She picked up her mug of coffee and sipped at it. "What's this country going to be like? A lot of people died with the flu. Things will have changed."

"Yeah, you're right; there will be a lot of changes." He put down his fork and looked around the cabin. "I'm going to have to pay particular attention to the garden that I plant this year. There are going to be food problems for sure." He picked up the cup of coffee. "And I'll have to build a better cabin than this. I don't know whether my previous cabin can be rebuilt."

"What about the world? Just listening to the radio, you know it will all be different."

"Our standard of living has probably been set back a hundred years. We can just hope that there will be enough memory and knowledge so that it won't take a century to catch up." He put the cup down and chewed on a crusty piece of bread. "You know, maybe there are still some plusses, even if that sounds macabre. There will be a lot fewer stresses on the environment. More fish, less pollution, less global warming."

He looked over at Cat and she quickly looked down at her plate. "I wonder how many people that I know are still alive," she said.

"Yeah." He pushed the food around on his plate. "My sister Elizabeth is a nurse in Spencer. My brother is in the army. I don't even know if Shamus is alive, and he was my nearest neighbour."

After a couple of minutes of silence, he finished the food on his plate and started to clean up, taking the dishes to the dry sink that he had built.

"I suddenly don't feel very hungry but I guess I should eat it," Cat said. She finished her meal and picked up from the table. "I'll finish here while I'm waiting for the bread to rise, if you want to go back to the sap."

He dried off his hands and headed for the door. "We could talk about planning for the future tonight if you want." He stopped at the door and turned around. "There will be a lot of changes, Cat, a lot of changes. But it will never be as bad as what you've been through already. At least I don't think so."

He was returning to the cabin later when he heard a wailing sound that was out of place in the woods. He froze and listened to the faint noise. It was centred at the shack. He hurried closer trying not to spill sap. He paused again. Was it the radio? No, it wasn't noon yet. It almost sounded like bag pipes. Then as he got closer the sound became more distinct. It was the wail of a harmonica.

He opened the door to the shack to find Cat blowing a riff on the harmonica. She saw him and slipped into "This Land is My Land." He realised that his mouth was hanging open and shut it with a snap.

Then he sang along with the song until Cat had finished.

"You play the harmonica," was all that he could say.

"Yeah, I do. I found this in your pack when you were sick and I played it to bolster my spirits. I had forgotten about it until I was feeling down today. I had put it in my pack and forgotten all about it."

"That's wonderful. I've been trying to learn to play too, but not very well I'm afraid."

"When I found it I assumed that you played, and I was a little embarrassed to play in front of you. I figured that you played as well as you do everything else."

York grabbed Cat and gave her a big hug. "Will you teach me to play? The best that I can do is Twinkle Twinkle."

"Glad to. I'll help to get the sap on and then we can play together."

* * *

The warming weather brought an accompanying hope for an early spring. This hope was crushed by a late winter blizzard that roared through the woods for two full days and confined them to the cabin except for forays to the toilet or to gather water.

On the first morning after the storm, York travelled the routes to the sugar trees, breaking trail and firming the ground around the camp. The sugar season would continue for a while longer and they would need the syrup later in the year.

Even snowed-in during the white-out conditions of the blizzard, their spirits had been on cloud nine. Warmth, shelter, sustenance, and music nurtured the two of them as winter clawed at them in vain.

CHAPTER 22

27 March

York was driving along the Wolf Ridge Road, relishing once again the breeze in his hair and the sun on his face. He had thought that he would never again enjoy the open road, that sense of release that he always got from just driving. He had been able to recover his vehicle and gas was no longer a problem. The silver Jeep TJ whined a little when he down shifted from fourth gear as he approached the turn. A little too fast, but there was no other traffic on the road, or at least there shouldn't be.

The tires squealed a little as he entered the curve. His speed slowed from the gearing down and from the friction of the directional change. The squealing continued, however, and then actually began to increase. Strange. The tires began to scream as he came out of the curve. The scream did not ease as he hit the brake pedal and pulled to a halt in the middle of the road. Then the tires screamed his name.

"York! York, help!"

He was groggy from sleep as his feet hit the floor. He lurched to the left and smashed against the table. He was aware of the sound of breaking glass as a jar fell. The sound melded into another scream from outside the cabin, a scream rising in volume and pitch until it was unnaturally truncated.

He threw the door open and rushed out practically into the arms of the bear.

Cat lay on the ground, broken and cast aside. The crimson stain around her looked garish against the pristine snow but it matched perfectly the nail polish worn by the bear. Cat did not move.

The bear, still erect, moved one step toward him and swung his left forepaw like a club, a spiked club, black and brown and red. York lunged backwards. His stockinged feet slipped on the packed snow just outside the door. The paw fanned the air by his right ear as he landed on his butt. He rolled to the left as the bear advanced toward him. The bear had to return to all fours to make any speed and York scrambled behind the open door, momentarily out of sight.

His rifle was in the cabin. There was a window right beside him, the only window in the shack, but it was too small for him to crawl through.

The door smashed against him, mashing him between it and the wall of the cabin. He lost his wind and braced himself for the next blow. His head exploded in lights as the next crunch of the door blasted his shoulder, hip, and skull at the same time. He braced himself again, trying to protect his head this time. His ribs felt fractured on the right side. He was being trashed like a junked Chevy in a crusher.

His right arm was trapped against his side. Every breath drove a searing lance into his chest where the ribs had fractured. The haft of his belt knife was scraping his right wrist.

The pressure eased a little then was reapplied. The bear was leaning against the door, tenderising his next cutlet.

"Oh Cat, why did it have to end this way?"

The pressure eased, but his ribs screamed. Again the pressure, a sharper blow to the door this time, forcing his arm against his side again. His wrist scraped on the knife but when the pressure eased again his hand did not come away empty.

The feel of a weapon in his hand changed his purpose. He might be prey but he would not give up. As he died he would not go quietly.

He braced for the next blow, listening. He smelled the sour

odour of the bear. Again the wood crushed against him. He could not stand this much longer.

So what! What did it matter? Cat gone. The last vestige of joy swept from his life. His life was a mirror of the world around him.

The pressure from the door eased. He reached out with his left hand and swept a large clump of snow off the windowsill. With a lunge against the door, he screamed and catapulted the snowball into the bear's face.

The bear reared back and gave him just enough time to dash around the corner of the cabin.

He grabbed a branch of the maple tree that crowded the shack and, with ribs ripping at him, swung up onto the roof.

"Never try to outclimb a bear," he whispered to himself.

He could see the bear's eyes scanning the rooftop as its head cleared the edge of the gable.

The bear continued to climb toward a large limb that overhung the roof.

It inched onto the branch, and with a lurch landed on the roof and lunged toward him.

He clenched the knife in his left hand. Splinted his right arm against his chest. Took one step and dropped over the edge of the roof at the front of the shack.

His feet slipped as they made contact with the ground but with a paratrooper roll he broke the fall. On hands and knees he scrambled past the splintered door and into the cabin.

Without having to look, he reached above the doorway, seized the rifle and brought it to the ready, levering a round into the chamber. He backed from the door as he worked, trying to establish some separation and a field of fire.

A black shape shut out the light from the doorway and he fired the first round from the hip, at the centre of mass.

The bear jerked and he worked the lever of the rifle, chambering another round.

He adjusted his stance, slipped in something that had spilled as he lurched out of bed, staggered, fell, triggered off a shot and hit the floor.

He rolled to his right, levering the action again, and swung the barrel back toward the door. The doorway was empty.

He leaped to his feet fighting back the pain in his chest and crept toward the doorway. Nothing.

He stepped to the threshold and looked each way down the wall of the cabin. Nothing.

He took five quick steps straight ahead then whirled around prepared to fight. Nothing.

In the distance to the left of the cabin he saw the bear lumber into a thicket and disappear from sight. He raised the rifle, sighting on the foliage where the bear had disappeared, but there was no target. He lowered the rifle.

"Stupid Bear! Take a claw to a gun fight!"

He turned slowly. Even though he didn't want to find her, he couldn't avoid it. She had been a source of joy in his dissolving world. Now she lay shredded and still. Beside her he slumped to his knees and reached forward. He needed to touch her while she was still warm.

He bundled her into his arms. And she moaned. She moaned! She was alive. He wouldn't have thought it possible, looking at her injuries.

CHAPTER 23

27 March, late morning

He carried her into the shack and gently lowered her to the cot. She moaned with the movement but did not awaken. In his mind he was back three months carrying her into safety in his cabin. So much had changed in that time. She was now no longer just a stranger from a snowstorm. Now emotion was threatening to overwhelm his thinking as he tried to help her after this latest outrage. He should have left her at her fiancé's house. He should have left her at the military camp. He should never have let her venture out alone. She would be OK now if he had done any of those things.

He threw more wood into the stove and lit a couple of candles to add more light to the shadows. He pulled away her clothing and started to sponge the wounded areas with warm water and a clean towel. She had a scratch from her left ear to the corner of her mouth. It was not very deep, but her left arm was badly cut. She must have got her arm up to protect her head when the bear took a swipe at her. He opened the first aid kit and applied some antibiotic ointment before wrapping her arm with two field dressings. Those thick absorbent dressings would keep that wound clean and dry.

He then turned to the wounds on the chest wall. On her right side there were three deep lacerations about eight inches long arranged in parallel and leading from back to front. The bear had taken a sideways swipe at her and connected with three claws. There was frothy blood at the centre gouge and more bubbles appeared as he watched.

He knew from the bubbles that the wound extended into the chest cavity and that he needed to prevent air from getting into the chest through the chest wall. He applied antibiotic ointment and used one of the waterproof coverings off the field dressings to cover the wound. He then cinched it in place with two more field dressings.

What worried him the most was her breathing. It was shallow and laboured and she had a pink froth at her lips as she gave a weak cough. He made her as comfortable as he could, covered her with all their blankets, and slumped into the chair to watch.

After an hour he checked the wounds. There was no bleeding. He fed the fire again then grabbed the rifle and went outside. There was no sound, sight or smell of the bear. He recalled the way that the bear had jerked when he had fired the first shot. The animal was wounded without a doubt, and would likely die in the woods and never bother them again. Still he would be careful.

That night he stayed awake tending Cat. She moaned a few times and on one occasion she called his name very clearly but she did not wake up. In the morning he redressed her wounds with the exception of the chest wound. He did not want to take the chance of letting more air into the chest cavity so he left the dressing in place.

Examining her again, he found a large bump on the back of her head. This was likely why she was unconscious; she must have struck her head when she fell. He watched over her all that day and the next night. His own chest pain eased quickly. If his ribs were broken, they had not displaced. He found that he was able to breathe much more easily.

In the morning she was fevered and delirious. He dressed her wounds again and kept her clean and warm. He worked around the shack and tried to awake her knowing that she needed fluids soon or she would become dehydrated. On one occasion she swallowed sips of water and he provided about a cupful, spoon by spoon, before she stopped swallowing. He tried several more times and had water and warm broth available, in case she would take more. Her fever persisted and her breathing became more laboured.

The following morning he checked her wounds and listened to her breathing, and then came to a decision. If she stayed here, as she was, then she would surely die.

The options were few. As far as he knew there were no open roads, or vehicles travelling on them. The cabin was close enough to a couple of roads that any traffic on those roads would have been heard. That was especially true if they were plows or snow blowers. There was no way to summon help, and from what they had seen in the last month it would likely be a long time before help was a telephone call away. That meant that they needed to travel by foot.

The medical help available was likely in Spencer at the clinic or at the reception centre. From what he had seen of the flu, and the rapid way that it had spread, it was unlikely that the flu was still active. Probably everyone that was going to be infected had been so already. Like a forest fire racing rapidly through an isolated forest the flu had probably consumed all of its fuel. A few sparks might remain but it had probably burnt itself out.

There was another possibility. Doc Simpson lived closer than Spencer although in the opposite direction on the main road. With all of his patients either recovered or dead, the doctor would spend at least some of his time at his own house. If there was no electricity the clinic would be closed anyway. There was no wood heat there. He knew that the doctor had a wood stove. They had discussed the relative merits of beech and maple for heating when the doc had decided that he was going to put in a stove.

The doctor would need medication and equipment if he was going to be able to help Cat and that would probably be in Spencer. York had a pretty good first aid kit though. The Doc had helped him put it together so at least some of what he would need might be there. He would have to carry the kit as well as transport Cat. She had not revived, so she would have to be ferried on the toboggan. If he started now, then he could be ready to go by noon, and with a little bit of luck he could get to the doctor's house by dark.

He brought the toboggan into the cabin and padded it with a

deer hide that he had brought from the burned cabin a few days ago. It would provide good insulation from the cold and also a measure of padding and comfort.

He dressed Cat in her parka, boots, and gloves and placed her tenderly on the toboggan, then covered her with all of the blankets. He lashed her to the toboggan and pillowed her head on his parka. He would not need the parka right away as it was a mild day, and for what he had in mind he wanted to be well ventilated.

He put a bit of food in the pack along with all of the medical supplies that he could carry, and a thermos of warm broth. He checked the magazine on the rifle and slung it over the pack on his back and stepped into his snowshoes. He manhandled the loaded toboggan out the door, latched the door firmly, and started down the trail.

This would be a speed trip and because he was towing the toboggan, the shortest route was unfortunately denied him. He could not go through the woods with the toboggan and its cargo. The only option was to go to his cabin, then down the lane, and out the road to the main highway. By that route it was about fifteen kilometres to Doc Simpson's house. Who knew if Doc Simpson was even still alive but that was the only reasonable goal at this time. If he was lucky he might meet some assistance on the way and could modify the plan if a better opportunity presented itself.

He followed the path through the woods and out into the fields south of his cabin. In an hour he stopped in his own yard to check Cat. She remained unconscious but securely lashed to the toboggan. He pushed on down his lane and out onto the road. He even managed a bit of a trot going downhill then thought better of it not wanting to get overheated; he had a long way to go yet. He passed Shamus MacGregor's farm but there was no sign of life.

Farther down the road he stopped to rest, and inadvertently looked up onto the hillside at the old family homestead. He saw the old Victorian house, or rather what was left of it. There were two brick chimneys still standing but the rest had been burned to the ground.

He did not feel as anguished as he thought that he should. Finally he had the house back in his possession and it had been snatched from him again. He felt a slight sadness but there was no pervasive sense of loss like that he had experienced when he had returned from Afghanistan. He realised that he now missed his cabin more than the house, and he missed Cat most of all. There was a stirring of anger, though, that the house had been burned. There was likely a footprint with a Nike mark in it around the grounds of that house as well.

He turned his back on the homestead. Those problems were best dealt with at another time. He checked Cat again and then started down the road. Another two hours passed and he reached the main highway, where he stopped to check his passenger and saw that her eyes were open. He sank to his knees beside her in the deep snow.

"Hi there. Are you cold?"

She moved her lips but no sound came out, just a wheeze and a little blood at her lips. He put his finger to her lips and wiped away the blood.

"Don't try to talk. We're on our way to the doctor's house."

"I'm sorry," she managed to gasp out in a whisper. There were tears in her eyes.

"Stop!" he said. "You have nothing to be sorry about. I'm the one who failed you."

She tried to shake her head and he held her face between his hands. "Don't say anymore. This is no time for an argument. I have warm broth. Can you drink?"

She wheezed out, "No, where is your parka?"

"It's your pillow. You're keeping it warm for me until I need it. I'm plenty warm and I couldn't wear it until we get stopped anyway."

He slipped the rifle off his back and placed it across Cat's knees on the toboggan. He took off the pack and retrieved the thermos. He helped Cat to sit up part way and slowly fed her some of the broth, stopping when she began to cough. The pink froth looked redder than it had previously. He waited for the paroxysm of coughing to end and then settled her back onto the toboggan. He tightened some of the lashings and settled the pack and rifle back on his shoulders in preparation for the next leg of the journey.

"What's that terrible smell?" she gasped. "Do I have gangrene?"

"No you don't have gangrene. You have a cut on your face

and bad ones on your left chest, and lots of other scrapes and bruises. You had a bump on the head and have been unconscious for a couple of days."

"Then what's the bad smell?"

"Do you remember the deer hide from the venison we've been eating?"

She nodded.

"Well you're lying on it. It doesn't smell very good until it's been cured, but now it's keeping you warm."

She nodded and closed her eyes. He watched her breath for a few seconds then set off at the best pace he could muster.

He swung to the right when he arrived at the highway and then started down the wide snow filled road. About five feet of snow he estimated. No sign of a plow or a vehicle track. He thought that he heard a snowmobile in the distance but the sound was soon gone. Just let those bastards try to interfere with him now. He leaned into the traces that he had rigged for the toboggan and started the uphill climb that faced him for the next five kilometres.

They had come down the same slope a month ago when making the last move toward his now burnt cabin. He had been thankful for gravity's assistance at that time, but he cursed it on this occasion. He had to stop every fifteen minutes for a breather, as the toboggan bit into the snow and put a huge strain on his shoulders. The breaks became longer as he tried to recover from each successive effort. On one occasion he waited so long that he began to get a little cold and he thought about his parka, and then rejected the thought. He needed to push ahead. Bundled as she might be, Cat was still in serious risk of becoming hypothermic since she was not moving. He felt her face and it was cold, but she opened her eyes.

"Are you cold?" he asked.

She nodded her head yes. He knew that there was no solution to that problem except to get her help in a warm place. He resumed the trek forcing himself to go all the way to the top of the slope before taking the next break.

His heart was thumping in his ears when he finally stopped. There was a kilometre of level ground, then another kilometre down a side road to the doctor's house. Would it still be standing? Would there be anyone there? Anyone alive?

He pointed his snowshoes where they needed to go and turned off his mind. An hour later they were at the side road. This was the point of no return. There were other houses farther down the main road, but if he went to the doctor's house he would not have the endurance to return to the main road without rest and warmth. The trip to the doctor's house was still the best course of action, he reminded himself. He was glad that he had thought this all through while he was fresh. His fatigue would affect his judgement now.

Other houses were unlikely to be a source of medical care for Cat and she would die for sure without proper care. She might be dead already. York saw her breathe and headed down the side road toward the doctor's house. He stopped twice in the first five hundred metres and three more times in the next three hundred. He was nearing his own limit of endurance having towed the heavy toboggan almost eleven miles through deep snow, carrying a heavy pack on his back.

Guess I'm not in as good shape as I used to be, he thought. He leaned into the traces again and the toboggan did not move. Another jerk and it began to inch along behind him as he moved up the slope for the last hundred metres. He considered going ahead without the load but did not think that he would have the strength to come back and continue the journey if there was no help available.

His ankles hurt. He had stumbled several times and whenever he did he struck the side of one snowshoe against the opposite ankle. He fell and was barely able to get back to his feet. That can't happen again he told himself or neither of us will make it. He started again, gasping for breath. The wind stirred and he exhaled against his face. He was nearing the top. There should have been wood smoke on that breeze if there was life at the house still out of sight ahead. He sniffed again. Nothing. Maybe there was electricity.

That hope was dashed when his line of sight crested the hillside. The house was there. At least that was a plus. But there were no lights, no smoke from the chimney, no sign of inhabitants.

He was in despair. No doctor meant that Cat was going to die. He would be able to survive and could eventually make the return trip to the sugar shack. Why would he even want to? There was little there to draw him back.

He tugged the toboggan to the front door and stopped, gasping for breath, chilled all the way through. He steeled himself for the next required efforts, to find a way in, then to drag Cat inside and try to generate some warmth. He should have stayed at the sugar shack. At least there was warmth and food there.

He bent down by Cat. She flickered her eyes open in response to his touch on her cheek. "Hang on, Cat. We're there and I'll have you inside and warm in a couple of minutes." He'd burn furniture if he had to.

He was dreading opening the door, dreading what he might find inside. Empty was one thing. If there were bodies and feasting rats he was not sure that he could deal with that right now. When Cat died he would dig a grave for her and bury her out of reach of animals even if he had to do it in the frozen earth with his bare hands.

He trudged around the side of the house. There was a door at the back but no tracks in the snow and all was quiet. He walked back to the front, took off his snowshoes and beat the snow off of them on the porch railing. He stepped up onto the porch and tried the knob. It was locked. He took out his belt knife. The handle would crack the window by the door and he could reach in to unlock the bolt.

Just before he swung the knife, the door opened.

CHAPTER 24

30 March, evening

York froze then regained his composure and threw himself to the left. Most people were right handed and if carrying a rifle had more difficulty swinging it to their right. He wanted to take advantage of that extra second of time to get out of the killing zone and get set to fight back. He repositioned the knife to an underhand grip and braced his feet. With his left hand he groped for the rifle on his back.

"York? Is that you?" asked Elizabeth peering around the doorway.

"Yeah. Yeah it's me," he stammered. "I didn't think there was anyone here."

"We thought you were dead," she said. "Come in. It's not much warmer in here but it's a bit better. Where's your coat?"

York pointed to the toboggan then started down the steps. "I'll pull this up closer. Actually I think it will pull right through the door and we can get her in easier that way."

"Who is she York?" Elizabeth stood on the porch and reached for the traces as he manhandled the toboggan up the steps.

"Do you remember the woman I found in the ditch and she had the flu?"

"Back in January when all this started?"

"It's a long story," he said. They dragged the toboggan into the hall.

"Hello, York," said Doc Simpson coming from down the side hall.

"Doc, can you help me out? A bear attacked her and she has an open chest wound. I think the right lung is collapsed."

The doctor hurried to Cat's side. York stripped away the blankets and the three of them lifted her off the toboggan and carried her into the first bedroom and laid her carefully on the bed.

"Man, it's cold in here," York said. "I thought that you had a woodstove."

The Doc and Elizabeth looked at each other and then Elizabeth nodded. "Come with me, York," she said.

He followed her out into the kitchen then into the attached garage. She pointed to a tiny pile of wood on the floor beside the Doc's Impala. "Grab that, York, and we'll light the stove. If we need more, there's wood furniture."

"Where's the rest of your woodpile?" he asked, knowing the answer already.

"That's all there is. There has been no electricity for over a month and we've used the wood a few sticks at a time to keep from freezing. We have no way of getting more. There's an axe but the snow is too deep to move in the woods."

He picked up an armful of wood and headed back into the house. "Let's get a fire going, sister of mine," he said. "I can solve your fire problems without burning all your furniture."

He had a blaze going in the wood stove in two minutes and returned to the garage to bring in more wood, to fill the wood box by the stove. His sister put a kettle on to boil. He realised that he was making a mess of melting snow on the floors and slipped off his boots, setting them behind the stove to keep them warm. He padded in his sock feet down the hall to where Cat was lying.

Doc was examining the chest wound. He had a stethoscope around his neck. He was bent over sniffing at the wound. "York, you did a great job with these wounds. There is no sign of gangrene but she has a high fever. There's likely some infection just because of the mechanism of injury. You were also right about the collapsed lung. She needs to have a chest tube and some antibiotics to give her any chance of survival." The doctor stood up from the bedside. "She is also getting dehydrated. Has she had anything to drink lately?"

York told him about the last three days. The doctor was incredulous to hear that they had left York's property at noon.

"Doc, when can you start to work on her?"

"That's a problem. I have no medicines or instruments here. I have nothing but my stethoscope. There are instruments at the clinic but there are no medications. The influenza cleaned us out entirely."

"I may be able to help there as well, Doc." York went to the hallway, picked up his rifle and stood it in the corner, then carried the pack into the sick room. "Do you remember the list that you helped me with? Well here is the most of it."

Doc looked at him, shook his head, and started to unload the pack. York handed a couple of packages of foodstuffs to Elizabeth, surprised at the way she examined the bundles. She left the room and he helped Doc to sort out what was available to use for medical care.

"York, the problem is that she needs a chest tube. Her right lung has collapsed and will not reinflate because there is air in the chest cavity on the right side." The doctor rifled through the medical supplies a second time. "You don't have a chest tube here. I could make do with the other instruments that are here, especially since there is already an open wound; but there is no chest tube."

"What does a chest tube look like, Doc?"

"It needs to be about a foot or more long and it needs a valve or a water trap at the end to let air out of the chest but not back in. Wait. We don't need the valve. You've got rubber gloves there, and I can jury rig a valve with a glove. The tube is the only problem."

Elizabeth came to the door carrying two cups of tea. "What kind of tube are you looking for?" She gave a cup to York and then one to the Doc.

"Something that we could use for a chest tube." The doctor took a sip of the tea. "We don't need the valve, just something about 16 French, about a foot or two long."

She thought for a moment then left the room. She returned a few seconds later carrying a short, soft rubber hose with a shower attachment on one end and fitted with a cup to go over a faucet on the other end. “I saw this in the bathroom when I first got here. It was attached to the sink.”

“I used to use it to wash my hair when I had a bath instead of a shower,” the doc said. “That’s a great idea. We can sterilise it and with the ends cut off it will do the trick.”

He gathered up all the pieces that he would need and headed for the kitchen. York bent over Cat and whispered in her ear. She gave a ghost of a smile, and he stood up and followed the Doc and Elizabeth.

“York, what in the world happened? How did she get injured by a bear?”

“I’ll tell you about it sometime.”

“Well there’s something that we have to talk about right now, York,” the doctor said. “I want you to know that there is no guarantee that this will work for her. If there has been a lot of damage to the lung it may not re-inflate, even with the chest tube. If that is the case only surgery can help and even then it’s not a sure thing.”

York stood still and silent for a minute then said, “I understand. Just do your best and if there’s anything that I can do to help just ask.” He picked up his teacup and drained it. “Have you got plain water?” he asked.

“That we do have plenty of,” said Elizabeth. She opened a crock on the table and with a small dipper filled his cup.

For the next few minutes they boiled instruments and the expedient chest tube. Doc and Elizabeth reviewed the procedure they would follow. Doc cut a finger out of the glove and with suture thread he bound the finger securely to one end of the sterilised tube. He then sliced the tip of the finger so that it was open when pressurised but would seal one side against the other if a negative pressure was applied. He dissolved a broad-spectrum antibiotic tablet in a small amount of water. York then went in to see Cat and coaxed it into her one sip at a time.

The house was much warmer by then and Cat seemed more comfortable although she still shook with rigors. He could see the froth at her lips as she coughed and he knew that she was still critically ill.

The Doc entered Cat's room and explained to her what he intended to do. She murmured consent. They cleared away a working space and she was rolled onto her left side. York went around the bed so he could be facing her while the doctor and nurse carried out the procedure. He held her hand, and saw her wince when the local anaesthetic was injected.

He and Cat looked into each other's eyes and he whispered encouragement. She would squeeze his hand every once in a while and on one occasion he saw her contort her face and she clamped his hand like a vice. Then Doc and Elizabeth were bandaging her up and she drifted off to sleep.

"It's working OK," the doctor said. The glove finger would occasionally open a little then seal back tightly together.

Elizabeth left the room and came back with several pillows and cushions and they propped them around Cat to keep her half on her back and half on her left side. She was still breathing with the left lung only, but they could not lay her on the right side for fear of kinking the chest tube. They cleared the instruments and debris out of the room and together cleaned up.

Doc gave instructions for antibiotic use and danger signs that should prompt him to be called, since they would take turns caring for her, and then they all retreated into the kitchen. York was exhausted and asked for a cup of tea before grabbing a spot to lie down.

"I'm sorry," said Elizabeth, "but I used the last tea bag that we had when I gave you that last cup. We don't have very much at all."

He remembered the way that she had looked at the packages of food. He also understood why she looked a little different to him. Her cheekbones had been accentuated by weight loss and she was gaunt and pale. He had been so consumed by his concern for Cat that he had not paid attention to much else. Looking at Doc he realised that the two of them were starving. He went to his pack and got out the thermos bottle.

"There's broth in here that needs to be heated." He carried it to the stove and took down a saucepan. "I'll trade you for a glass of that cold water. I'm still a little dehydrated from the walk here. Do I understand correctly that the two of you have not had a lot to eat lately?"

"The last time that we ate was two days ago," said Doc. "That was a bit of porridge and a small tin of green beans. We have enough for the same about three more times." He slumped into one of the kitchen chairs. "We've been trying to make things last until the roads open. People have gone for fifty days without food in the past so we might make it."

"Elizabeth, why don't you open those packages that I gave you?" York said. "There's fresh bread and jam in them. There's tea here in the pack," he said rummaging around. "There's a cooked venison steak here in this package. Save the plastic bag. They may be hard to come by for a while."

"York, how come you have all this?" Elizabeth asked. "How is it possible?" She got a teapot from the cupboard and with one teabag began to make a pot. "Your cabin burned down. We heard about it from Shamus. How have you even survived?"

"It's a long story and I promise to tell it all, but I'm really bushed right now. I'm going to have that cup of tea, and then is there a place that I can sleep?"

"You can have our room," Elizabeth said, then she blushed a little and looked at Doc.

"York, your sister and I are an item," he said getting up and walking over to put his arm around Elizabeth's shoulder. "We were thrown together almost day and night for a month of hell while the flu raged." He gave her a squeeze. "Well it just seemed that we belonged together and when it became apparent that there was a lot of surviving left to do, I couldn't imagine being separated from her. I love her and have asked her to marry me when this all comes to an end. I hope that you approve." He stood motionless watching York.

"Doc, I approve wholeheartedly." York grinned and walked over to shake his hand. "Elizabeth, congratulations, I think it's wonderful." He gave her a hug, which she returned tentatively at first then stronger. "I also want to apologise for my behaviour for the last few years, Elizabeth. I acted like an ass. Please forgive me. I'd like to have another chance to be a better brother."

Elizabeth clung to his neck and sobbed in his arms.

"Doc, I'm sorry. I didn't mean to get your fiancée all upset."

"York, you have no idea what a weight you have lifted from her shoulders. Come on; let's have that cup of tea."

Elizabeth wiped her eyes and York got a skillet down from the rack and put it on the stove. He had the venison sizzling before he went into the living room and crashed on the sofa. The other two protested but he was asleep shortly after making Doc agree that he would call him in four hours so that he could sit with Cat.

He tossed and turned and he thought of Cat. He thought about his brother Russell, wondering where he was at this time. He would like to talk to Russell again and apologise for the years lost there as well. He was up and about before Doc came to wake him, and he sat with Cat for the next four hours. There wasn't anything to do except to watch for the danger signs that Doc had mentioned and be available to help if she needed anything. This was different from the last time that he had cared for her when she was ill. The feeling was different.

He spent part of his sitting time planning the next few days. Partly it was to take his mind off of Cat and partly it was because he disliked being without a plan. There were some basic survival problems here and he felt that he was just the one to solve them. Doc and Elizabeth were the best ones to look after Cat, and he could make all their lives better by doing other things.

He woke Elizabeth when six hours had passed and the first glimmer of light was in the sky. He was already dressed in boots and parka.

"I'm going for firewood," he told her, whispering to try to avoid waking Doc. "I'll be gone for a few hours probably, depends on what I find."

In the garage he gathered the ropes from the toboggan and grabbed a small bucksaw. The axe that Elizabeth had pointed out was very dull, better for splitting than cutting. He went out the back door of the garage, put on his snowshoes and headed into the woods to the right side, the south side of the house.

The mild weather yesterday had released the snow that had accumulated in the trees with the last storm. He pushed into the evergreens and began foraging for downed timber that had been held off the ground. Kindling would not be a problem. There was lots of squaw wood on the trees at the woodline. About thirty meters inside the woods he came to the power line. The road to the house had a curve in it and it must have been cheaper to angle the wires cross-country in a straight line instead of following the road.

He headed down slope, following the power line, and found the first of the downed trees that he was looking for. It was an old spruce and would provide lots of kindling and cooking wood. He needed some hardwood to provide the BTUs to heat the house. He continued down the power line, and about fifty feet before it intersected with the road again he found an old yellow birch that had a rotten core and had toppled in a windstorm. It was held off the ground by a large branch about thirty feet up the trunk.

He unslung the saw and started to work. In about two hours he had several pieces sawed and towed to the road. He walked to the house, stopped long enough to ask how Cat was doing and to get a long drink of water.

He dragged the toboggan down the hill and loaded wood to the limit of his strength. Working on snowshoes it was best to make several small trips instead of a few heavy ones. By the end of the day he had enough dry wood split and stacked in the garage to keep them warm for a month. Another pile remained outside to be split. He stowed his tools in the garage and went into the house.

Nobody was in the kitchen and he took off his boots and walked toward Cat's room. He heard Doc and Elizabeth talking. He rounded the corner and his heart leapt. Cat was sitting on the side of the bed.

All three turned toward him. Then all three tried to talk at once, and then stopped.

"How are you?" he asked Cat.

"I'm OK," she whispered. She tried to hold up her hand and it sank back onto the bed.

"Her lung has reinflated and her fever has broken," said Doc.

"She has really just come around in the last half hour."

"She insisted that she wanted to get up to the bathroom," Elizabeth added.

"How about if we carry her in that chair as far as the bathroom?" asked York, pointing to the chair by the bed. "You and I are strong enough to carry her, Doc."

Doc nodded and they soon had her at the doorway to the bathroom. He and Doc walked to the kitchen to await the call for return transportation.

"Doc, there's now enough firewood to do until the snow is gone although not necessarily until the cold is gone. There's lots of cooking wood not far into the woods on the south side of the house." York poured two cups of tea from the kettle on the stove. "What we need now is food."

Doc nodded agreement.

"If I can borrow your snowshoes I'll go get it.

"This house is still the best place for all of us now, if you don't mind the extra company for a while," York continued. "I have all the food we need at the cabin, and at the sugar shack where we've been staying, so I need to bring supplies here. I need to go soon and then probably a trip once a week."

"Can I help?" asked Doc.

"Thanks, maybe a later trip. Cat needs your skills right now. He sipped at the tea and then sat in one of the chairs. "If it's OK with you I'll sit with her for the next little while then get some sleep. I'll leave before first light and make a round trip tomorrow."

"You're kidding," Doc exclaimed. "That's thirty kilometres on snow shoes with a load."

York smiled. "Well not exactly. I'll have an empty toboggan one way and I'll be able to go cross-country on the outbound leg. I know that country well and there is a lot of open treed terrain. The area had most of the softwood cut off of it about sixty years ago so there's plenty of room to manoeuvre an empty toboggan through there. That will save me three miles although the terrain is not as smooth as the road."

Doc shook his head. There was a call from down the hallway

and they trooped back to provide sedan chair service. To their surprise Cat was already back in bed, sitting propped up on several pillows. Elizabeth was giving her nursing skills full rein as she smoothed and tucked in the bedclothes and fussed over Cat's chest tube placement. Cat was beaming. "I made it back by myself," she said. Her voice was more than a whisper, but not much more.

"All right, there's been enough excitement for the day," Elizabeth said. "There's been enough showing off around here. York, you and Josh get out of here while I get Cat settled for the night.

"Good night, Cat," Doc said.

York lifted his right hand in a tentative wave. He was rewarded with a weak smile and an unheard whisper. Then he left the room.

* * *

The next morning he was on the way at four o'clock, with pack on his back and toboggan towing behind. The other three said goodbye at the door. Cat was very unhappy that he was going by himself.

The stars were crisp and clear as he headed down the roadway. The evening had been clear also with no promise of precipitation in the crimson sunset. He had his parka open wide and he took advantage of the downhill slope to make good time. He reminded himself, however, that an accident could be the end of him as well as the three who now depended upon him for their survival.

At first light he had covered the eight kilometres to the Old Connector Road and by sunrise he was well into the woods heading on a compass course as straight as an arrow for his burned cabin. He had decided that he would leave the sugar shack untouched for now. The cabin had the frozen foods in the inoperative freezer. That food should be used before the spring thaw so he would draw from that source first.

He arrived at about nine in the morning and spent an hour collecting supplies from the freezer and the basement. He filled the pack, and with a couple of apple boxes he heaped enough food onto the toboggan to do them a couple of weeks if they were careful.

As he was leaving the ruins he thought again about the Nike running shoe. He had not wanted to slow himself down, or carry the heavy rifle all the way from Doc's house to here and back, so he had left the rifle with the other three. It would also provide a measure of protection. He knew that Elizabeth could shoot the rifle. Their father had taught them both the basics of survival skills.

He also did not yet wish to open the arms cabinet. There were months of wet weather ahead and those rifles and ammunition could be very important to them all for food gathering in the months to come. He had no wish to expose them to moisture and condensation.

Still he felt uncomfortable with only his belt knife at hand. He thought of the bear again. No, that was just nerves; there would be no rematch there. He re-entered the ruins and took his bow from its cabinet along with a full quiver of hunting arrows. He lashed these to the toboggan and headed down the lane, reprising the route that he had taken with Cat two days ago.

Their previous track was still visible. The toboggan was lighter on this trip but the pack was heavier. The urgency was gone, however, and he felt good as he steadily travelled along the smooth surface. He stopped for ten minutes after about the first hour and drank from the thermos of tea. He had not opened it on the outbound leg to prevent it from cooling. He wanted it hot and stimulating to help with the more demanding return journey.

At Shamus's place he stopped and studied the house. He was well ahead of schedule. He pulled the toboggan off the road, retrieved the bow and quiver and trekked up the lane towards the house and barn.

CHAPTER 25

1 April

There was no sign of life from Shamus's house. He scanned the area for any evidence of what had happened to the old man. The doorways were blocked by snow and he struggled up to try first the front door then the back. The back door yielded entry and he found Shamus dead on the divan in the living room. There was no decomposition of the body, because of the cold. York covered him with a blanket, promising to return to complete a burial.

He searched the house. There was quite a bit of canned food in the cupboards and the freezer was full. Shamus had died of the flu, old age, or a heart attack, but not of starvation.

He left the house and went to the barn. Inside were six healthy highland cows and one bull, well nourished by the large stack of hay that adjoined their stall. The air inside was warmer than outside thanks to the heat given off by the cattle. There was a large amount of manure in the stall, but not as much as he had expected. The stalls had been cleaned not more than a few days ago. The animals were skittish as he approached.

Shamus had arranged a series of forty-gallon drums along one side of the barn. He had been fond of travel and although he used to ask York to check on his animals, he had always tried to ensure that they were well fed and watered without much intervention. The barn well was pumped by a windmill, and had automatic fill and shut off floats powered by twelve volt batteries. That ensured an adequate supply of water even if unattended. He broke the thin skin of ice on the water tank closest to the door. The rest of the tanks were open. Shamus had continued to feed and water his stock even after he had died.

He soothed the cattle and left the barn. He would have to come back in a day or two and clean out their stalls after he had finished his more urgent chores. The cattle were valuable and needed to be cared for until he could ascertain their ownership. He had a momentary thought of opening their pens so that they could run if the Nike Man should appear, then he thought better about it. He couldn't save the whole world.

He returned to the road and readjusted pack and toboggan harness, and then pulled his load toward the main highway. He was very tired when he struggled into the yard at Doc's house. The round trip had taken him twelve hours including his side trip to look for Shamus. His shoulders ached from tugging on the toboggan.

Cat met him at the door, and Elizabeth's protests could be heard from behind her. He was surprised at the embrace and a little embarrassed at the kiss and the tears that greeted him. He returned the hug, but afraid of disturbing her chest tube, he disentangled himself to carry in the supplies.

Doc and Elizabeth stared at the powdered milk, the packages of frozen meat and vegetables, and the jars of preserves and maple syrup that he stacked on the kitchen table.

"Leave it to York," said Cat. "Send him into the woods with a Swiss army knife and he'll build a mall." York shot her a glance, not knowing if he was being mocked or not.

They feasted and celebrated that night and talked for hours. He could escape the chore no longer, and was forced to tell his experiences for the last few weeks. Cat added details, usually where he was making light of some feat.

"I know that you have always been one for being prepared for everything," said Elizabeth, "the ultimate Boy Scout. But how did you even know to start preparing for this disaster?"

"Just stuff on the news, and a visitor one day. Do you remember the young lad that I brought into the reception centre the night I found Cat in the ditch?"

"Vaguely," said Elizabeth.

"He was a Mormon and he had come to my cabin a few days earlier. I chased him away but he left some tracts behind that gave me some ideas about all of these preparations." He paused. "I don't suppose you know if he made it."

Doc and Elizabeth looked at each other, and then back at him. "He died the next day," Doc said. "I know now who you are talking about. He told me that you had spoken to him and told him that he had made a difference in your life. He said that because of that he felt he could die in peace."

"I'm sorry," Elizabeth said.

"He had guts," York added. He got up and went out onto the front deck and stood for a moment looking up at the stars. The night was cold, clear and fresh, so different from the school gymnasium that he had fled so many weeks before. "He had guts," he said again, and then he returned into the house.

The other three looked at him as he came into the warm kitchen. He recognised worry on their faces.

"It's all right," he said. "I just needed a breath of fresh air. I'm not used to all these fancy furnishings and such and needed to return to my roots."

"We'll buy that for now," Doc said, "but if you need to talk don't let it fester."

"No problem, Doc. I think I'm about ready for bed. At least my shoulders tell me so."

"That's a good idea for all of us." Elizabeth surged to her feet. "Cat you need to get settled. Come on and I'll get you tucked in after I change that dressing."

York collapsed on the sofa in the living room and felt himself drifting.

*   *   *

He awoke and lay quietly for a while. It was well past dawn. He felt very comfortable just lying on the couch, wrapped in a quilt, contemplating the next series of moves in this survival chess game that they had all been thrown into. His back and shoulders complained a little.

His life in the last few days had become one of mixed blessings. He was overjoyed that he and Elizabeth were again brother and sister. He was angry with himself for having driven her away for so many years. He had been devastated by the injuries that Cat had received, believing that he could have prevented the attack if he had been more careful. He was now elated at her rapid recovery. He was comfortable with their present supply of food, fuel, and lodging but he knew that tough times were ahead.

"Those things will have to wait until they need attention," he said to himself as he threw off the quilt and bounced from the couch. His legs and shoulders complained a little louder, still feeling the effects of his previous exertions.

He tiptoed down the hall to the room where Cat slept. The door was open so that they could hear her if she called. He peeked around the corner and stared into her open eyes.

"I heard you coming."

"Guess I'll have to be quieter next time. How are you feeling?" He pulled up a chair beside the bed.

"Much better." Without apparent discomfort she adjusted her position in the bed. "You saved my life again. How am I ever going to even the score with you?"

"I'm not keeping score."

"Maybe not, but I am."

"Well, you can just keep giving me harmonica lessons for free and we'll call it even."

"It'll likely take a few days before I can blow the harp again."

Silence filled the room.

"Cat, I was so worried about you. And I blame myself for letting this happen to you."

"Don't say that. There was nothing that you could have done any differently. You brought us through situations where I'd have died a dozen times over."

"Yeah but..."

"No buts. Shit happens and sometimes you can't stop it. I'm happy to be alive, happy to be here and happy to be with you."

"Yeah but..."

She raised her hand and he stopped.

"OK, I hear you," he said. You know, you're one full-of-surprises lady."

"What do you mean?"

"In Sloat's office you were like a wolverine at the guy's throat." He grinned at her, not having the heart to tell her that the house was in ruins. "Then it turns out you play the harmonica like a pro, the harmonica no less. Nobody plays the harmonica. Then you go dancing with a bear and live to tell the story."

Cat reached out and took his hand. She stared at him for a few seconds then lowered her eyes. "I'm full of all sorts of surprises, York. You've found a few of them but I'm not sure if you want to know the rest."

"What do you mean?"

Elizabeth's voice fractured the moment. "Are you in there bothering my patient?" She made more noise, that was obviously deliberate, and then appeared around the corner.

"Good morning, you two. I hate to interrupt but my patient requires antibiotic and a dressing change."

"That's OK, I know when I'm dismissed," he said. I'll go find trouble to get into elsewhere."

"Call me later, York. I want to go to the mall," Cat said behind him.

He went to the kitchen, stoked the wood stove and put the kettle on to boil. He sliced off thin strips of venison from a loin slab that had been in the last load that he had towed from the cabin. He set the meat to simmer in a fry pan. With flour, powdered milk, powdered eggs and sugar he prepared a simple pancake batter, added some frozen blueberries and then tended the meat. With the boiling water he made tea, and then opened a jar of maple syrup that he and Cat had made earlier. The maple season had been cut short by the bear attack. "I'll have to remember to go back and take the spiles out of the trees," he muttered to himself.

"You've been living alone too long," quipped Elizabeth as she padded into the kitchen stretching and yawning. "You're starting to talk to yourself."

"Just planning my day. Want some breakfast?"

"It smells delicious. I was surprised at how little I could eat last night before I was full, so don't cook a lot for me."

He set the venison on a warming plate on the back of the stove and then poured some pancake batter into the frying pan. The blueberries popped and sizzled as the batter cooked.

"How's Cat?" he asked.

"Her lungs are clear and I think things are healing nicely." Elizabeth got up and poured a cup of tea for herself and one for him. "You really like her, don't you?"

"Well, she's kind of grown on me," he replied. Then he frowned. "She's a person that I can talk to for hours, Elizabeth. We were through hell and back, sort of like you and Doc. But at other times we seem so different. I belong in the woods and I'm more comfortable in the country than the city. She seems so out of place in these situations and at times I think that she just wishes that she could have her old life back." He flipped the pancakes out onto a plate and placed the plate and the jar of maple syrup in front of Elizabeth.

"She looks at you like a puppy looks at its master whenever you come in the room." Elizabeth took a bite of pancake and rolled it around in her mouth. "Oh this is so good. So do you love her?"

He turned back to the stove, hiding his embarrassment. "Jeez, Elizabeth. Go slow, eh. We're just getting back to talking to one another and you're already acting like we're sisters at a pyjama party."

"I'm sorry if I embarrassed you."

He swung around and leaned back against the counter, then poured a cup of tea for himself. "That's OK. I'm just not used to talking out loud about my feelings." He purposefully didn't answer the question, but the question still echoed in his mind.

He looked over at Elizabeth to find her carefully watching his face. She grinned at him. “I think that answers my question.” She pushed herself away from the table and picked up the plate and teacup, heading for the sink.

He took the crockery from her hands and blocked her way to the sink. “I’ll look after those. Breakfast is on me today. It reminds me of being back in my cabin.”

“Well that’s fine with me.” She stood on tiptoes and gave him a peck on the cheek. “It was a wonderful breakfast. Thank you so much. I’ll go and finish tending to my patient.”

“And I’ll fix some breakfast for her. I suppose that Doc is still sleeping.”

“Yes and I’ll let him sleep for a while.” Elizabeth headed down the hallway toward Cat’s room.

York turned back to the stove and poured some more batter into the pan. While the pancake started to sizzle he searched for a tray and began to put together a room service package for Cat: cup and saucer, small teapot, milk pitcher, maple syrup pitcher, and a plate and cutlery for the pancakes. He whistled a meaningless tune and flipped the pancakes, then removed them golden brown from the pan.

He picked up the tray, grabbed a linen napkin from the sideboard and headed down the hall. This time she wouldn’t hear him coming. As he approached the door to Cat’s room in his sock feet he could hear the two women talking. He stopped dead in his tracks.

“Oh Elizabeth, he’s so coarse. At first I saw that and it put me off, but he helped me out in a couple of tough spots, and I then pretended that the rough edges didn’t matter. But as I spent more time with him I realised that I didn’t belong with him. I think that I was just one more trophy or conquest to him. What is it that they say in the army, one more objective?”

“Are you sure that it’s all over, that there is no salvaging anything?” Elizabeth queried.

“I’m sure. I’ve seen him for what he really is. Simple, short sighted, charming at times, but not really a man that I would want to spend my life with. There’s still some nostalgia for some good times together but...”

He returned to the kitchen. He put the tray on the table, moved the frying pan to the cool spot on the stove, and pulled on his boots. He opened the door to the garage, grabbed an axe and headed to the woodpile.

He lit into the chunks of maple and ash like the tide approaches a beach; slowly, inexorably, never wavering, gradually consuming the pile, without pause or attention elsewhere. His shoulder muscles began to burn and his hands were aching where he gripped the axe. He would set things to rights here, and then he would head to his shack and make plans for his own life.

It was good to be able to rely on yourself.

CHAPTER 26

2 April

The woodpile had melted before his onslaught. There was sufficient wood to heat the house and cook the food for at least a couple of months, and if the spring were a warm one maybe it would last for three.

He paused to collect his thoughts. There were still a few things that he needed to do to ensure that the other three were able to survive until the thaw. After the wood was finished, he would make more trips to the cabin for food. If he and Doc were to each make two trips with packs and the toboggan, they could get sufficient supplies for the rest of the winter and the early spring. He would have to teach them how to jerk the frozen meat so there was a means of preserving it as the weather warmed. Heaven alone knew when there would be electricity to provide refrigeration.

He scanned the yard. The snow was diminishing day by day and the long lane was open to gravel along part of its length. The roads were going to be open soon. There was still no sign of buds opening on the maple trees, so maybe he could still get in a few days of maple sugaring before the sap became bitter.

Spring would bring a whole new set of problems. Water was

plentiful now with lots of snow to melt, but when the snow was gone, it would be a long trek to the nearest stream and the water would have to be boiled. No electricity meant no pumping of water from the well. A new well would have to be dug not drilled, a well that was shallow enough to be serviced by a hand pump, or perhaps a windmill set up like Shamus had in place.

There would be plenty of food for all of them for the spring and summer but gardens would have to be planted without the benefit of seed catalogues, tillers, or fertilisers. He knew that the following winter would be very difficult as more and more of the old supplies were exhausted. But then again, maybe there would be electricity by next winter. Maybe the food distribution system would be back in operation. He snorted and returned to splitting wood.

It was almost noon when Elizabeth came to the front door. "York, you're going to kill yourself. Come in and take a break. There's lunch made."

He drove the axe deep into the beech log that he was using for a chopping block, and then arched his back, stretching muscles that were pleased by the interruption. He turned toward the house then suddenly wheeled back to the log and wrenched the axe from its grip.

"Elizabeth, get back in the house. Lock the doors. Get my rifle and stay out of sight."

He sprinted to the woodline in front of the house, cursing the footprints that he was leaving behind. He could hear the snowmobiles coming closer as he gained the cover of the woods. There was no doubt in his mind who was riding the snowmobiles. He crept farther into the woods and then doubled back toward the corner of the tree line where the laneway emptied into the dooryard. If somebody followed his footprints, he would have lots of warning as they went past to his left. He crouched amongst some small conifers.

Maybe he should have run to the house, to the rifle. But on the other hand he had a probable position of surprise, to the rear of the killing zone and behind anybody who would be watching the house. Elizabeth could handle the rifle. How much killing there would be was a good question. He could put the axe to good use in close quarters but it was no match for a rifle or handgun. How many of them were left from the night that York and Cat had stolen the snowmobile?

The snow machines stopped and idled just out of his sight down the lane. He heard snippets of conversation above the "pop, pop" of the motors. "Rooftop... tracks here... snowshoes..." then "...check it out... cover you...."

He had counted on the bandits roaring into the yard full speed and perhaps providing an opportunity for surprise and confusion. He was not expecting a well-ordered advance to the house.

There was movement in the trees across the driveway and he froze, watching out of the corner of his eye. A man in military dress, with no cap, moved quietly through the woods and stopped almost opposite him. The man carefully observed the house then stepped to the edge of the trees and waved in the direction of the snowmobiles. He heard the machines rev up as he watched the man shift his rifle from his left hand back to his right.

The snowmobiles roared up the driveway and stopped in a spread out line astern with the lead vehicle opposite where he crouched concealed. Two of the sleds carried two riders. The lead rider, like the others, was wearing a snowmobile helmet with a tinted face shield. He flipped up the shield to talk to the scout. "Go back to your machine and take up a position covering our rear."

York had seen that face before and recognised the voice. He braced himself. This was not going to be easy but had to be done. He stepped out into the lane and every eye turned toward him as he shouted.

"You always were a sucker for an ambush!"

The lead snowmobiler swung his leg over the seat as each of the others brought a weapon to bear on York. "At ease," the leader quietly said to the others, motioning for them to lower their weapons. "If he had wanted to hurt you, you'd all be dead by now, even if he's only carrying an axe."

He walked toward York and stopped toe to toe in front of him. The face that peered from the helmet was gaunt and weathered. It had been a hard winter for everybody, York thought.

"Hello, Russell," York said holding out his bare right hand.

Russell looked down at the extended hand, paused, looked up at his face, and then pulled the trigger mitten off of his own right hand. He grasped his hand firmly and with his left hand gripped York on the right shoulder.

"It's been too long, brother. I'm glad you made it." Russell led the two away from the noisy snowmobiles.

"You, too. It's been a tough grind. Thanks for the map and the small pack. They came in handy."

"No problem," said Russell. "I heard that it was you in the camp. I had left to get some transport for you. I was planning on letting you escape from my custody but I needed to arrange for a snowmobile to be available."

"Jeez, why didn't you let me know?"

"I couldn't very well walk in and tell you in front of the sentry not to escape yet." Russell stopped and faced him with a grin. "Just like you always said though, try to plan for every eventuality. I put together a small pack to give to the girl. Just in case. Where is she by the way?"

"She's inside." He scowled then pointed toward the house. "Why don't you and this motley crew come in for lunch. We have plenty for everybody."

"Thanks, but we are on a recce patrol to Spencer, show the flag, maintain a law and order presence, you know, all that 'aid to the civil authority' crap that we used to hate to practice."

"Well, I've got all sorts of intelligence details for you: lay of the land, friendly casualties, enemy activity, and all sorts of stuff that your CO would love. I can probably give you a trip's worth of data, not to say that there won't also be info in Spencer."

Russell paused a moment then turned to the warrant officer who was on the fourth snowmobile. "Warrant, lead the patrol to Spencer. Banks can take my sled. Take Griffin and the rest with you as well. With who we have here, we don't need a guard. I'm going to stay here until you return. Be back in two hours. Then we'll go back to headquarters. I think that there's good info here but we still need to cruise through Spencer."

"Roger that, sir," said the senior NCO. "Banks, grab the OC's sled and lead down to the highway. Then right toward Spencer. Double file. Spread out."

The soldiers swung the snowmobiles around as the front door of the house opened and Elizabeth dashed off the deck into the yard. "Russell, that is you! I knew it was you."

Russell and his sister embraced and Elizabeth was in tears. They walked hand in hand to the porch where Doc stood watching.

"Russell, this is Doctor Joshua Simpson, my fiancé."

Russell stopped short, looked at Elizabeth, and then stepped onto the porch. "Any fiancé of Elizabeth's is a friend of mine," he said pumping Doc's hand. "And I didn't even get an invitation to the engagement party. I hope I get one to the wedding."

"You will," said Doc. "This is really getting to be a Lancaster family affair around here."

There was a pause, then Elizabeth glanced at York, but it was she who broke the silence by introducing Cat as a friend of his.

"We've met before, under less comfortable circumstances," said Russell shaking her hand.

"Where?" asked Cat, then before anyone could answer, "The soldier back at the army camp. You're the one who gave me the packsack with the map and the food in it." She launched herself at Russell and wrapped her arms around his neck and gave him a big kiss. "Thank you so much. You're York's brother? He told me about you, sort of."

"I'm glad you survived the winter. I told you to stay with him and you'd be OK," said Russell glancing at him.

York remained motionless beside the others. Elizabeth grabbed Russell and ushered them into the house as Doc and Cat trooped after them. York then stepped off the porch and headed toward the garage, wiping some snow from the axe. He picked up a few sticks of split wood and carried them in the other arm. He was just about to enter the garage when the door opened for him.

Russell was there to take the axe from his hand then walk back to the yard for another load of wood. They worked together soundlessly for about ten minutes, carrying wood and stacking it. Then Russell stopped and wiped his brow leaning against the garage.

"Well, I suspect that you and I have enough war stories to tell each other for a year thanks to this flu thing. How was the winter?"

"It's a real long story, Russell. It'll take more than a few rums to tell it all."

"Your lady is really nice. She seems to think a lot of you."

"That's just show. I helped her out of a jam a couple of times and she's grateful, but I'm not her type. I think that I'm not quite sophisticated enough for her."

"Shit, that's not the feeling I got inside just now." Russell broke a splinter off a piece of birch and chewed on it. "They're putting something on the table that smelled awfully good. Elizabeth was beaming about her catch and it sure seemed to me that Cat was bragging you up pretty well."

"Just your imagination. I've heard her and Elizabeth talking when they thought nobody else was around. I know which way the wind blows."

They stood in silence for a few seconds.

"She seemed to like you, Russell. Maybe you should take a shot at her." He regretted the words as soon as he had said them. "I'm sorry! I didn't mean that. I heard about Ashley. I'm sorry that she died, sorry for you and her both."

Russell didn't say anything for a while. "Yeah it was hard. She was pregnant. We were going to have a baby. We were really happy but she always felt terrible about you, and so did I." Russell walked over and stood in front of him. "I wish that it had never happened. We thought that you were dead. I swear to you that I would never do anything intentionally to hurt you, and I'll damn sure never again look twice at any woman that you have ever dated, spent time with, or even met twice. You're too important to lose a second time."

The door to the kitchen opened and eased the moment.

"Will you two get in here and have some lunch? Save the war stories for later," Elizabeth exclaimed grinning from ear to ear. She reminded York of a younger version of his mother.

The laughter gave way to subdued conversation as Russell brought them up to speed on the catastrophic events of the last few months. The United States had suffered at least eighty million deaths, Canada seven million. Around the world the figure was only a guess but was widely talked about as two billion.

To this date there were no international communications except through Ham radio operators and some government radio facilities. Most of the world was without reliable electric power. Cities were ghost towns and most of the survivors were in the rural areas. There was no petroleum supply except in isolated pockets as the governments had confiscated any known stockpiles.

The spring was expected to bring relief from the cold and dark but also to bring disease from rotting corpses, loss of clean water, and depletion of the stored food. For some people the worst was yet to come.

Doc reached over and took Elizabeth's hand and raised it to his lips. Russell sat and stared at his coffee cup.

York ignored Cat. He needed to re-establish in his own mind that this was a friendship only, and it was easiest for him if he paid little attention to her. On one occasion he caught her looking at him rather dolefully, but he looked away. He assured himself that he was not driving her to the coast again, even if he ever got his Jeep back. He had other fish to fry and he meant to get on with his life. It was good though to sit around the table with Russell and Elizabeth. It felt like it should feel. He could be happy with their company.

CHAPTER 27

2 April

York heard the snowmobiles coming up the lane. “That was a fast trip,” he said as he went to the front door.

The bullet ripped a splintered hole in the door and he dropped to the floor in the ragged shaft of light that now pierced the dark hallway. The report of the weapon indicated a high powered rifle.

“What the hell are those yahoos of yours doing, Russell?” he shouted. “Everybody stay down.”

“That can’t be my guys,” Russell shouted back.

“What is happening?” “Why are they doing this?” “What should we do?” There was confusion in the dining room.

“Russell, my rifle is in the corner by the fridge. There are extra rounds in the cupboard overhead. Watch the back.”

York rolled and crawled to the far end of the kitchen, locked the door leading to the garage, and snatched his bow and quiver from beside the stove. He inched his eyes high enough to peer at an angle out the kitchen window. There were three snowmobiles in the driveway. Two men were visible by the machines. As he watched, a white pickup pulled into the driveway, struggling in the snow with four-wheel drive engaged. The driver and passenger got out and stood by the truck.

“Hey, in the house! Anybody there?” shouted the truck driver. “Hey, Doc, are you in there?”

"Russell, there are four out front and at least one unaccounted for."

"Roger that. I don't see anybody out back."

"Hey boss," called one of the men out front. "I hear voices inside. There's somebody in there."

"Doc, we know that you're in there. We don't mean you any harm. We just want to talk to you. Open up."

York finished tying his bootlaces and glanced out the front again in time to see the fifth man emerge from the woods fastening his belt. Two of the men harangued the new arrival about his obvious recent activities. York took the opportunity to scurry into the dining room.

"You two stay down," he motioned to Elizabeth and Cat. "Russell, why don't you give your pistol to Doc. I'm going out the back door and into the woods. Doc, go to the hallway and answer them, keep low and keep them talking but whatever you do, don't open that door. I know them. They've tried to kill us already and they're the ones who have been burning places all over the county."

"Don't go out there, York," said Cat. "It's too dangerous."

He snorted and headed for the back door. "Doc, you better start that conversation. I need the cover. Russell, I'm going to the south. I'll try to lower the odds from behind them. Maybe then they'll quit or we can hold out until your cavalry arrives back here." Maybe I can keep the soldiers from being surprised, he also thought.

"What do you want?" he heard Doc shout from the hallway.

"Hi, Doc, me and the boys were looking for a little help. Can we come in?"

York scanned the back of the house from the window in the doorway and then eased the door open. If there was anyone watching the back then he would be a sitting duck, but he doubted that the invaders were that thoughtful, organised or ambitious.

He was right. There was nobody to be seen. He tripped the lock on the door and pulled it closed behind him. As he did he heard Cat.

"We have a harp lesson tonight, York. You be there."

"Now what the hell am I supposed to do with that?" he said to himself.

The snow had melted away from the foundation of the house and there was a clear walkway to follow to the corner. I just hope the snow in the woods is not still deep, he thought.

"Who's in there with you, Doc?" one of the men out front called. "We're not dummies, you know."

York forced that conversation, as well as Cat's last shouted words, into the back of his mind as he concentrated on getting to the woods unseen. It was only a matter of time until the geniuses out front realised that there were other entrances to the house. He wanted to be undercover in the woods and fighting back before they split up. He chose the old footprints that he had made on his last trip into the woods to gather kindling. He was in the open as the next rifle shot blasted the morning.

He thought that he had been seen, but there was no crack of a passing bullet, and he realised that the shot was not intended for him. He gained the cover of a fir thicket and melted into the woods.

He paused to look around and plan his route. He needed to get into action before the gunplay escalated. The snow was drifted in spots but it was passable without snowshoes. He fitted an arrow and started to his right toward a spot where he could engage the enemy. There was another rifle shot followed by a scream from the house.

"Boss, there's a woman in there. There's a woman. Don't shoot anymore. We can use a woman."

"Link, you and Harry go around back, check it out."

York crouched and waited as one of the two men moved by him toward the back of the house. He wondered who had been hit in the house. As long as Russell was all right they had a fighting chance. The two scouts had split up, one going around each side of the house instead of one covering the other as they moved. He lifted the bow judging when the man would be unseen by the others still in front of the house.

"Screw you," he whispered as he loosed the hunting arrow at the scout.

The arrow hissed through the air and ripped into the scout's neck. He dropped like a felled tree but with not a sound in the snow.

York glanced to the left. One of the three men out front was looking in his direction. He remained motionless and the man looked away. He froze and waited for the inevitable second look. Sure enough, the man glanced back quickly in his direction then turned his attention back to the house. York eased farther back into the woods. He had only a few seconds until the other scout came around the house to discover the dead man in the snow.

He moved farther toward the lane opening, to place himself behind the men out front. Finding a reasonable firing position he prepared another arrow and loosened the others in the quiver. Things would happen quickly from here on in. He aimed at the centre target. That man was the best selection for a first shot simply because he was a tougher second shot. He waited for the shout that he knew would come.

The second scout announced his discovery with a yell. All three men out front responded to the shout by looking to their right. He loosed the first arrow into the back of the centre man. As that target was falling, he nocked the next arrow. As the right hand man was turning to look at his companion, he loosed the arrow into the second target's left side. The arrow glanced off the stock of the rifle that the man was carrying. Instead of diving for cover the man swung in the direction from which the arrows had come and raised his rifle.

York forced himself to aim well and loosed the third arrow into the same target's heart as the man fired the rifle. The bullet cracked overhead. The man fell, skewered by the arrow. York scanned for the others and saw nothing so he turned and quickly ran farther back into the woods.

He twisted and turned, changed direction like the buck from six months ago, and sought a position of relative safety to stop and reorganise his thoughts. After about thirty seconds he readied another arrow and again froze. He listened. Not a sound could be heard except a breeze in the branches.

There were five men initially and three were now out of the fight. At least the first and last that he had shot were dead, the second was dead or wounded. He had used four of his eight arrows and there were two men left. He would not get as easy shots again. His enemies were armed and were now hunting for him.

If he moved he could give away his position. The snow was noisy in spots. He could not just sit and wait for them to come to him. If Russell was injured, the others in the house might not be able to defend themselves. If the remaining two bandits went about it the right way then they could take the house and he could not allow that. On the other hand, when he was moving he was much more vulnerable, and a rifle was a more efficient killing weapon than his bow.

Where were the two remaining enemy? The scout was assuredly in the same area where he was. He would have moved into the trees beside the house and then moved toward the head of the lane.

The other man, the man on the left out front, was lost from view from the moment that he sent his second arrow on its way. The man had not crossed the killing zone so he had either run around the far side of the house or into the woods close by the west side of the house. That was by far the most likely. The man was probably on the other side of the lane thinking things through just as he was doing. Neither of the enemy would be happy about trying to find him in the woods. He had a distinct advantage; he was alone and did not have to worry about accidentally shooting a buddy.

After another five minutes of careful observation and listening he arrived at a plan. He would try to engage the scout first, before he had a chance to link up with the other man. That was the best chance to even the odds and to prevent the house from being overwhelmed.

"Hey, Slasher! Where are you?"

The call came from the woods close to the house. He had guessed correctly where the scout was located. The voice was loud and was stained with panic.

Nerves will get a man into trouble faster than stupidity, he thought. He started slowly in the direction of the voice. The second man, Slasher, did not reply. That would be too easy, he thought. He crept forward.

"Hey, Slasher, where are you?"

A rifle boomed, a rifle that was familiar to him, his own .45-70. It was followed by a scream, then a second higher pitched shot, then the boom again. Then there was silence for thirty seconds.

"York! This one's down," he heard Russell shout. "I've been counting. If you want to change the plan let me know, otherwise I'll continue as we decided. Everyone is OK in here, just a splinter wound earlier."

He felt like laughing. Russell was a good man to go to war with. He had taken the opportunity to engage the enemy when he came in sight. He had told him everything that he needed to know, while telling the enemy nothing important. He was maintaining the plan but was flexible if needed.

He turned 180 degrees and focused on the last man. There was no sound in the woods. There was no hint of the enemy location. He waited another thirty seconds, then picked his route in advance and sprinted to the west and south toward the power line. It was a cleared lane through the woods that would give him a measure of security by expanding his field of view in a couple of directions. It was also a field of fire that was particularly of benefit to his bow because arrows were easily deflected by the smallest twig.

He gained the concealment of a fir thicket and resumed his watching and listening. He moved to the edge of the thicket and then to a multi-trunked tree that offered him concealment, cover from fire, and a location from which he could see and shoot down the powerline.

An inexperienced hunter hated inactivity; he relished it. It was easier to observe and listen when motionless. It was safer than thrashing through the woods into the sights of the enemy. He thought about climbing a tree then rejected the idea. Without scouting the fields of view and fields of fire in advance, the position in the tree could be a death trap.

He checked his watch. It was noon, but his bladder was empty, he was not hungry, and his boots were warm and dry. He was patient and could afford all the time in the world. He scanned the tree lines along the power right-of-way, then the woods around him. He listened to the whisper of the wind, the creak of the trees, and the sounds of the early spring wildlife.

He knew that back in the house Russell would have organised a watch and a defence. They were safe there with only one assailant still in action. He wondered who had received the wound. The scream and the comments from the men outside would indicate that it was one of the women, but Russell had said that it was not serious and Russell would not have lied to him. He hoped that it was not his sister. She didn't deserve that kind of treatment. But neither did Cat. Even if she did not think very highly of him, she was still a good person and had been through enough already.

He caught himself drifting into reverie and jerked himself back to the task at hand, staying alive. He continued to scan and listen.

What about the last statement from Cat, about the harmonica lesson? He knew what he had heard this morning. Was she just toying with him? Or just trying to make him feel OK as he went out to fight? What was that all about?

A squirrel set up an angry chatter to his right down the power line. Another encroaching squirrel could be the cause, but it could also be the first clue to trouble in the offing. He forced himself to put Cat into the background, and focussed all of his senses on the task at hand.

At last he found the first true indication of threat, cigarette smoke, a faint hint of tobacco wafting on the breeze. Careful soldiers never smoked on operations. The smell of tobacco smoke was a dead give away; and even stale tobacco smoke on your clothes, from a cigarette a few hours before, could reveal your position from several hundred metres away.

The wind was coming from his right. He adjusted his position so that he could train his bow in that direction, and kept low, out of sight and still.

A shadow moved in the tree line farther down the right of way. The shadow was out of tune with the other movement caused by the wind. He continued to be aware of the woods around him but focused on the tree line. A glint of light moved in the trees and he focused even more closely. There was a gap of several minutes where no movement or sound was noted. Only the odour of cigarette was constant.

He widened his field of attention to take into account the potential movement of the man across the power line. After a couple of minutes there was a rustle of bushes and York's quarry was visible just behind a screen of budding alders not thirty meters away.

There was no shot possible with bow and arrow at that range, with the alder branches ready to divert the best-aimed shot. He would not get a second shot, just a volley of rifle fire in return. He had to await a clear chance for a kill or a disabling shot. The longer he waited, though, the greater the chance that he would be discovered himself. Then there would be little hope. Who the hell cares anyway, he thought.

He continued to watch the man out of the corner of his eye. He believed, as many hunters do, that a steady gaze would alert the person being observed; that they would know they were being watched. In fact he felt that he himself was being watched, even though the man was actually looking up the power line toward the house.

His target then did the unexpected, the man stepped out into the cleared right of way. He was unprepared for such a move, as it made no sense to him. If the man was crossing then he should have run or crouched as he crossed. If the movement was to look along the open area, then that was best done from cover.

York made his move. Arrow in place along the bow, he shifted his stance, remained squatted, and took aim. The man seemed to sense danger and turned toward him as the arrow was loosed. The arrow caught the man in the left shoulder and he bawled with pain. The man then raised the rifle in his right hand and triggered a shot at York that splintered the tree at his side. He felt a smack on his left arm and looked down to see the bow smashed in his hand.

He turned to dash into the thicket out of sight of the rifleman, and tripped on the quiver that he had laid beside him. Oh how stupid. Now I'm going to die because I didn't clear away my kit. He glanced to his right through the trunks that had recently been his hiding place, bracing himself for the next bullet that would be on the way. He stared straight into the eyes of the other man and into the muzzle of the raised rifle. He caught a sour scent and wondered if that was what people called the smell of fear.

Then with a hideous roar, the black monster careened into the gunman at a full run. The rifle discharged into the air. Neither York nor the bear were endangered by the shot but both of them were stirred by the blast. He melted back into the woods. The bear began to slash at the man with his claws and paws, then grabbed the man in his jaws and shook him like a cat with a mouse. The screams were hideous and he used the sound to cover his withdrawal to the lane and then directly to the house.

He hailed the house from a distance. Transiting back into friendly lines was one of the most dangerous parts of any patrol into enemy territory. He wanted no errors now but he also wanted out of the woods until he was properly armed again. There were still screams from the woods. Then all was silent.

"Shit York, what did you do to that guy out there?" Russell asked as he came out into the dooryard. "You were always the silent one."

"Oh the stupid ass took a gun to a bear fight," he replied.

Russell looked at him with a puzzled expression on his face and York added, "It's a long story, brother. Let's have coffee and I'll start at the beginning."

He looked down at the two men who were lying dead by the pickup truck. One was face down in the mud. His feet were dressed in running shoes, running shoes with a Nike logo in the footprint. York kicked at the foot closest to him. "Nice shoes."

He walked with his brother toward the house.

"Oh by the way, York, you need to change your tune a little."

"What do you mean?"

"That conversation that you heard when Cat and Elizabeth didn't think you were listening? Well it seems that our sister and your girlfriend weren't talking about you. They were talking about some loser named Don or Ron or something."

York paused in the dooryard, and then resumed walking. He turned his head to look at his brother walking beside him. "Are you positive about that?"

"Yeah, I asked them outright what was going on. You know me, no finesse at all."

He paused again, and Russell halted beside him.

"Are you OK with that, York?"

"Yeah, no problem."

They walked together toward the house.

ABOUT THE AUTHOR

Retired from the Canadian Army, an Infantry Officer and a Medical Officer, Kendrick Lacey brings to his writing a wide ranging knowledge, and a disparate blend of life experiences. His varied pastimes today include boating, travel, and cabinet making. Kendrick practices and teaches medicine in small village New Brunswick.

Order Form

Flu Shot
Kendrick Lacey M.D.
ISBN: 1-894372-35-2
$19.95 CAN / $15.00 US

The following discounts apply for orders of 10 or more copies:
Bookstores and Retail Accounts: 40%+
Wholesalers: 46%+
Educational Institutions: 20%
Public Libraries: 20%
Medical practitioners/corporate clients: 40%

All orders must include applicable sales taxes.

Allow $3.00 S&H for single copies and $5.00 for multiple copies

Quantity	Unit Price	Amount
______	$19.95 CAN $15.00 US	__________

Applicable Discounts __________

Applicable Sales Taxes __________

Shipping and Handling __________

TOTAL ________________

QUICKFAX or
e-mail your order:
Fax: (506) 632-4009
E-mail: dcpub@fundy.net

DreamCatcher Publishing
105 Prince William Street
Saint John, NB, Canada E2L 2B2
WebSite: www.dreamcatcher.ca